Herbert Greenhough Smith

The Romance of History

Herbert Greenhough Smith

The Romance of History

ISBN/EAN: 9783744675666

Printed in Europe, USA, Canada, Australia, Japan

Cover: Foto ©Andreas Hilbeck / pixelio.de

More available books at **www.hansebooks.com**

THE
ROMANCE OF HISTORY

MASANIELLO	BAYARD
PRINCE RUPERT	LITHGOW
BENYOWSKY	JACQUELINE DE LAGUETTE
TAMERLANE	VIDOCQ
MARINO FALIERO	LOCHIEL
CASANOVA	

BY

HERBERT GREENHOUGH SMITH

LONDON

RICHARD BENTLEY & SON, NEW BURLINGTON STREET

Publishers in Ordinary to Her Majesty the Queen

1891

CONTENTS

MASANIELLO	1
PRINCE RUPERT	29
BENYOWSKY	55
TAMERLANE	93
MARINO FALIERO	118
BAYARD	137
LITHGOW	166
JACQUELINE DE LAGUETTE	190
VIDOCQ	218
LOCHIEL	259
CASANOVA	288

THE ROMANCE OF HISTORY

MASANIELLO

MASANIELLO was born at Amalfi in the year 1622. His father was a fisherman, and the child first saw the light among the nets and baskets of a little hut on the sea-coast. His birth was attended by an augury. It is said that an ancient monk, whose glittering eyes and snowy beard had gained for him, among the village folk, the reputation of a prophet, once visited the cottage, and having looked long upon the child as it lay asleep in its poor cradle, broke forth into a prediction that the boy would some day rise to more than kingly power, but that his empire would be brief and his fall sudden. The seer who uttered such a prophecy deserved his fame. The story of Masaniello—the most romantic story in the history of mankind—fulfilled the oracle; with what exactness, and by what events, we propose to call to mind.

The boy was brought up to his father's trade. When he was about his twentieth year he left Amalfi and crossed the bay to Naples. There he took a garret in a house which overhung a corner of the great market square, and married a girl no richer than himself; and thenceforward every morning, as soon as the sun rose up behind the black peaks of Vesuvius, his boat was to be seen dancing over the blue waters of the bay.

The life of a fisherman is hard and poor. Masaniello went barefooted. His dress was the common dress of the fishermen of Naples—loose linen trousers, a blue blouse, and a red cap. But his figure, though not tall, was striking; his face was handsome; his eyes black, large, and glittering; and there was about him a peculiar air of self-reliance, the index of a bold, capable, and fiery mind.

For about four years he lived quietly; in poverty, yet not perhaps in discontent. But the Spanish Viceroys who ruled Naples, and who had long waxed fat upon the taxes, were yearly sucking deeper of the people's blood. A tax was set on fish, a tax on flour, a tax on poultry, wine, milk, cheese, salt. At last a tax on fruit, the fare on which the lower classes chiefly lived, brought the city to the brink of a revolt. Yet it is probable that, even then, without a leader, the popular excitement would have died away in empty threats and mutterings. At this crisis, the agents of the Government happened to fall foul of Masaniello. A basket of his fish which had not paid the tax was seized and carried to the castle. The same day his wife was stopped as she was carrying in her apron a small quantity of flour, was dragged to the receipt of custom, and being found to have no money, either to pay the duty or to bribe the agents, was locked up in a cell.

They had better have hanged a hundred lazzaroni on the gibbet in the market-place. Masaniello was stung to madness. From that moment his sole thought was of revenge.

The most tremendous weapon known to man was ready to his hand—a city on the verge of riot. His measures were soon taken. In appearance they were harmless, even trifling ; but in truth they were most dexterously planned. He began by collecting in the market-place a knot of boys. To each of these he taught a phrase of words, and gave a little cane, bearing on the top a streamer of black linen, like a flag. Soon five hundred, and at last two thousand, of these volunteers, were going up and down the city. In the hovels of the lazzaroni, among the stalls of the fruit-sellers, before the gates of the toll-houses, under the windows of the Spanish nobles, everywhere their slender ensigns fluttered, and the pregnant words were heard : " God be with us, and Our Lady, and the King of Spain ! But down with the Government, the fruit-tax, and the devil !"

Masaniello's scholars made a vast sensation. A few of the spectators mocked and jeered ; but the seed was scattered in no stony soil. It sprang up and flourished ; and in three days it was ready to bear fruit.

It was Sunday, July 7th, in the year 1647. The day was the festival of Our Lady of the Carmes, a day which had for centuries been held in celebration of an ancient victory achieved against the Moors. It was the custom on that day to erect in the market-place a wooden castle, which was defended by a company of boys, while another company, half-naked and painted red, with turbans on their heads, in imitation of the Moors, assailed its battlements with a storm of apples, melons, cucumbers, and figs. This spectacle, which usually ended in a free fight and uproar, was, as might have been expected, excessively popular among the lower classes ; and that morning, at the hour at which the fruit-growers from the villages began, as usual, to pour into the city, the square was already thronged with thousands of spectators.

The performance had not yet begun; the crowd was waiting, idle and unemployed, ready to welcome any manner of excitement; when suddenly a startling cry was heard. One of the fruit-sellers had refused to pay the tax!

The man was Arpaja of Pozzuoli, Masaniello's cousin. The plot had been arranged between them. On being called upon to pay the duty, Arpaja flew into a rage. "God gives us plenty," he exclaimed in a loud voice, "and our cursed Government a famine. The fruit is not worth selling; let it go!" And with the words he kicked over his baskets, and sent the gourds and oranges rolling on the ground.

At that instant, as the crowd stood breathless in excitement, a voice sent forth a cry of "No more taxes!" The voice was Masaniello's. The crowd caught up the words; they swelled into a thunder. In an instant the rebellion was afoot.

Andrea Anaclerio, the elect of the people, rushed out of his palace, and threatened Arpaja with the whip. But a storm of sticks and melons flew about his ears; a large stone struck him on the breast; and he was glad to fly for refuge into the chapel of Our Lady.

Masaniello sprang upon a fruiterer's table. The crowd already recognised their leader. He began to speak; and he spoke with a certain rude and fiery oratory which moved his hearers more than eloquence. He bade them rejoice, for the hour of their deliverance was at hand. St. Peter, once a fisherman, had beaten down the pride of Satan and released the world from bondage; so likewise would he, Masaniello, another fisherman, strike off the bonds of the most Faithful People. Let them pay no more taxes; let them win back with fire and sword the ancient Privilege of Naples, the right of freedom from all taxes, which the Spaniards had infringed. His own life might fall; his head might ride aloft upon a pole. But to die in such a cause would be his glory.

There is no rhetoric which thrills its hearers like that which gives the echo to their passions. The crowd broke into a fierce shout, and turned with exultation to the work of ravage. The first object was the toll-house in the square. Faggots drenched with pitch were hurled in at the windows; a lighted torch was added; and the building in a few minutes was a pile of raging flames. Then there was a cry for arms. A ponderous beam was brought and wielded by strong men, the gates of the Carmine Tower were beaten in, and the crowd rushed eagerly upon the pikes and halberds. Clubs, knives, and bars of iron were pressed into the service; and the mob, thus armed, preceded by the banner-boys of Masaniello, turned in their wild justice towards the palace of the Viceroy.

Their way lay past the prison of St. James. They halted there to burst the doors and to add the prisoners to their number.

At length they reached the palace. The guards who stood at arms before the gates were swept away. The Viceroy, Ponce de Leon, Duke of Arcos, and those about him, strove to secure themselves behind the inner doors. But the barricades were broken in. The Duke was hunted like a thief from room to room, and forced at last, at the peril of his life, to drop from a back window by a rope, and to fly in a close carriage to the castle of St. Elmo.

Then the palace was sacked from floor to roof. A great fire was kindled in the street. Rare and costly furniture, hangings, pictures, jewels, golden dishes, goblets stamped with the proud arms of Ponce de Leon, were hurled out of the windows, and piled into the flames. Yet in all this, and throughout the whole revolt, there was no private theft. These riches were held as things accursed, as treasures purchased by the people's blood, and worthy only to be sacrificed in the hour of their revenge.

And now the people, drunk with the giddy wine of vengeance, required no further rousing. The time had come for discipline, for order, and restraint; and Masaniello turned with all his vigour to the work. Then was seen the power of a commanding mind. In a marvellously short space of time, the mob became an army. Parties, each led by its own captain, and missioned to its separate duty, began to go forth through the city; searching the armourers' shops for weapons; tearing down the Spanish standard from the Carmine Tower, and planting in its place the ancient flag of Naples; marching through the streets, with trumpets singing and drums rolling, collecting volunteers; bursting open the prisons of St. Maria and St. Archangel; dragging the cannon from the bastion of San Lorenzo, and setting the great bells pealing an alarm. As often as the Spanish soldiers met with a detachment of the rioters, a fierce fight arose; lives were lost on both sides; but the guards were always overpowered. All business became suspended. The shopkeepers shut up their shops, and joined the rebels. The nobles, and the farmers of the taxes, with beating hearts and faces white with terror, barred themselves inside their palaces. Only a train of monks, in stoles of white, with censers in their hands, ventured, about the hour of Vespers, to issue from the Convent of St. Paul, and to pass with prayers for peace along the streets.

When night fell, Masaniello was at the head of fifty thousand men. Nor did darkness check the course of his proceedings. Thousands of candles, torches, cressets, watch-fires blazing at every corner of the streets, made the city as bright as day. Recruits came streaming in without cessation. And all night the work went on.

As soon as day began to break, new swarms of volunteers, equipped with sickles, pitchforks, scythes, and even spits and pokers, came pouring in from all the country round. But the arms most used that day were links and torches. A platform was erected in the market-place ; and there Masaniello sat, and gave his orders. The toll-house in the square was now in cinders; but in different quarters of the city there were several others. Masaniello drew up a list of these, together with sixty of the proudest palaces in Naples, which their owners had enriched or built out of the produce of the taxes. All these were ordered to be burnt ; and throughout that day, and far into the night, parties were going forth un- ceasingly with faggots, pitch, and torches. Women and children helped the work with sacks of straw and cans of oil. In every quarter of the city some haughty edifice, the home of a Mirabello or an

Aquavana, was turned into a heap of smoking ruins. Treasures of all kinds, and of untold value, perished in the flames. Pictures of the Madonna and the saints were alone held sacred, were preserved, and hung up in the churches. Nothing was taken by the people. So strong on this point was the public feeling, that one of the rioters who ventured to pick up a silk scarf was instantly dragged into the market-place, and hanged by a fierce crowd.

Meanwhile, the Viceroy had stolen secretly from St. Elmo, and was now shut up in Castel Nuovo, which was kept by a strong guard. From the castle he sent out his orders. But the few bands of guards which he could spare were entirely useless; and in truth the Duke was in a desperate pass. He tried tactics; and he tried devotion. He sent out the Duke of Maddaloni and the Prior of Rocella with a piece of parchment, which he pretended was the Privilege of Naples. But the crowd immediately found out the trick; the Prior was hooted, and the Duke came near to being torn in pieces. He then bethought himself of St. Gennaro; and in the chapel of the great cathedral, the chapel in which, three times a year, the holy head, enshrined in silver, is still laid upon the altar, while the priest lifts up before a crowd of pilgrims the vials of sacred blood, the august relics were displayed. The saint, however, wrought no miracle; and the Viceroy passed the night in agonies of uncertainty and trepidation.

While the Duke was quaking in the castle, Masaniello's power was rising higher every hour. He was already, indeed, in everything but name, the governor of Naples. The proud and beautiful city was at his feet. The haughty cavaliers of Spain durst not wag their fingers; for the number of his followers was now at least a hundred thousand. His throne of timber in the market-place was surrounded by battalions of armed men, ready to carry out his slightest orders. Beside him, at a table, six clerks were constantly employed in writing out his edicts. One of these proclamations, which is recorded, shows that Masaniello possessed, like all born leaders, a falcon's eye for details. The nobility were ordered to walk out without their cloaks, monks to put off their cassocks, and ladies to wear no skirts that swept the ground; for in all such garments arms might be concealed. The Law Courts were shut up. Criminals of every rank and station were dragged before that strange tribunal at which Masaniello was both judge and jury. In one corner of the market-place a gibbet was set up; and the course of justice was of the admirably swift and ready kind which characterised the judgment-seat of Minos—

> " Sempre dinanzi a lui ne stanno molte :
> Vanno a vicenda ciascuna al giudizio ;
> Dicono e odono, e poi son giù volte."

So vast was the first change in Masaniello's fortune! Two days had sufficed to raise him from the task of mending nets and hawking mullets, to a throne as absolute as Zim-Zizimi's.

The Viceroy was secure within the castle; but the castle was kept in a close state of siege. No provisions could pass in; and the Duke, and the scores of lords and ladies who had found refuge with him, were beginning to feel miserably in want of meat and poultry, fruit and wine and snow. A spy brought word that Masaniello was preparing a new list of palaces to be set in flames that night. The Duke's mind had been wavering; he saw no hope in holding out; these tidings turned the scale; and he gave way.

It was the afternoon of Tuesday; Masaniello was sitting on his bench of judgment; when a packet from the Viceroy was put into his hand. He tore it open before the crowd. It contained the true parchment of the Privilege; and in a letter which accompanied the parchment, the Duke expressed his willingness to grant, without reserve, the prayer of the most Faithful People.

The populace received the news with raptures of

delight. It was rapidly arranged that the Viceroy, with the chief officers of state, should meet the people on the morrow in the Carmine Church, when the treaty should be ratified on oath, and a solemn service held in celebration. The insurgents were still kept under arms. But to all appearance the revolt was at an end. The remainder of the day passed quietly. All the city, in joyful anticipation, looked forward to the morrow.

But this spirit of contentment was destined to be roughly broken. Masaniello's chief subalterns were Genovino, a fierce old monk, and Perrone, the captain of a crew of bandits who had their dens among the gorges of Vesuvius. The latter, who had joined the cause in the confident belief that his five hundred desperadoes would enjoy a thieves' paradise among the treasures of the palaces, had been bitterly deceived, and was at heart a traitor. His opportunity was soon to come. That night he had an interview with the Duke of Maddaloni and his brother, Don Carafa. From that meeting the bandit carried off a heavy bag of gold. Nor was the treasure paid for nothing. Judas had received the price of blood. It was agreed that on the morrow, during the ceremony in the church, and in full view of the spectators, Masaniello should be shot dead.

The morrow came. At noon the great church of Our Lady was crowded to the doors. Perrone's bravos, to the number of three hundred, were scattered here and there among the crowd. A gorgeous canopy had been set up before the altar, above the crimson cushions of the Viceroy and the Bishop. Masaniello was standing on the altar-steps, a bare sword in his right hand, surrounded by a host of lords and cardinals, conspicuous, among robes of scarlet and tunics laced with silver, by his fisherman's shirt and his cap without a feather. The Viceroy had not yet arrived; but the music of his bugles could be heard approaching. This was the moment on which the conspirators had fixed. Perrone suddenly held up his hand; and from different parts of the church seven carbines were instantly fired point-blank at Masaniello. Two of these were so near him that the flash of the explosion singed his blouse. The others struck the altar at his side. Yet, wonderful to state, not one of the seven balls so much as grazed him.

The bandits had relied with confidence on the fall of Masaniello, and the confusion and dismay of his adherents. Their error cost them dear. When the smoke cleared off, and he was seen still standing on the altar-steps, their hearts misgave them. And they had good cause for terror. The crowd, raging with fury, turned upon them; and in a moment the church was ringing with the din of battle. The desperadoes, men whose whole lives had been passed in fighting, now fought like wild beasts brought to bay. But the contest was not equal, and they fought in vain. Soon, above the roar of voices and the clash of arms, were heard the yells of wretches being torn in pieces in front of the great altar. A part escaped into the adjoining convent; but these were quickly hunted out and butchered. A few got clear away into the mountains and plunged into the darkness of their dens. Perrone, who was seized alive, but covered with wounds, was dragged into the square, and impelled by threats of torture to reveal the authors of the plot. He had just gasped out the names of Maddaloni and Carafa when he fell back dead.

Two hundred poles were set up in a circle about Masaniello's throne; the corpses of the traitors were beheaded; and soon the fierce head of a bandit grinned on every pole. Two poles, higher than the rest, were placed before the platform, and left vacant. One of these waited for the head of Maddaloni; the other, for the head of Don Carafa.

The Duke had taken refuge in the monastery of St. Efrem. A spy warned him that his hiding-place was discovered. He stole out of the convent in a monk's gown and cowl, mounted a swift horse, struck the spurs up to the rowels, and galloped for his life to Benevento. He was just in time. The crowd, failing to find him in the convent, burnt his palace to the ground, and turned in search of Don Carafa.

The Don was less lucky than his brother. A monk from the convent of Zoccolanti was seen stealing towards the gates of Castel Nuovo. He was seized, and a note found sewn into his sandal. It was from Carafa to the Viceroy; he was hiding in the convent; and he implored the Duke to send a guard, with cannon, to protect him. The convent was instantly attacked. Carafa, in a friar's frock, sprang out of a window, rushed into a cottage, and crawled under a bed. The woman of the cottage made a signal to the crowd; and in a moment Carafa was dragged out, and hacked to pieces. His head was borne in triumph to the market square and set up in its place; his right foot, en closed in a kind of iron cage, was fixed beneath it; and under the ghastly effigy was written this inscription: "This is the head and foot of Don Carafa, traitor to the most Faithful People."

Seldom has a more terrific spectacle of warning made the blood of men run chill.

The plot had failed. Masaniello was stronger

than ever. His escape was regarded by the people as a miracle. At the time of the attempt he had happened to be wearing, suspended by a ribbon from his neck, a coin, on which was stamped the image of the Virgin. It was plainly to this talisman that his life was owing. Henceforth he was regarded with a double honour, as the champion of the people and as the favourite of Heaven.

All thought of the Privilege had, for the time, been driven from men's minds. It was evening when the Viceroy, who had shut himself up again in Castel Nuovo, sent out a letter to disclaim all knowledge of the plot. He was probably sincere; for the Duke, had he conspired against an enemy, was more likely to have planted a stiletto in his back than to have shot him in the open. His protest was accepted. Masaniello returned word, that he proposed to ride next morning to the castle, and to have some private conference with his Grace about the public weal.

That day marked the height of Masaniello's power. As soon as it was known that he proposed to ride in public through the city the people prepared for an ovation. The houses were decked as for a day of festival. Garlands of flowers and myrtle-branches strewed the streets, and twined round every balcony and doorway. Gorgeous arras, tapestries, and banners of rich stuffs, hung out of all the windows; and every point of outlook, on window, roof and balcony, was alive with eager gazers. The procession started from the Carmine Church. First came a band of heralds, waving flags and blowing silver bugles; then troops of mounted soldiers, glittering in coats of mail; and then a company of boys and young girls, gaily dressed, with baskets in their hands, tossing a shower of flowers before the hero's horse. Masaniello had, that day, put off his humble garb; and the people with delight beheld their leader in a suit of silver satin, a hat with a gay plume, and a sword bestarred with jewels, prancing upon a steed as white as snow equipped in gold and azure. Behind him came the carriage of the Cardinal, and the sedan of his chief counsellor; and the cavalcade moved slowly to the castle, with the splendour of the pageant of a king.

Masaniello was received at the castle gates by the Captain of the Duke's Guard. He alighted, and attended by the Cardinal ascended the steps towards the entrance. In front of the portico he turned, and in a loud voice charged his followers, that if he failed to reappear within an hour, they should burst with fire and sword into the castle, and demand the reason. At this hint of treachery the people shouted fiercely. Masaniello, as he turned away, drew out of his breast a scroll of writing. It was the parchment of the Privilege. And at that sight, more eloquent than words, the great crowd roared again.

Whatever treason Ponce de Leon might be hatching—and the suspicion did him no injustice—he received his visitor with the most gracious smiles. It was agreed, without a word of cavil, not only that all taxes should be taken off, and that a free pardon should be granted to the rebels, but that Masaniello should maintain his men in arms until assent to the agreement could arrive from Spain. Finally, with many assurances of his esteem, the Viceroy pressed his enemy to accept the rank of Duke St. George, at the same time hanging round his neck, with his own hands, a chain of massive links of gold. Masaniello, having gained his ends, professed himself the Duke's most humble servant; and in this pleasant comedy the time· slipped fast away. Presently a roar was heard outside the castle. The hour was over; and the people, mindful of their pledge, were preparing, without more ado, to burst in at the gates.

Masaniello, with the Duke beside him, came out into a balcony before the palace. At the sight of

their leader safe and sound the people broke forth
into loud and long huzzas. The sight was one
which might have swelled with pride the heart of
any king. Masaniello was not loth to show the
Duke some token of his power. He called for
cheers; and the vast sea of heads below them
roared in succession at the names of Our Lady,
of the King, of the Duke of Arcos, of the Cardinal,
and of the most Faithful People. When the shouting was at the loudest, Masaniello laid his finger on
his lips; and in an instant there was the silence of
the grave. Finally, he bade the crowd disperse;
and forthwith, as if by miracle, the Largo was
left empty. The Duke could hardly trust his eyes
as he surveyed the scene.

The Cardinal had invited Masaniello to reside
in his own palace; and, in the Cardinal's carriage,
he drove thither from the castle. Throughout that
night the bonfires blazed, the guns thundered, and
the bells pealed merrily in all the steeples. And
Masaniello's power was at its height.

At its height, during two days, it remained. His
men were kept in arms; and he ruled the city like
a conqueror. It had been arranged that the ceremony which Perrone's plot had broken off should
be renewed on Saturday, the 15th of July; and on
that day, amidst a scene of pomp and splendour,

the Privilege was ratified on oath before the altar of the Great Cathedral.

And now the old monk's oracle was half fulfilled. Masaniello "had attained to kingly power." Was the latter half of the prediction now to come to pass?—was "his empire to be brief, and his fall sudden"? A strange and awful answer was at hand.

The Duke of Arcos was nursing in his brain a scheme of vengeance which, for ingenious and inhuman villainy, would have been heard with rapture by a crew of Dante's fiends. This scheme was now mature. That night, after the proceedings in the church, he arranged a splendid supper at the castle, at which Masaniello and his wife were the chief guests. There, either in a glass of wine, or as others say, in a ripe fig, Masaniello swallowed a strange poison, which had been compounded by the Duke's physician, Don Majella. This drug was not intended to take life; its effect was more terrific; it was of the nature of "the insane root, which takes the reason prisoner." The victim, when he sat down to the banquet-table, was a man of great and striking powers of mind, pre-eminently cool, wary, resolute and sagacious. When he rose up from it he was a madman!

The effect of this atrocious scheme was soon

apparent. The supper ended; the guests departed; and nothing unusual was observed. But early the next morning the people in the streets were startled at the spectacle of Masaniello, in a ragged shirt, and with a stocking on one leg, running at full speed towards the castle. At the entrance, he demanded audience of the Viceroy; the guards, who knew him, durst not bar his passage; and he made his way into the Duke's presence, crying aloud that he was starving. The false and smiling Ponce de Leon looked upon his handiwork with glistening eyes. Food was brought; but the wretched man would now touch nothing. A new whim had seized him; they would go, the Duke and he together, to Posilippo, and spend the day in pleasure. The Duke eluded the proposal on the score of pressing business; and Masaniello sailed alone in the Duke's gondola. Forty boats of minstrels came behind him. Crowds of gazers, lost in wonder, watched his progress from the shore. During the voyage he amused himself by flinging handfuls of gold coins into the water, and shouted with laughter, as the sailors dived to fetch them. At Posilippo, he ordered a rich feast to be set out; and it is said that before the boat's head turned at evening towards Naples, he had drunk twelve bottles of *Lacryma Christi*, the rich and giddy wine which ripens only on the ranges of Vesuvius. Reeling with the effects of wine and poison, he was taken to his bed. The next morning he was raving. He called for a horse, and with a bare sword in his hand, rode furiously about the streets, slashing at all who ventured to oppose him. At length, he found his way to the sea-shore. At sight of the sea he threw himself from the saddle, and shrieking out that he was in flames, rushed, dressed as he was, into the waves. But all the waters of the ocean could not quench the fire that burnt him up. As soon as he emerged, he broke into fresh freaks of violence. He swore that he would fire the city; he hurled himself, sword in hand, upon the bystanders. His own friends were forced to seize and overpower him, to bind him with a chain, and to lead him to his house, where he was placed under a guard.

The plot had been most cunningly contrived. There was nothing to excite suspicion; for the madness of the victim was easily ascribed to over-strain of mind and body, to days of ceaseless vigilance, and nights without repose. Masaniello might now be murdered almost with impunity; not as a rebel to the state, but as a dangerous madman.

Four hired men were ready to put a finish to the work of treason. Their names were Michael

Angelo Aidozzone, Andrea Rama, and Carlos and Salvator Cattaneo; the last two, brothers. Early on Sunday morning these four men repaired, with carbines in their hands, to Masaniello's house. They looked in at the door; but, to their surprise, the object of their search was nowhere to be seen. His guards were asleep; his chain lay on the floor. The madman, by whatever means, had gained his liberty, and disappeared.

Several hours were spent in fruitless search. All traces of the fugitive had vanished. Nor was it till late in the afternoon that he was seen again.

It was about five o'clock; the service in the cathedral was drawing to a close; the Cardinal was preaching to a vast assembly; when a ghastly, ragged figure, with wild eyes and matted hair, was descried upon the steps of the great altar. The figure carried in its hand a crucifix, to which, at intervals, it muttered and gesticulated. It was some time before the ghost was recognised. But it was Masaniello.

The Cardinal went up to the intruder, and, with great tact and management, induced him to be led away into the adjoining convent. He went calmly; for his violent humour had given way to a strange apathy, and he was now as docile as a child. He had not many minutes left the church when the four assassins entered it together. They soon learnt what had occurred. Attended by a small band of their own party, they followed the track of their prey into the convent.

Masaniello had retired alone into a quiet quarter of the cloisters. He was leaning from a window, and looking out across the waters of the lovely bay, over which the wind of evening was now beginning to blow coolly. The sound of footsteps roused him. He turned round quickly, with the words, "Who wants me? I am here." Before he had time to speak again, or to make any movement of defence, the four assassins raised their pieces and fired upon him in a volley. All four shots took effect. He fell back, dying, against the stonework of the window, and sank thence to the ground, with the faint cry, "Ah, ungrateful traitors!" Almost before the words were spoken, the rattle was in his throat. In another moment he was dead.

Salvator Cattaneo threw himself upon the body, and severed the head from the shoulders with a knife. A spear was brought, the head was fixed upon it, and the band of conspirators, bearing it aloft, rushed out into the streets.

Nothing could illustrate more strikingly the tremendous power which the dead man had wielded than the sensation which was excited by the tidings of his death.   The news spread like wildfire through the city.   His own followers seemed struck with stupor; his enemies went wild with fierce delight. One band rushed forth into the market-place, and took down from their place of infamy Carafa's head and foot.   Another hastened to the convent, sought out the headless body of their enemy, and haled it by a rope out of the cloisters.   The Viceroy left the castle and rode to the Cathedral, where doubtless he gave thanks to St. Gennaro for having blessed his plot.   Soon all the horde of smaller tyrants and oppressors began to crawl in swarms out of their cellars, caves, and convent cells, to feast their eyes upon the sight of the head of the terrible fisherman going up and down the city on a pole, and to have a kick at his carcase as it was dragged along the kennels.   At length the head was fixed upon a spike above the gateway of the Holy Spirit; and the body was hurled into a ditch near the Nolana gate.

Such was the fall of Masaniello.   But it was his fate to illustrate, beyond example, the mutability of human things.   And the last scene of the strange drama was not yet.

The great mass of the people still revered the name of their deliverer.   The savage violence of his madness had troubled and estranged them.   But his death struck them with consternation ; and in a few hours nothing was recollected but his greatness. Night had not come before tens of thousands were murmuring his name with blessings, and calling upon each other, with tears of shame and rage, to remember all they owed to Masaniello. The hearts of his enemies, which had been thrilling with delight, began to feel a chill; and soon their bands, which had been going up and down so gaily, vanished like mist before the gathering of the multitude. That night, preparations were set on foot for a burial worthy of a people's hero ; and before morning all was ready.

The corpse was taken from the ditch into which it had been thrown. The head was brought down from the pinnacle above the gate, and fastened to the shoulders by a thread of silver. The body, washed and drenched with perfumes, was laid, clothed in a vestment of white linen, upon an open bier, and carried to the chapel of Our Lady, where it was placed in front of the great altar. A crown was fixed upon the head, and a sceptre set in the right hand; and thus, in pomp and splendour, as at the burial of a king, the corpse of Masaniello lay in state. For many hours the crowd continued to stream past the spot ; a rain of flowers fell ceaselessly upon the body ; and the tolling of the bell, and the mournful music of the organ, were mingled with the constant sound of weeping.

At length, when the sun was sinking, the bier was placed upon a lofty car, and drawn by coal-black horses through the streets. Five days before, along that very road, the hero of the hour had passed in triumph, amid the blaze of banners and the shouting of the crowd. Now, black hangings drooped from every window; faces dark with sorrow crowded both sides of the way. Before the hearse a thousand priests, in stoles of white, walked with censers in their hands and crosses lifted; behind it, muffled drums and trumpets played a solemn march. Then came a company of men-at-arms, with spears reversed and colours drooping; and then thousands, and tens of thousands, of the people.

The solemn pageant wound its way through all the quarters of the city. At length it turned again towards the church. The organ broke forth into the last majestic service of the dead. A stone was lifted in the marble pavement; and there, with more than royal splendour, amidst the blaze of torches and the strains of solemn music, the dark house closed for ever above the dust of Masaniello.

PRINCE RUPERT

THE history of England contains few figures of a more peculiar interest than that of Rupert, Prince of Bohemia and General of the Cavaliers. The interest which belongs to his story is the interest of romance. The life of Rupert is an epic—as wild, as stirring, and as eventful as that of any of the heroes of Homer, of Mallory, or of Ariosto. In truth, with these old champions of the legends he had much in common. The interest which the details of his life excite resembles the interest excited by the exploits of Achilles, of Roland, or of Lancelot of the Lake. Like them, he moved in a constant whirl of wild adventure; like theirs, his fame is not the fame of a great general—of the brain that devises and the eye that foresees—it is the fame of the free hero who fights for his own lance. But no Homer, no Ariosto, has seized on Rupert's exploits and left them "married to immortal verse."

What may be called the first division of his life —it ended with the field of Naseby—is that part of it which bears conspicuously the colour of romance.   In its main events the story of that period is as follows :

Rupert was born at Prague in December, 1619. His race combined the splendours of two proud houses.   His mother was the daughter of a king of England ; his father, Frederic, King of Bohemia and Palatine of the Rhine, traced his grey line through Otho back to Charlemagne, and beyond him, through the dusk of ages, to the fierce Attila who was called the Scourge of God.   Rupert's birth was celebrated at an hour of passing peace. But the fiery cloud of war, then wandering over Europe, was already drawing threatfully towards his father's kingdom.   Soon the savage chime of arms began to be heard about his cradle.   The banners of Maximilian were seen shining on the slopes of the White Mountain.   The battle of Prague was fought—and lost.   The beautiful city fell.   Frederic and his queen were forced to fly ; and when at last, after months of hardship, they again found refuge, it was to look no more upon the palaces, the gardens, the bazaars, the proud spires, and the wandering waters of the fairest city in the world, but upon the dykes and fens of

Holland. The royal exiles found asylum in a palace at the Hague; and there for many years they continued to reside.

Rupert and his elder brother were sent to the University of Leyden. Rupert hated the classics; but his passion for reading books on the science of war caused him to pick up French, Spanish, and Italian readily. In the feats of the gymnasium he was soon without a rival; while his aptitude for arms was such, that at fourteen he was judged capable of commanding a regiment. With the pistol he became a deadly shot—a curious proof of which is said to be still existing at St. Mary's Church, at Stafford, where, many years after, on a wager with the King, he sent two bullets in succession through the weather-cock on the spire. Field sports of every kind were his delight. His mother had always been pre-eminently fond of hunting, and the boy, during his holidays, was sometimes allowed to join her parties. On one of these expeditions, Rupert and a favourite hound outstripped the rest of the party and became lost to sight. When the company reached the spot where they had vanished, nothing was to be seen but a pair of boots sticking out of a hole in a bank. The astonished hunters pulled at the boots, and presently pulled out the Prince, the Prince pulled out the hound, and the hound pulled out the fox. Nor were foxes' tails his only trophies. While he was still at Leyden, the Prince of Orange held a tournament for the knight-errants of his court. Rupert entered the lists, overthrew all his opponents, and was crowned at the close of the day, amidst the notes of trumpets and the shouts of thousands of spectators, by a fair lady, with a garland of flowers. He was then not yet fifteen.

It was the succeeding year that Rupert came, for the first time, to England, on a visit to the court of his uncle Charles. That court, then at the height of its gay splendour, was regarded by every sovereign in Europe with envy and despair. A king of fine artistic taste, a beautiful and pleasure-loving queen, had combined to make of it a sparkling and amusing world. It was a world in which genius was the slave of beauty. Vandyke was painting there the beautiful and noble faces, and filling his canvas with the peaked beards, the flowing locks, the plumed hats, the scarves, the ruffs, the lace collars, and the rich armour, in which his soul delighted. Ferabasco was setting knights and ladies dancing all night long to the strains of his bright and joyous music. Inigo Jones was laying out his terraces. Ben Jonson was displaying his masques.

It is true that even then, outside the palace walls, an angry sea was rising. But, hitherto, the sun continued shining, though the tempest muttered in its caves.

Into this world of pleasure Charles received his nephew kindly, welcomed him to all the amusements of the court, and even promised to provide for him. But it was not very easy to decide how this was to be done. Several plans were suggested. Laud, with fine insight both into Rupert's character and into the good of the Church, proposed to make him a bishop. Then, on Rupert's surprising refusal to deck himself in lawn sleeves and a mitre, a plan was projected for sending him as Viceroy to Madagascar, with charge to send home every year to England an argosy of oranges, sugar, spices, turtle-shells, and gold. Why this scheme fell through does not appear. Rupert himself was eager to accept it; but, for whatever reason, the expedition never sailed. It was then resolved that Rupert must pick up an heiress—and the daughter of the Duke of Rohan was the lady selected by the King. The match, however, came to nothing; and Rupert remained about the court, without any very settled prospects or position, hunting, dancing, masquing, sitting to Vandyke, and studying the fine arts, for over eighteen months.

In the meantime, affairs in Bohemia were changing. Frederic and his eldest son were now both dead. Charles Louis, the next in age, was heir to the kingdom of the Palatines, in which the rotten old Duke of Bavaria now sat. Frederic had spent the last ten years of his life in futile efforts to regain his crown; and, at his death, that mission had devolved upon his heir. But the Duke was shadowed by the banners of the Empire; and the army which, with infinite exertion, Louis had at last succeeded in collecting, did not, including a detachment of the Swedes, exceed four thousand men. With this array, however, such as it was, he resolved to fly at the throat of the old robber; and his plans for the attempt were now mature. Rupert flung himself eagerly into the enterprise. Bidding adieu to masques and hunting-parties, he crossed over to his brother's camp, and plunged at once into the smoke of war. He was placed at the head of a regiment of cavalry; and presently found himself, under the flags of battle, marching against Lemgo.

The road lay past a grim and scowling fortress, the garrison of Rhennius. Rupert, burning for battle, and careless of his enemy, was unable to resist the sight. He determined to assault the fortress with his troop of horse. The cavalry of the garrison, in twice his numbers, rushed furiously out at his approach; and then, for the first time, the spectacle was seen—a spectacle afterwards to be witnessed with wonder and terror on many a famous field—of Rupert riding at the charge. The enemy was swept away like chaff. A few fled back over the drawbridge and rushed into the town. There was not much more of real resistance than a rabble of camp-followers might have offered to the charge of the Tenth Legion.

Rupert, with colours flying and bugles singing, left the garrison to its meditations, and rejoined the cavalcade. The chief command of the expedition had been committed to Count Conigsmark; the Swedes were under a Scotchman of the name of King. Of these two officers, King was a traitor, who was only looking for an opportunity to forsake the cause; while the Count's sole thought in drawing up a battle was how to place himself most safely in the rear. It was under these auspicious leaders that the Palatines at length found themselves in sight of the spires of Lemgo, but cut off from that city by a large and dangerous body of Austrian horse.

The conduct of the two commanders, now that a battle was imminent, was exactly what might have been expected from their respective characters. King posted his infantry and artillery at a spot where they were likely to be useless, and refused to stir. Conigsmark selected a narrow defile, in which he drew up his forces in four lines, his own being the rearguard and well within the shelter of the gorge.   Hardly were his lines in order, when the Austrians, in close column, dashed upon him. Their onset broke the first line instantly; and its flying masses, hurled back upon the line behind it, wrecked that also.   The third line, which now came into action, was thus exposed at once to the rush of fugitives from its own side, and to the charge of the enemy's horse.   This line was Rupert's.

The shattered lines, instead of meeting the assailants with a charge as fiery as their own, had chosen to encounter the attack on their own ground. This was an error which Rupert was in little danger of committing. On seeing the ranks before him waver, he turned round in the saddle, and shook his drawn sword in the air. Instantly the spurs flew into the flanks of his five hundred. The charge that followed swept the enemy headlong out of the defile into the open plain.

The splendour of this exploit was extreme. It is half pitiful, half ludicrous, to relate the cause which made it unavailing. It had now become the duty of the rearguard to dart forward in support of Rupert's charge; and, had this been done, the chance of victory might have been recovered. But the disaster of the foremost lines had been enough for Conigsmark; and the Count, with a white face and a beating heart, was already retreating up the gorge at the top of his speed. Rupert was left alone and unsupported in the midst of tenfold odds. King looked on with unconcern; the enemy had time to rally; fresh troops were hurried up; and though fighting every foot of ground with desperate courage, Rupert's men were gradually forced back into the gorge. Soon parties of the enemy began to gather on the hills above them, and to steal downwards among the boulders in their rear. Nothing so much resembles the spectacle which followed as some wild story of the ancient legends. Rupert's position was desperate; his friends had forsaken him; he was caught between the devil and the deep sea. At the foot of the only standard which still reared above the tempest the colours of the Palatines, he fought till every man about him fell. Then, collecting his strength for a final effort, he burst through the swords of his assailants, and put his horse at a stone wall. The exhausted beast refused the leap, and fell back upon his haunches. Before he could recover himself a score of cuirassiers rushed up, and Rupert was a prisoner.

His first experience of the field, thus ended, singularly resembles that of every field in which, in

after years, he played a part. That day was fatal
to his cause ; but it covered his own name with glory.
And such was to be Rupert's fate through life.   He
never charged an enemy whom he did not scatter to
the winds.   At Rhennius, at Lemgo, at Worcester,
at Edgehill, at Marston Moor, at Naseby—it was
everywhere the same.   It was his singular destiny to
fight for the falling flag on every field, and to emerge
from every field with added glory.

He was now the captive of the Empire.   His
prison was appointed in the ancient Tower of Lintz
—a rock-built, battlemented donjon, black with age,
which looked gloomily upon the waters of the Danube.
Except for the loss of liberty, however, he was put
to no great hardship.   It is true that Ferdinand,
nettled at his abrupt refusal either to ask for pardon,
to turn Catholic, or to fight under the Austrian banners, put him for a short time under guard ; but
generally he enjoyed the freedom of the castle and
the castle gardens ; and in course of time he even
obtained leave of parole for three days together,
during which he was free to pay visits in the neighbourhood of the castle, to hunt the chamois among
the perilous crags which overhung the river, or to
track, among the windings of the lower valleys, a
fox, a wild boar, or a stag of ten.   Nor was the
ancient Tower a dungeon wholly given up to gloom.

Count Kuffstein, the governor of the castle, was an old soldier, with whom it was no hardship for a younger to exchange a story, or to sit down to a flask of Rhenish; while his daughter, Mademoiselle de Kuffstein, was a lovely girl, whose beauty and spirit consumed the hearts of numberless adorers for ten miles up and down the Danube. Such society, even in a prison, makes time fly; and, moreover, Rupert, even when debarred from hunting, discovered several means of lightening the burden of captivity. He studied chemistry; he played tennis; he practised with a rifle; he tamed a hare, as a present to the Lady of the Tower; he improved, with the same object, a device of Albert Dürer for drawing perspectives. He also spent much time and patience in training a magnificent white dog, of a very rare breed, whom he called Boy. This dog, who afterwards accompanied him in all his perils, became in time as well known in the field as his master, and almost as much dreaded; for when Rupert's name had grown to be a sound of terror in the ears of the Roundheads, his dog was regarded by the superstitious among them as a familiar spirit, who brought him unvarying success. Various extraordinary opinions arose respecting his nature and power. Some declared that he could swallow the deadliest poisons without injury. Some held that he was, in reality, a Lapland lady, who had been changed 'by enchantment into an animal. Some believed that he was a powerful wizard, and some that he was the devil. One thing, however, is certain — that no wizardry had rendered him immortal; for, to Rupert's infinite regret, he was killed at last in the battle of Marston Moor, in the act of pulling down a Roundhead.

The Prince had need of all his devices to kill time; for his captivity was long. Three years were wasted in negotiations for his release. At the end of that time he found himself at liberty, without other condition than his word of parole that he would not again take arms against the Empire.

Those years had covered England with a gloom that deepened. Charles had now advanced to the verge of war. The Queen was in Holland, employed in pledging the crown jewels, and endeavouring to raise supplies. Henrietta sent for Rupert, informed him that the King had appointed him General of the Horse, and was then expecting him in England. Rupert put hastily to sea in a small vessel called the *Lion*, which was driven back by a tempest and nearly wrecked. He again set sail, and landed at last at Tynemouth in the dusk of an evening which, though the month was August, was as cold as winter. Impatiently refusing to delay his journey for an instant, he threw himself on a horse and rode forward.   In the midst of a dark and frozen road the horse slipped, his rider was thrown violently against a jagged edge of rock, and dislocated his shoulder.   The limb was set by a surgeon who was luckily discovered within half a mile of the spot. But Rupert, to his great vexation, lost some hours.

At length, in spite of every misadventure, he came up with the King.   The place was Leicester Abbey.   The time was evening—the evening which preceded a momentous day.   War had not yet been finally declared.   But the next morning, upon a rising ground within the park at Nottingham, the King unfurled his standard.   An omen attended the ceremony which would have appeared to a Roman soothsayer as full of warning as a sacred chicken which refused its food, or a bullock found at the sacrifice to be without a heart.   No sooner was the standard raised than a fierce tempest blew it down. Again the heralds raised it ; and again, as if the ancient elemental powers viewed with indignation the folly of man, the tempest bore the standard away. At last it was secured with strong cords to the flag-staff on the turret of the ancient castle, and the little blood-red flag of battle which streamed above it was seen shining afar out over the windy vale of Trent.

And now, in awful and splendid succession, the

scenes of the Civil War begin to pass before us. At those scenes we shall glance rapidly, beholding, as in the rolling pictures of a panorama, a few of the varied aspects of Rupert in the field.

The Royal Horse, to which he found himself appointed, consisted of a few ranks of ragged troopers, ill-equipped with corselets, casques, and even swords. At the head of these, Rupert rode out of Nottingham. For a month he scoured the country day and night; he stormed garrisons, taxed cities, despoiled the tormented Puritans of horses, saddles, swords, carbines, pistols, armour, doublets, plumes; and at the end of that time rode into Shrewsbury at the head of more than three thousand followers, all mounted on good horses, armed with good swords, glittering from head to foot in coats of mail, gay with crimson cloaks, gilt spurs, and dancing feathers, and burning for battle with all the spirit of their chief.

With some five hundred of these troops he was resting, on an autumn afternoon, in some meadows outside Worcester. The day was sultry; the men were hot and wearied; and they were glad to take off their armour, which had become heated by the sun, and to lie down at full length in the deep grass, under the shadow of a clump of lime trees. No enemy was suspected to be at hand; no watch was kept; and the first signal of danger was given by a trooper who chanced to lift his head out of the deep herbage, and whose eye was caught by the sparkle of a coat of mail emerging from a narrow road which led towards the meadows. The alarm was just in time. A thousand horse, the picked troops of the enemy, clad in complete armour, had stolen upon them in the silence of the autumn day, and were on the point of sweeping down upon their drowsy groups. Rupert snatched a sword, leapt into a saddle, and dashed bare-headed upon their ranks. His men flew after him. Four hundred of the enemy were killed on the spot, or swept into the river and drowned. The rest flew back into Pershore in a panic of fear. While the sight of their white faces and bloody spurs was striking terror into the people of the town, Rupert, with six standards, and a rich prize of horses, went leisurely back to pick up his armour under the lime trees. He had only lost five men.

Two days later he was riding out alone, for the purpose of reconnoitring the position of the enemy. Their camp was posted on Dunsmore Heath. On the road he came up with a country fellow, who was sitting on the shaft of an apple-cart, and flogging his horse in the direction of the camp. Rupert bribed the man with a guinea, put on his smock-frock and slouched hat, took his seat on the shaft, cracked his whip, and proclaiming in a loud voice that his apples were the finest and the cheapest in the world, drove coolly into the heart of the enemy's encampment. There he inspected their position at leisure, sold his apples to the troopers, and drove the cart back to its owner, who was holding his horse in the road. Then, taking off his disguise, and giving the man another guinea, he bade him drive in turn into the camp and inquire of the soldiers, " How they liked the apples which Prince Rupert had sold them ? "

A month later, the full force of the King's army met the full force of the Roundheads at the battle of Edgehill. Rupert's share in that great action may be summed up very briefly. He won one portion of the battle. His allies lost the other.

On the morning of that day the royal troops were drawn up on the brow of the steep rising which looks down upon the Vale of the Red Horse. Below them, a wide plain stretched towards the town of Kineton ; and from the streets of the town the Roundhead army came streaming forth into the open ground. First came Stapleton's cuirassiers, glittering in bright armour ; then the troops of Denzil Holles, of Lord Brook, and of Lord Mandeville, in scarlet, in purple, and in blue. Rupert looked upon their hosts with glistening eyes. The day was Sunday; the time was the middle of the afternoon; the church bells were ringing among the elms on each side of the valley; and among the enemy the forms of the dark-robed preachers could be seen, moving with eager gestures between the armoured ranks. On the King's side, the prayer of one brave man has been preserved for us: "O Lord, Thou knowest how busy I must be this day; if I forget Thee, do not Thou forget me!" Such was the simple and noble prayer of Lindsey.

Rupert, at the head of his cavalry, rode slowly down the steep. The rest of the King's army followed, and gathered in the plain. It is said that its plumed and glittering ranks were watched from the hills by a spectator whose name is written on the scroll of fame in letters more lasting than their own. From the slopes above the valley Harvey, the discoverer of the circulation of the blood, is said to have watched, for many hours, the progress of the battle through a glass.

As the guns began to roar, Rupert, at the head of his brilliant troop, dashed forward at the charge. The ranks before him were swept back into the town in hopeless rout. Ramsay, their leader, drove the spurs into his horse and galloped towards St. Albans. Lord Wharton fled headlong into a saw-pit, from which he peeped out at intervals at the

Cavaliers despoiling his baggage, and thanked heaven that he was safe. Rupert, while his men were engaged in completing the victory and collecting the spoil, rode back, with a few attendants, to the field. He expected, as was natural, that what his wild energy had found so easy his allies had not found impossible. But the event had proved far otherwise. When he reached the field, he found the remnants of the two armies still engaged in a bitter struggle. The ground was strewn with the dead and dying; the royal standard was taken; and only a few noblemen were left about the King.

Rupert had no men with whom to charge. Night was falling; and before either side could claim a victory, darkness parted the contending armies. Lord Wharton crept out of his saw-pit, and made off to his own party. There was no moon; a biting wind was blowing; and Rupert and the King sat all that night beside a fire of brushwood, which they kept burning on the hill-side. When day dawned, the two broken armies, like two wounded wolves, lay glaring at each other, neither daring to renew the fight. When night again fell, Essex drew off his shattered forces, leaving the empty name of victory to the King.

In reality, the only victor of that day was Rupert.

The King retired to Oxford; and gradually his

court, which was now settled there, began to re-assume some likeness of its ancient splendour. Rupert had rooms in Christchurch ; and thence was to be seen, for many months, darting out at intervals, over the ancient bridge at Magdalen, to skirmish with the enemy, or to head the storming parties at the walls of towns and garrisons. At Brentford, which was the first to feel his power, his cavalry was stopped by redoubts of stones, and by barricades of carts, waggons, tables, chairs, and beds, through which poured a ceaseless fire of musketry. Rupert headed a troop of foot, tore the barricades in pieces, rushed into the breach at the head of his cavalry, and swept the enemy out of the streets. At Lich-field, for the first time in English warfare, he employed a powder-mine. The walls of the Cathedral close, within which the enemy was ensconced, were too strong for his artillery. Rupert drained the moat, constructed a mine, and filled it with five barrels of powder. While he was thus engaged, the Puritans looked over the walls in fancied safety, or entertained their leisure, after the curious fashion of the godly, within the walls of the Cathedral. They hunted a cat about the nave, baptised a calf at the carven font, pulled down the images of saints and prophets, smashed the painted windows and the gilded organ-pipes, broke up the communion plate, and set all the bells in the steeple ringing in derisive peals. In the meantime the mine was ready. Rupert waited for the fall of evening. The match was applied; a tremendous explosion was heard; a yawning gulf, filled with smoke, appeared in the walls; and the besiegers rushed in through the ruins. The enemy, in terror, instantly raised a white flag on the Cathedral, and surrendered. Rupert allowed them to march out under the honours of war.

On a Sunday morning in the middle of June his trumpets were heard ringing among the cloisters and quadrangles of the ancient city; and presently, amidst the cheering of the people, Rupert and his cavalry were seen riding out across the bridge and through the city gates. He first fell upon Lewknor, an outpost of the enemy, where he seized a great number of horses, arms, and prisoners. Thence he pushed on through Chinnor, where he stormed another outpost, and came up with the main body of the enemy at Chalgrove Field. There he drew up his cavalry in a wide cornfield bounded by a hedge; and in this position he waited, while the enemy, pouring down the slopes of Gelder's Hill, advanced on the other side of the dividing barrier. Presently their skirmishers began to fire their carbines between the roots of the low fence of thorn. That sound was Rupert's signal. He instantly rushed over the hedge at the head of his men and scattered their ranks to the winds.

It was in attempting to resist this charge that Hampden received the wound that caused his death. No reader of Macaulay will have forgotten his pathetic picture of the dying patriot, as " with his head drooping, and his hands resting on his horse's neck, he moved feebly out of the battle." Within six days he was a corpse.

In the meantime Rupert rode back to Oxford. His troops were followed by a long train of prisoners, horses, captured standards, and baggage-waggons heaped with spoil. The huzzas of the townspeople and the smiles of the court ladies which greeted his return, could not be said to be undeserved. Within a space of forty-eight hours from the time he started he had ridden fifty miles, taken two outposts and many standards, fought and won a pitched battle, killed both the officers who opposed him, left a great number of the enemy dead on the field, and lost of his own party only five men.

Some time after this, Lord Essex, with a body of troops, was passing through the forests of Auborn Chace, eager to reach Newbury before the King. No enemy was suspected to be at hand, and the earl rode carelessly through the flowery glades. The turf was soft and spongy, and the fall of a horse's hoof awoke no sound. Very suddenly a troop of riders, noiseless as a flight of phantoms, appeared among the distant beechen boles and came sweeping over the turf upon his ranks. The ghosts were Rupert and his cavaliers.

A sharp encounter followed. Essex was beaten back to Hungerford, and the King reached Newbury before him.

At sunrise the next morning, the two armies marched out to the encounter. The strife was bitterly contested. All that day the fight went on. Night fell; the losses on both sides were deadly; yet the victory was undecided. The King, with the fragments of his army, retired into the town. The enemy, equally broken, prepared to snatch a few hours of rest, for the trumpets were to sound for retreat at break of day. But twelve hours of desperate fighting had not sated Rupert. In the silence of the night he stole about the sleeping town, and mustered, by the gleam of the watch-fires and the torches, a small band of men and horses. Moving out with these in the grey light of morning, he caught the enemy in a defile, as they toiled away beneath their baggage, cut down a great number of them, and would have killed or taken many more, but that his men were dropping out of their saddles with weariness, and their horses falling down at every step.

It is in such adventures, of which these are but specimens of events that happened daily, that Rupert is best seen. In the great battles of the war, though his personal achievements were not less, his glory was eclipsed by the disaster of his allies. It is not by these that we can judge him rightly. And yet we cannot bring ourselves to turn away without one glance at the two great fields which were to follow—the fields of Marston Moor and Naseby.

Marston Moor! No battle-scene in history is more impressive than that which is conjured up before the mind at the name of that famous field. As we pronounce the words we see again, as we have seen them in a hundred pictures, as we have read their story in a hundred pages, the sombre circumstances of that great fight. We see the sun setting in angry splendour, dyeing all the clouds with blood; we see the fields of yellow rye in which the Roundheads were drawn up, and the gorse-bushes and the broken ground which was the station of the King; we see the air dark with brooding storm; we hear the fierce hymn rolled from the ranks of the Roundheads, mingled with the boom of thunder; we see Rupert, in his scarlet cloak, facing the grim battalions of the Scots; we see Cromwell, yet an unrisen meteor, praying at the head of his fierce host; then we see the wild charge of Rupert, and the ranks of the Tartans whirled away before him like the leaves of winter; and then, in the gloom of storm and darkness, the heart of the King's battle breaking before Cromwell.

It was Rupert's constant fate—and it was so at Marston Moor—to find that while the enemy had been flying like deer before him, his companions had been flying before the enemy; and so it was to be again at Naseby.

It has been often stated that in that last great contest of the war, Rupert faced the forces of Cromwell, and was beaten back. This is an error. Rupert and Cromwell—the unconquered champions of their parties—never met. It is true that at Naseby Rupert eagerly sought Cromwell; but Cromwell had taken the right wing, while Rupert believed that he was stationed on the left. Rupert on that day, as ever, scattered his opponents to the winds. Then believing, as at Edgehill and at Marston Moor, that the victory was won, he rode carelessly back to the field, and reined his horse on the crest of the overlooking hill. He instantly discovered his mistake. There in the vale below him he saw Cromwell, at the head of his men, with his helmet knocked off, and the blood streaming down his face from a wound above the eye, driving the Cavaliers in wild disorder among the low bushes of a rabbit warren. He saw the King strive to rally his men for a last charge. He saw an attendant lay his hand on the King's bridle, and turn away his horse's head.

Of what followed we are able, from descriptions which have come down to us, to form a singularly exact idea.

Rupert spurred his horse into the press, and fought his way to the King's side. They rode together from the field. On the crest of the rising ground which overlooked the plain they drew rein for a moment, and cast a last glance at the scene below them. The Roundhead soldiers, drunk with victory, covered the whole field with a raging flood of men and horses. Such of their own party as were not riding off the ground were either lying among the heaps of slain or huddled together in groups of guarded captives. Mingled with the sombre banners of the Puritans, in which five Bibles were displayed against a ground of black, there could now be seen shining above the hosts of the victorious enemy the crimson folds of the Royal Standard, and the snow-white silken ensign of the Queen. From that sight the two spectators turned away their eyes, and rode silently together into the falling night.

The war was over. Rupert had ridden his last charge in England.

The scenes at which we have been glancing, briefly and rapidly as they have passed before us, may have perhaps attained the purpose of denoting in what light the figure of Rupert ought to be regarded. He is usually dismissed by historians with the remark that his character lacked the essential qualities that make a general great—foresight, patience, tactics, discipline. But it is not as a great general that we think of Rupert. The interest which surrounds his figure is of a different kind. He is one of the free seekers of adventure. His forerunners are the ancient heroes of romance : Achilles whirling in his chariot ; Eviradnus darting into the cave of Hugo the eagle-headed ; Roland, with his sword Durandal, defying the ten kings. Such are the fit comparisons of Rupert in the field —such are the companion pictures which arise before the eye of fancy, as it views his black flag flying over conquered cities, or his white plume shining in the front of battle.

BENYOWSKY

OTHELLO'S narrative sums up, with singular exactness, the story of the strange career which we are now about to trace. The history of the Count de Benyowsky is a tale

> "Of most disastrous chances,
> Of moving accidents by flood and field,
> Of being taken by the insolent foe
> And sold to slavery."

It is a tale which, as it tells

> "Of his redemption thence,
> And portance in his travel's history,"

whirls the reader round the globe, through every kind of peril and adventure, through scenes that change at every instant like the aspects of a dream. It is this swift succession of events, so varied and so striking, that imparts to Benyowsky's story its peculiar colour of romance. He is the Candide and the Monte Christo of real life.

He was born in the year 1741 at Verbowa, the family estate in Hungary, was baptized by the names of Maurice Augustus, and, as the son of a magnate, was brought up at the court of Vienna. The fortunes of his early years were well adapted to call forth his character. His father was a general of the Emperor's Horse; and the boy, being destined for the same profession, received at fourteen the rank of lieutenant, marched against Prussia, and fought in four pitched battles before he was seventeen. While he was absent in Lithuania, his father died, and he became the Count de Benyowsky. But his brothers, during his absence, seized on his estate. He instantly flew home, raised and armed a party of his vassals, and drove off the birds of prey. But the interloping heirs had friends at court. He was accused as a rebel and a rioter. His castle and domains were taken from him by the State and given over to the clutch of the usurpers. In anger and disgust he turned his back upon his country, and having a desire to study seamanship, repaired to Amsterdam, and thence to Plymouth. There he found time to learn, not only how to sail a ship, but how to play a game of chess, and how to twang the harp.

He then resolved to see the world; but as he was about to step on board a vessel bound for the West Indies, the States of Poland sent him an appeal to join their confederation against Russia.

His bold, restless, and adventurous spirit leaped at the proposal. He crossed to Warsaw, took the oaths, and held himself in instant readiness for action. But before he was required to draw his sword he chanced to fall into a fever, while staying at the house of a gentleman of Zips named Hensky, was nursed back into health by his host's three daughters, fell in love with one of them, and married her. The honeymoon was scarcely over when he was summoned by the States to Cracow, which a Russian force was marching to besiege. Without venturing to tell his bride where he was going, he tore himself from her embrace, and rode away upon that fatal enterprise which was destined to prove fruitful of so many strange vicissitudes.

Benyowsky was now twenty-seven ; a soldier and a sailor, master of a handsome face and figure, a constitution made of iron, a manner which, according to occasion, could sway the minds of men or steal away the hearts of ladies, a ready wit, a tongue which spoke six languages with equal ease, a spirit to which peril and adventure were as the breath of life. Such a man was likely to turn out a dangerous enemy. And so the Russians were to find.

He arrived at Cracow just as Count Parrin, with the Russian force, appeared before the walls. He was at once appointed colonel-general of the cavalry ;

and speedily his troop of horse became a name of terror. Provisions from the first were scarce, and soon ran very low. Benyowsky dashed out of the town, stormed and took the fort of Landscron, and fought his way again into the city with thirty prisoners, a herd of oxen, and sixty baggage-waggons heaped with grain. The Russians, stung with rage, drew close their lines of siege. In vain. Benyowsky, with his troop, stole out at dead of night, swam across the Vistula, gained the open country, collected waggons in the villages, and loaded them with spoil. The point was then to lodge them in the town. It was three o'clock at night, and a dim moon was rising. Benyowsky placed the convoy with a party under Baron de Kluscusky, set himself at the head of the remainder, and dashed upon the camp. The Russians, as he expected, flew forth like angry hornets. His charge was beaten off, half his little band were killed or taken, and he himself was cut down from his saddle, wounded in two places, and secured. But meantime the Baron had slipped softly through the lines, and the waggons were all safe within the city.

Benyowsky was ransomed for a thousand pounds —a disastrous bargain for the Russians—and returned into the town. When next he issued forth, he was alone and in disguise ; but six hundred troopers were prepared to join him at a given signal. He made his way to Lublau Castle, beguiled the governor with a glib pretext, and looked about him at his leisure. His plans for seizing on the fort were ready, his six hundred men were on the march, when their commander let the secret slip within the hearing of a spy. The spy flew with the tidings to the governor. Benyowsky was instantly made captive, and sent in irons to the Russian general.

A band of his own troops released him on the road. At the head of these he set himself to scour the country, his ranks swelling as he went. The Russians, in reprisal, put a price upon his head, and sent out a party to secure him, dead or living. Benyowsky kept his scouts on the alert, concealed his infantry in a wood beside the road near Sokul, and himself lay watching with his troopers opposite, behind a little hill. All one day and half the night he lay in ambush. At length, in the grey light of morning, the scouts came rushing in. The enemy, three thousand men, were marching down the road. Benyowsky watched his moment, darted out of his retreat, and killed or captured the whole party.

At last a troop of Cossacks came upon him by surprise at Szuka. They had with them a howitzer, stuffed to the muzzle with old iron, stones, and rubbish. This piece was fired off in the skirmish, and Benyowsky was struck down by the hail of missiles. Stunned, bruised and bleeding from no less than seventeen wounds, he was seized by the exultant enemy, and carried off in chains.

And then began his tribulations.

Wounded as he was, no surgeon was allowed him. He was fed on bread and water; he was forced to march all day in heavy chains. His guards at first were bound for Kiov; but discovering when they reached Polone that their prisoner was dying, they were obliged to leave him in the hospital. As soon as he began to mend, his chains were once more fastened on him, and he was conducted to the dungeon of the city fortress.

The dungeon was a den, far underneath the ground, where eighty captives were cooped up together. No ray of light could penetrate the darkness; sighs, groans, the noise of clanking chains alone disturbed the silence. The den was never cleaned; the foul air cherished pestilence; and in one corner stood a pile of noisome corpses, which grew larger day by day. Within this fetid hole, dolorous as a pit of the lost souls in Malebolge, Benyowsky wore away three weeks of living death.

On the twenty-second day of his captivity the survivors, leaving thirty-five dead bodies in the den, were led forth into the Place of Arms, where several hundred prisoners were assembled. These were chained in rows together, and started on the march to Kiov. The hardships of that journey were such as would have tasked a strong man in full health ; and Benyowsky was half-famished, wounded, limping on a crutch. The roads were steep and rugged ; but the prisoners were beaten forward by the guards like cattle. To increase their miseries, the commander of the guards turned out a greedy thief, who stole the prisoners' bread, sold it, and put the proceeds in his pocket. At nightfall, he accepted from the villagers, among whose huts the prisoners ought to have been quartered, petty bribes to leave them undisturbed ; and Benyowsky and his fellow-captives were lodged on the bare ground and left to shiver in the snow and rain. The result was such as might have been expected. The road was strewn with dead and dying. Out of near nine hundred prisoners who left Polone, less than a hundred and fifty scare-crows crawled, half-alive, into the gates of Kiov.

Benyowsky, on arriving, fell into a fever, and for ten days was raving in delirium. The moment he began to mend he was sent forward to Cazan. There he was lodged in the house of a goldsmith named Vendischor, and found himself at liberty to move about the town, to pay visits and make friends.

A bold idea struck him; he would organise in secret all the exiles in the city, attack the governor and the garrison, and regain his freedom *vi et armis.* He went instantly to work. One by one conspirators were sworn; the design grew, and promised well; when one night two of the intriguers quarrelled. One of them went straight to the governor, revealed the whole plot, and named Benyowsky as the leading spirit.

The next night, about eleven o'clock, as Benyowsky was just stepping into bed, a loud knocking was heard at the street-door. He lighted a candle, wrapped himself in a dressing-gown, went downstairs, and opened the door. An officer with twenty soldiers stood without, who had been sent to take him. A curious freak of fortune saved him. The officer, who did not know his features, took him for a servant, and demanded whether the Count de Benyowsky were within; then, without waiting for an answer, he snatched the candle from his hand, and darted up the stairs to seize his prisoner. Benyowsky, left alone below, took in the situation at a glance. He drew his dressing-gown about him, and slipped away into the night.

He hastened to the house of Major Wynblath, one of the companions of his plot. The two resolved to risk their lives on a bold venture. They stole

out of the town, procured horses at the nearest village, and giving out that they were officers with
despatches from the governor of Cazan, got safely
to St. Petersburg. There they found a skipper due
to sail next day for Holland. They booked a passage
with him for five hundred ducats, and arranged to
meet at midnight on the bridge across the Neva.

Midnight came ; the fugitives were at the bridge.
The skipper was behind his time ; but in a few
minutes they descried him coming. He appeared to
be alone ; but as he stepped up to Benyowsky, twenty
soldiers started out of the darkness at his back
knocked them both down, and made them fast. The
honest skipper had been seized with a suspicion, and
had sold his passengers for a round sum to the
police.

Benyowsky, separated from the Major, was conducted to the fortress and locked up in a solitary
cell. The place might have been a dungeon in the
Tower of Famine. For three days not a soul came
near him. He had neither bread nor water. When
at the close of the third day a gaoler entered with a
pitcher and a crust, he found a gaunt-eyed spectre,
weaker than a child.

The ghost was dragged before the Council,
questioned, and again remanded to his cell. But
his fate was sealed. Ten days later, in the dead of

night, an officer with seven soldiers opened the cell-door, clothed him in a dress of sheepskins, loaded him again with chains, and led him forth. Outside the fort, a two-horsed sledge was waiting. Benyowsky was placed upon it, a soldier took the seat beside him, and the horses instantly flew forward into the darkness of the night.

By the tinkling noise of sledge-bells on the road behind him, the Count judged that he was not alone; and when day dawned he discovered that the train was one of sixteen sledges, which were carrying six prisoners, under a guard of Cossacks, across the vast Siberian regions of eternal ice to lifelong exile in Kamchâtka.

The distance from St. Petersburg to Kamchatka is, as the crow flies, full four thousand miles. The journey through that arctic wilderness was, at the best of times, a task of many months and of the bitterest privations. Sometimes the exiles were so happy as to pass a night among a nest of Tartar huts; but in general they encamped among the snow. When provisions were in plenty, they broke their fast on fish or horse-flesh, with a pitcher of mare's milk; but more than once they were reduced to birch-bark sopped in water, while the horses fed on moss. At first their course lay over boundless level plains of snow, broken here and there by grim low hills and swept by icy whirlwinds, over which they passed in sledges, sometimes drawn by horses, sometimes flying at the heels of elks. Then the road ran through gigantic woods and over mountains where no sledge could travel, and where they tramped on foot, frozen with the cold and dropping with fatigue. On one such mountain-top two of the conductors sank down beside the way, and never rose again. Thence they moved through rugged passes where the sledges could be only drawn by dogs. To drive a team of dogs requires much practice; and so Benyowsky, who knew nothing of the art, discovered to his cost. More than once sledge, team, and driver went rolling down a precipice together from a height of sixty feet. Luckily, the snow was soft and yielding; and man and beast were hoisted out again, scared, bruised, and shaken, but with no broken bones.

At last, in spite of every misadventure, they arrived at Okotsk on the coast, whence they were to cross by ship to the peninsula of Kamchatka. They embarked; the ship weighed anchor; but scarcely was she out of sight of land when the captain and the officers broached a brandy-cask, and speedily were all as drunk as pipers. The mate was in the hold in irons; and in this position of affairs a storm sprang up, which raged with increasing fury every hour. The crew were helpless; no officer was capable of giving orders. In the middle of the night, the mainmast sprung. The captain, roused by the uproar, came tumbling up the hatchway from his drunken sleep, was struck by the falling wreck of spars, knocked down the steps, and broke his arm. The shock aroused him to a sense of danger; and, finding that the Count could navigate the ship, he gave him charge of her, and went below. All that night Benyowsky kept the ship before the wind. Next morning the gale slackened. A stay was stretched from the mast's stump to the bowsprit; a foresail was rigged up; and Benyowsky, finding the ship manageable, began to think of attempting to escape. He first endeavoured, but in vain, to gain the crew. Then he placed a lump of iron on the binnacle, which falsified the compass, insomuch that the ship appeared to sail due east, when in reality she was sailing south. How this device might have succeeded is not known; for unluckily a gale of wind sprang up from the southwest, which drove the ship directly to Kamchatka, and into the harbour of the river Bolsha.

The prisoners were disembarked, and taken up the river in a boat to the town of Bolsoretskoy Ostrogg. Here they were conducted to the fortress, and the rules of their life in exile were explained to them. They would be set at liberty, supplied with a musket, a lance, powder, lead, an axe, knives, tools for building cabins, and provisions for three days, after which they were expected to maintain themselves by hunting, in the dreary wastes, ermines, wolverines, and sables. Every exile was compelled to report himself once daily to the guards ; and disobedience to a guard was punished by starvation.

The little village of the exiles was situated at a league's distance from the town. It consisted of eight cabins, in which lived fifty men and women. Thither the Count and his companions were now led, and were received into the huts of their fellow-exiles until they should be able to build cabins for themselves. Benyowsky was quartered in the hut of M. Crustiew—a person of much influence among the exiles. That evening, as they sat before the fire, with brandy, tea, and caviare beside them, Benyowsky began to sound his new companion on the chances of escape. Crustiew had a few books in his cabin, among which was *Anson's Voyages*. It was natural that such a book should have suggested the sole project of escape which in truth was possible. To attempt to cross the awful wilderness through which they had come thither was quite hopeless. But Crustiew believed that it might be possible to seize a ship, and to escape by sea. Benyowsky listened; and from that moment the design was never absent from his mind.

Next day the governor, whose name was Nilow, sent for Benyowsky to the fort. An agreeable surprise awaited him. Nilow, hearing that the Count spoke several languages, desired to appoint him tutor to his family, which consisted of three daughters and a son; Benyowsky being still to occupy his cabin in the exile village, but to be exempted from the duties of his comrades, and to receive the pay and rations of a soldier.

The Count accepted the proposal with great willingness. But the scheme had a result which neither he nor Nilow had foreseen. Next day he met his pupils, gave them their first lesson, and afterwards amused them with an account of his adventures. The youngest girl, Aphanasia, a lovely damsel of sixteen, listened as Desdemona listened to Othello, and with a like result. Aphanasia fell in love with Benyowsky.

Chance, as it happened, was to throw them still more intimately together. Aphanasia's mother desired her to learn music, and Benyowsky undertook to be her music-master. Unfortunately, the Count could only play the harp; and no harp existed in the whole peninsula. Benyowsky, in this predicament, volunteered to make one. He formed the frame of wood, twisted strings of deers' gut, and produced an instrument which, although in his own phrase "not very lively," enchanted all the people at the fort, and Aphanasia most of all. She and her harp thenceforward were inseparable companions; and her passion for the giver fed itself in secret, and grew stronger day by day.

Nilow, a drunken brutal despot, had betrothed his daughter to a rich Kuzina, as drunken and as brutal as himself. ؛Benyowsky heard this story. He could not marry her himself; but he determined, if it were possible, to rescue her from the Kuzina, whom she detested heart and soul.

Meantime, he chanced to make acquaintance with a Hetman of the Cossacks named Kolassow, who had lost large sums in playing chess for wagers. Discovering that Benyowsky was a skilful player, Kolassow matched the Count against two wealthy merchants, Casarinow and Csulosinkow. Benyowsky was to play a set of fifty games against whatever champions these two might choose to bring. The games were played; the stakes were heavy, and Benyowsky and his backer swept in several thousand roubles. But this result, though gratifying, was one which very nearly cost the Count his life.

Csulosinkow was the first who took his losses

badly. One night he lay in wait, together with his cousin, as Benyowsky was returning to his cabin. The pair sprang out upon him, armed with knives and bludgeons. Benyowsky had no weapon but a stick, and at the first onset he was badly wounded. By good fortune, with one blow he split the cousin's skull; and at that Csulosinkow fell upon his knees and roared for mercy. Benyowsky let him go,—and himself crawled homeward to his cabin, where during the next ten days he lay in bed. The cousin died.

Casarinow took a stealthier method of revenge. On New Year's Day the prisoners arranged a humble festival among themselves. Casarinow sent them, on the occasion, a present of some sugar, which the exiles put into their tea. The sugar had been poisoned; and in a few minutes the whole company were rolling on the ground in horrible convulsions. Benyowsky, who had only sipped his cup, found himself quaking like a man with ague. Copious draughts of whale oil gave the sufferers relief. But one of them, who had drunk largely, died on the spot, while another recovered only from the jaws of death.

The sugar was suspected. A sample, wrapped up in a piece of fish, was tested on a dog and on a cat. The animals went into strong convulsions, and in ten minutes both were dead.

Next morning Benyowsky called upon the governor, and accused Casarinow of the crime. Nilow was at first incredulous; but Benyowsky hit upon a simple proof. Casarinow was invited to drink tea at the fort that afternoon. He came; the tea was brought, and Casarinow was about to put it to his lips when Nilow mentioned, with a careless air, that he had received his sugar from the exiles, who had passed it to him as a New Year's gift. Instantly Casarinow turned as white as ashes. "Why, Casarinow," said his host, "you look ill. But drink; the tea will cure you." The wretched man put down the cup, and turned away. His guilt was manifest. Nilow made a sign, the guards rushed in, and he was seized and dragged away to prison.

This adventure was well over. But another cause of trouble was at hand. One of Benyowsky's fellow-exiles, Hippolitus Stephanow, had caught a glimpse of Aphanasia, and had lost his heart. Bursting with envy, he saw the Count rise into favour. Thenceforth, to plot and cavil against Benyowsky became the business of his life. He began by insulting him among the exiles; then he challenged him to fight. The Count accepted. The assailants met with broadswords, and Stephanow was speedily disarmed. Benyowsky spared his life; and Stephanow broke into a flood of gratitude, which afterwards, as will be seen, turned out to be worth nothing.

While these events were passing, the Count's resolution to escape had never for an instant faltered. He had formed, in secret, a council of the exiles, of which he was himself the ruling spirit. He was waiting only for an opportunity to play a desperate game; and at last the chance arrived.

A captain of the name of Csurin was in harbour with his ship, with which he was engaged to sail to Okotsk. Csurin had fallen in with a damsel of Kamchatka, whom he desired to carry off; but he durst not sail to Okotsk, where a process was abroad against him on a charge of having mutinied two years before. In this predicament Benyowsky gained his ear. It was not difficult to persuade a desperate man to share the lot of men as desperate as himself. It was agreed to man the ship with Benyowsky's comrades, and to escape, if possible, together in the darkness of the night.

The risks of the attempt were great. And everything depended on success. If the attempt failed, the adventurers would wear away the remnant of their lives in chains and dungeons, and the last state of their captivity would be bitterer than the first. Yet a chance so golden could on no account be missed. Benyowsky resolved to get on board, if it were possible, without awakening suspicion— but, if he were discovered and opposed, to fight to his last man, and either reach the ship or perish.

Preparations for the attempt at once began. But before everything was ready an incident occurred which nearly ruined all.

Ivan Kudrin, one of the conspirators, proposed, like Captain Csurin, to carry off a wife. The object of his choice was Aphanasia's maid. In deepest secrecy he told his charmer of his purpose. She, bursting with importance, revealed it to her mistress; and Aphanasia heard for the first time of Benyowsky's project of departure.

By this time, Aphanasia regarded Benyowsky as her lover. In this the Count was certainly to blame. His thoughts of Aphanasia, it is true, were those of perfect honour. He intended, if she chose to join the exile's wives, to take her with them, and to save her from her fate with the Kuzina. But he had never told her that he could not be her lover—that he had left a bride behind him—a bride whose image in his mind, through all his dangers, led him like a star. When Aphanasia, drowned in tears, now burst upon him, crying aloud that she was wretched and forsaken, he told her his proposal for her safety; but he still told her nothing more. It is not easy to acquit the Count of dealing lightly with a singularly pure and simple heart.

Aphanasia, however, was delighted. She vowed, not only to be secret, but to send him a red ribbon, should any sign of danger become apparent in the fort.

A few days passed—and the red ribbon came. By whatever means, the governor's suspicions were aroused. He was preparing to arrest the conspirators in a body !

The Count instantly made ready ; the exiles were assembled, arms in hand, in Benyowsky's cabin. It was a desperate enterprise ; and the hearts of the little band beat high within them, as they awaited the beginning of events which were to end in death or freedom.

The day—the 20th of April—was closing into dusk, when a corporal with four grenadiers was reported to be approaching from the town. The corporal came up to the cabin-door and called on Benyowsky to attend him to the fortress. The Count thrust his head out of a window and in a pleasant voice invited the corporal to step in and drink a glass of wine before they started. The corporal loved a glass of wine. He entered. Instantly the door was shut, four pistols were presented to his breast, and he was bidden, on his life, to summon his soldiers one by one into the hut. As they entered, they were seized and bound ; and in three minutes all five men were lying safely in the cellar.

Four hours passed ; it was nine o'clock, and almost dark, when a strong body of soldiery, armed with a cannon, was announced to be approaching. A single cannon-shot would have sufficed to blow the hut and all within it into atoms. Benyowsky called upon his comrades. Filled with the fire of men whose lives were in their hands, they rushed forth upon the foe. The soldiers, panic-stricken at that furious onset, left the cannon and raced like hares into the neighbouring woods.

Dragging the cannon with them, the conspirators stole forward to the fort. The sentinel, seeing in the dusky light a troop approaching with a cannon, imagined that his own companions were returning. He gave the challenge ; but Benyowsky, with a pistol in his hand, bade a prisoner return the counter-word. The man obeyed ; the sentinel let fall the drawbridge ; the exiles rushed across it, blew down the grating with a petard, and burst into the fort.

Then the fight was fierce and brief. Nilow, refusing to accept his life, was in the act of firing his pistol at Benyowsky, when he was struck down.

The guards, of whom twelve only had been left within, were killed or taken. And the fort was in the hands of the exiles.

By this time all the town was rising—at least three hundred Cossacks were in arms; and soon a storming-party, with Kolassow at its head, appeared before the gate. But the ramparts were alive with fiery eyes, the bridge was up, the castle-guns were roaring. Kolassow was compelled to change his tactics; he drew off beyond the reach of shot, to the heights which overlooked the castle, and prepared to starve them out.

But the Count was ready with a counter-scheme. No sooner was Kolassow gone, than he sent a band of men into the streets to gather the women and children together in the church. Nearly a thousand were soon mustered, and locked in. Chairs, tables, railings, doors, were broken up and piled at the four corners of the building. Three women and twelve girls were then despatched as envoys to Kolassow, announcing that unless the Cossacks instantly laid down their arms, the building would be set in flames and every soul within it perish.

Benyowsky had relied on the bare threat to prove effectual; but time passed, and still Kolassow gave no sign. Benyowsky bade a pile be kindled. In an instant, as the flames shot up, the heights became alive with handkerchiefs and white-fluttering flags of truce. Soon fifty Cossacks, fiery-hot with haste, came racing in advance, crying aloud that all the troops were following, and had laid down their arms. The aspect of the flames—mere idle menace as it was—had wrought like magic. The Count received into the fort as hostages fifty-two of the chief townsmen, and ordered the church-doors to be thrown open.

And now the Count was lord, not only of the castle, but of the town itself. He was able to complete at ease his preparations for the voyage.

He had, during the assault, received a wound in the right leg; and he was forced to lie in idleness for several days. Stephanow, his ever-watchful enemy, chose this moment for an act of spite. He sent Aphanasia a letter, informing her that Benyowsky was already married, and offering himself as the avenger of her wrongs.

Had Stephanow achieved the object of his letter, Benyowsky would have been but justly served. But Aphanasia's passion was of that pure, self-sacrificing kind which is more common in romance than in real life. She went to Benyowsky, showed him the letter, and demanded of him, in reproachful accents, wherefore he had feared to tell her all. Her only wish was to be near him; since she could not be his wife, she would be his daughter—or rather, for the present, she would be his son. In order that she might be more useful on board ship, she meant to put on a boy's dress. Aphanasia had her way. On the morning of departure she appeared on board, lovely, like Jessica, "in the garnish of a boy." In accordance with her change of sex, her comrades changed her name, and from that moment she was called Achilles.

It was the 11th of May 1771, when the exiles, ninety-six in all, embarked on board of the *St. Peter and St. Paul.* Every other ship in harbour, which might be used in the pursuit, was set in flames. The hostages were sent ashore, the flag of Poland ran up to the peak ; and a salute of twenty cannon, thundering from the port-holes, proclaimed that the bold slaves had gained their freedom !

And then began "the moving accidents" of sea.

The ship stood out of harbour among masses of rough ice, through which at times a way was only to be forced by firing cannon at the floes. At night, the deck was covered with a sheet of ice two inches thick ; and huge fires, flaming round the masts, were required to thaw the sails, which froze as stiff as iron. In spite of all precautions the vessel, battered by the floating bergs, sprang a leak ; the pumps had to be kept going day and night ; and before the rift was stopped the crew were dropping with fatigue. Then the water-barrels froze and burst; Benyowsky was compelled to limit the supply; and thereon Stephanow, still ripe for mischief, stirred up certain of the crew to mutiny. These men, in search of water, tapped a brandy-barrel by mistake, drank themselves into a frenzy, and staved in every water-cask but two. When, next day, the mutineers grew sober and realised their folly they turned on Stephanow in fury, and would have hanged him from the yards. The Count, however, once more saved the life of his insidious enemy; and Stephanow was made a scullion.

But the mischief was achieved. The ship was nearing warmer regions. No land was in sight; and food, as well as water, ran so low that a little bread made out of salted fish ground into powder was all that could be served out daily. Famine forced the crew to strange expedients. At one time beaver-skins, chopped into mince-meat, were stewing in whale oil; at another, twenty pairs of boots were boiling in the pot. On the 14th of July—nine weeks after their departure—the ship was still a fortnight from Japan; and the water was all gone.

And now, for the first time in his career, Benyowsky gave up everything for lost. Ill health, following on his wound, had shaken him; and he believed that he was dying. He resigned his office as commander, gave some last instructions, crawled into his hammock, and lay down to wait for death.

But in the middle of that night the Count's dog Nestor was seen standing on the forecastle, thrusting out his nose at the horizon, and barking like a dog gone frantic. Nestor was a prophet. When day dawned, a line of land was lying like a cloud on the horizon. It was a desert island, rich in fruit and game. In an hour the crew were shooting goats and boars, breaking open cocoa-nuts, and munching pine-apples and bananas in the wild and lonely woods.

The water-casks were filled; the ship's larder was replenished; and the sails were once more given to the wind. A fortnight later the ship sailed safely into Usilpatchar Bay; and the voyagers found themselves surrounded by almond eyes and yellow faces, gaudy fluttering dresses and twirling parasols.

Benyowsky waited on the king. He found that potentate seated on a yellow sofa in a rich saloon, apparelled in a robe of blue and green, and girdled with a yellow girdle. The king received the Count with great hospitality. The visitor was invited to a royal feast; and Benyowsky tried, but tried in vain, to eat a bird's nest with a pair of chop-sticks. In return, he taught the monarch how to use a musket, with which his majesty, to his infinite delight, killed a horse at the first shot.

The king presented Benyowsky with a jewelled sabre, a string of pearls, and a box of gold and gems. The ship revictualled; and the voyagers stood away for China.

Twelve days later they touched in passing at the island of Usmay Ligon. Benyowsky put to land in the ship's boat. A high sea was running; the boat was swamped, and the crew were swept into the surf. The Count was dashed upon a rock, and was with difficulty dragged by his companions to the shore, where for some time he lay senseless, and to all appearance dead. But brandy and assiduous chafing were at length effective. His eyes opened, and he returned to life.

The natives of the island had been civilised to some extent by a Jesuit missionary named Ignatio Salis, who had lived long among them. Ignatio was now dead; but his memory was still held in the profoundest reverence. His breviary, borne upon a carpet, was regarded as a talisman; his ashes rested in an earthen urn upon the altar of the nation's savage temple. The present chieftain was a captain of Tonquin who had been Ignatio's fellow-worker. This man, whose name was Nicolo, received the voyagers with great kindliness, placed huts at their disposal while the ship was undergoing some repairs, and did his best, indeed, to persuade Benyowsky to settle with him on the island. But for his wife at home Benyowsky might have yielded. He replied, in fact, that he must first see Europe, but that very probably he might then return.

At this the natives shouted with delight. Nothing could content them but that Benyowsky should select a bride among the native beauties, to whom on his return he might be married. In the court of Nicolo's house the old men of the tribe were seated in a circle. Seven women, veiled from head to foot, led forth into the circle the seven fairest virgins of the nation. The robes of these dark beauties were of silver satin, girdled with blue zones; their locks were loose and streaming, and were garlanded with flowers. Benyowsky was provided with a scarf, which he was enjoined to cast upon the object of his choice. The Count, with much apparent circumspection, cast the scarf at one of the fair seven. Instantly, her companions began to dance about her in a circle; and Benyowsky found himself betrothed to Tinto Volganta, which is by interpretation, the Luminous Moon.

Again the ship set sail. Two days afterwards she touched Formosa. An exploring party landed, and came across a tribe of natives, headed by a Spaniard, Don Hieronimo Pacheco, whose appearance must have strikingly resembled Robinson Crusoe's in his dress of skins. This man's history was itself a dark and strange romance. He had been a Grandee of Manilla, had surprised his wife in the embraces of a priest, had plunged his sword into the hearts of both, had fled in a small vessel manned by six of his own slaves, had landed at Formosa, and during the last seven years had been a savage chief. Don Hieronimo came on board the ship, and welcomed Benyowsky with great friendship. But meantime a party of the crew on land had come across a hostile tribe ; and presently the ship's boat was seen returning from the shore with several of the crew stuck full of arrows, and three men dead or dying at the bottom.

Benyowsky had not meant to tarry at the island. But the slaughter of their comrades roused the crew to fury. The Count and Don Hieronimo put their men together, descended on the hostile tribe, slew a vast number of them, and burnt their village to the ground.

Prince Huapo, one of the greatest chieftains of the country, seeing this achievement, offered Benyowsky a rich prize to march against his enemy, Prince Hapuasingo. The Count accepted this proposal, marched with forty men upon the nest of wigwams which Hapuasingo called his city, seized him as he was hiding, like Achilles, among his women, and brought him back a captive. Huapo, in his gratitude, presented Benyowsky with a massy pile of silver, gold, and jewels. This barbaric treasure the Count shared among his followers. "A generous gift "—as he remarks in point—" is worth a thousand speeches, of whatever eloquence."

Once more the sails were spread ; and thence the ship made way without adventure. A few days later, on the morning of the 22d of September, she sailed safely into the harbour of Mecao. The escape was finally accomplished ; the voyage was at an end.

Benyowsky claimed protection from the flag of France, and at once obtained a passage on the *Dauphin.* But before the exiles separated two misfortunes fell upon him. Stephanow, who had taken service with the Dutch Company, broke open the Count's chest, robbed him of all the presents and mementos which he had gathered on the voyage, sold them for a trifle to a Jew, and disappeared. This calamity, however, was nothing to the deep affliction which now overtook him. Aphanasia, the angel of his deliverance, his adopted daughter, was seized with a swift fever, sank, and died.

With this grief upon his spirit, Benyowsky

sailed for France. He landed, waited on the Duc d'Aiguillon, and was at once invited to enter the French service. The Count accepted the proposal, and sent off an equerry to bring his wife from Zips. Through all his perils and adventures—in the battle against Russia, in the den at Cazan, with the snow-surrounded sledges, among the exiles' cabins, in the lands of savage tribes—her form had ever been a pole-star, cheering, guiding, glittering before his inner eye. She came with all the speed that could be urged; and what that meeting was must be imagined.

The Duc d'Aiguillon, at the King's desire, proposed that Benyowsky should proceed to Madagascar, with the design of planting on the island a French settlement. No proposal could have better suited his adventurous spirit. A ship was fitted out; three hundred men were sent on board; and on the 22d of March 1773, the Count, together with his wife, set sail from Europe. It was the last and strangest venture of his life.

The ship first anchored at the Isle of France. The Count was armed with letters to the governor, who was charged to aid the expedition with all requisite supplies. But Benyowsky, on handing in his papers, found himself received with howls of rage. The merchants of the Isle looked jealously on the projected settlement, which threatened to interfere with their own trade. Impediments of every kind were brought against him ; and at length he was compelled to sail for Madagascar, without the stores he had expected, and with faint prospect of receiving more.

He landed at Louisburg in Antimaroa. And his calamities at once began.

That night the native chieftains, twenty-eight in number, came, attended by two thousand black retainers, to listen to his scheme. To this assembly Benyowsky painted in a speech of glowing colours the profit to be gathered from a trade with France. The dusky kings appeared to acquiesce, drank a barrel of the settlers' brandy with yells of approbation, and dispersed. But next day all was changed. A chief named Siloulout demanded to confer with Benyowsky in a neighbouring wood. The Count sent forward spies ; three hundred men were lying in an ambush, ready to murder him on his arrival. Benyowsky, with a troop, burst suddenly upon them, and sent them flying to the winds. Next day the river was dyed red with the heavy-fruited branches of the tanguin tree, which turned the water into deadly poison. Benyowsky cleared the river, burnt down all the tanguins in the district, and once more cheated his insidious foes. But thenceforward ceaseless vigilance was needed; and there were dangers against which no vigilance could avail. The climate, at that season, was, to Europeans, almost as perilous as a poisoned stream. A little village of log-huts was built with toil, together with a fortress and a hospital. The hospital was soon required. The air was charged with fever, the stores were poor, the stock of drugs was scanty, and the colonists, by some strange oversight, had with them no physician. At one time Benyowsky and his wife, both stricken by the fell miasma, were lying at death's door together. From the Isle of France no aid could be obtained. The recruits sent out, ostensibly to swell the little force, turned out to be thieves and cut-throats from the dungeons, or dying men out of the hospital. And in this position the tiny colony was compelled to keep perpetually alert against the Saphirobai and the Seclaves, two tribes which every day grew bolder and more insolent.

For several months the struggle was kept up with heroic resolution. But disasters thickened; the natives could be kept at bay no longer; the complete destruction of the settlers seemed inevitably at hand; when an event, unexcelled in strangeness among all the visions of romance, in an instant changed the scene as by enchantment.

Benyowsky had brought over from the Isle of

France an old half-crazy negress called Susanna, who had been sold in childhood to the French. Among Susanna's fellow-captives had been the daughter of the Ampansacabe, the supreme king of Madagascar, Ramini Larizon. The race of Ramini were both seers and kings. They traced their proud descent from a kinsman of Mahomet, the Great Prophet; and their power over their subjects was almost that of gods. Since the death of Larizon sixty-six years before, there had been no heir to take the rank and office. His daughter, indeed, had, during her captivity, borne a son; but the boy had become lost to sight; and the great and sacred name, at which fifty thousand dusky worshippers had once hushed their breath, now seemed to have become extinct for ever.

But now there came a marvel. The lost heir was rediscovered. By certain marks which could not be mistaken, Susanna, who had lived in serfdom with his mother, had recognised his person. A vision from on high impelled her to proclaim the tidings. Raving like a prophetess in frenzy she began to cry aloud a word which made the ears that heard of it to tingle. The lost heir was Benyowsky!

The strange hallucination spread like wildfire. The tribe of the Sambarives, to which the Ramini belonged, rose up in tumult. One of their chiefs,

Ciewi by name, was instantly despatched, attended by two hundred tribesmen, to invite the Count to take possession of his ancestral throne; and Benyowsky, at the very moment of despair, saw himself hailed king of fifty thousand savage warriors, every man of whom regarded him with an awe and reverence far stronger than the love of life.

He instantly accepted the position. The French had, in his eyes, betrayed and wronged him. He sent in his resignation to the Service, took off his uniform, and put on the skins and feathers of a savage king. The ceremony of his installation must have been a truly striking scene. Thirty thousand warriors were drawn up in a circle, tribe by tribe, in the midst of a vast plain, having the women in the outer ring. Before each tribe an ox stood ready for the sacrifice. Seven chiefs conducted Benyowsky from his pavilion to the plain; and as he came before them, the great multitude flung themselves together on their faces. The oxen were then slaughtered, the heads of spears were dipped in blood, and on these the warriors took the oath of loyalty by licking with their tongues the scarlet points. An aged chief placed in the new king's hand an assegai by way of sceptre; and once again the vast assembly fell together on their faces, before the feet of the great white Ampansacabe.

Nor was his royal spouse without her dignity. That same evening, before the beginning of the dances which were to last all night, the women of the tribes swore fealty to Queen Benyowsky, to obey her in all quarrels in which men had no concern.

Such was the last strange change in Benyowsky's fortune. He had been a captive in the lands of everlasting ice; he was now the sovereign of a kingdom where no snowflake ever fell. His power over his black subjects was supreme. It was for him to use it well. A scheme of great and wide beneficence arose before him. He resolved to civilise his nation; to found, in his own right, a trade with Europe; to bring into the island farmers, carpenters and blacksmiths, who should teach his people how to build and plough. With these objects, he resolved himself to visit Europe. The empire was committed to a council of the chiefs; a brig, the *Belle Arthur*, was obtained and fitted for the voyage; and amidst the tears and cries of the vast dusky throngs who followed with their eyes his fading sails, he put once more to sea.

At this point the Count's own *Memoirs*, which thus far we have been following, break off. The brief remainder of the story must be gleaned from various sources. The broken pieces, set together, come to this—

The ship reached Europe safely. But the Count could find no State prepared to aid him, at the risk of war with France. He then resolved to try America; and at Baltimore he made arrangements with a firm of merchants, who supplied him with a vessel, the *Intrepid*, of four hundred and fifty tons and thirty guns; in which, with a rich cargo, he spread his sails again for Madagascar.

His wife, who was in weakly health, he was compelled to leave at Baltimore. She never saw his face again.

Instantly on his arrival in his kingdom, he declared hostilities against the French. At the head of his black warriors, he first seized their storehouse at Angoutci. He then set off, attended only by a hundred men, to storm their factory at Foul Point. But the French had there a ship with sixty troopers, of which he had received no warning. On the morning of the 23rd of May 1786, they landed, and attacked him.

The Count had barely time to throw up a redoubt, defended by two guns, when the enemy were upon him. The affair was over in a moment. He who had escaped alive out of so many perils had now reached his last. As the French rushed forward, firing in a volley, a musket-bullet struck Benyowsky in the breast. He instantly sank back behind the rampart. His black troops, seeing their king fall, fled panic-stricken ; and the French soldiers, bursting over the redoubt, seized his dead body by the hair, and dragged it forth into the open ground.

TAMERLANE

A SPECTATOR standing on a minaret of the mosque
of Samarcand, in the summer of the year 1336, with
sight purged like Adam's when the angel touched
his eyes with euphrasy that he might view the
kingdoms of the world, would have surveyed, for a
thousand miles around him, the landscape of half
Asia :—north, west, and east, the boundless waving
grass-plains of the *Steppes*, with the herds and black
tents of the Tartars clustered on the banks of rivers,
or moving like dark clouds across the wilds; south-
east, beyond the mountain-walls, the pleasure-houses
of the Rajahs by the waters of the Indus, the pagodas
of strange idols, and the mausoleums, vast as
palaces, which starred the vales of Hindostan;
south-west, across the Province of the Sun, the
realms of the once splendid Caliphs, with the gilded
peaks of Bagdad lifted from its myrtles, and farther
still, beyond the silver thread of Tigris, the cedars
of Lebanon and the tomb of Christ.   Then the

gazer's eye, weary with wandering over countless kingdoms, might have alighted, in the plains of Samarcand beneath him, on the tents of a tiny shepherd-tribe, and a baby resting on its mother's knee. That child was Tamerlane—our hero; the boy predestined to arise like a destroying angel, to challenge every ruler in that vast expanse, from the fierce kings of Kipchak to the plumed and glittering hosts of Indian princes, and to take them all into the hollow of his hand.

The boy was born on the 8th of April 1336. His father, Teragay, was chieftain of the Berlass tribe, a clan of shepherd-warriors, whose village of tents wandered in the plains of Kesh. Teragay, a man of piety and quiet life, was the familiar friend of a sheik of noted sanctity, Shems-addin; and to Shems-addin the child was taken to receive its name. The mage chanced at the moment to be reading from the Koran—"Are ye sure that he who dwells in heaven will not bid the earth devour you? Lo, *it shall shake!*" As he pronounced in Arabic the last word, *Tamuru*, Shems-addin stopped and said, "The child shall be called *Timour*."

Timour grew up in his father's tent. Both the Berlass village and its population were what the vagrant Asiatic tribes have been from times before Attila. Their tents were pitched upon a chosen spot as long as pasture lasted ; when pasture failed, the village vanished, and embers, bones, and carrion vultures marked the place where it had dwelt. The tribesmen—shepherds, hunters, fighters, all in one— spent their lives on horseback, sometimes driving to fresh plains their goats and camels, sometimes shooting boars and antelopes, or hunting lions with their long Tartar bows, and sometimes flying in a cloud of dust to battle with a hostile tribe. Timour could ride and draw a bow almost as soon as he could walk. As a chieftain's son he also learnt to read, and at nine he could repeat the daily service of the mosque and spell a chapter of the Koran. At twelve his cast of character had already shown its ply. He was the little king of his companions ; his games were battles ; his playmates were his subjects, his soldiers, and his slaves. At seventeen, he was the boldest horseman and the keenest hunter in the tribe. But his vigour of body was less extra- ordinary than the fierce and restless workings of his mind. Nature had bestowed upon him the imagina- tion of a poet, almost of a madman. Sometimes he fell for days together into trances, which perplexed the wisest fakirs, during which he saw strange visions, and from which he could only be aroused by burning in the hand. Visions also, coloured by a vast ambition, often startled him from sleep. On one occasion, the Great Prophet stood before him and declared that seventy-two of his descendants should be kings. On another, he imagined that he cast a net into the sea, and dragged it to the shore alive with crocodiles. The interpretation, to his mind, was easy; the sea was the emblem of the world, and the crocodiles were the rulers of it. Another vision altered for a time his whole existence. He dreamed that he was sitting in a waste of rocks and thorns, surrounded by beasts, fiends, and frightful human creatures. These evil beings were his own bad passions. He started from his sleep in agitation, and for some months vowed himself unto austerity. He placed his conscience in the charge of sheik Zyn-addin; and the holy man bound round his waist his own shawl-girdle, and placed upon his finger a cornelian ring, engraven with the motto *Rasty va Rusty*—Righteousness and Salvation. Had this humour lasted, a vision would have changed the history of the world.

But it was not to last. Timour indeed throughout his life continued to see visions and dream dreams. Astrologers and seers, omens, verses drawn at hazard from the Koran, continued to the last to influence his most important actions. But it was not as an Ishan saint that he was destined to expend that restless energy of mind and body which would have made him the most holy dervish who ever shook his wild hair over his glittering eyes and danced and howled himself into a frenzy.

In one vision of this time, he found himself astray in a green wilderness, in which a palace rose amidst a garden full of flowers and fountains, trees and singing birds. Within this palace men on golden seats were sitting, with open books before them, wherein was written the destiny of every child of earth. Timour demanded to be told his own. But before the answer could be given he awoke—and, behold, it was a dream.

The record of those visionary volumes to which he sought to listen is the story which we are now about to call to mind. Their mysterious pages contained few more striking.

At the age of twenty-one, his father sent him as an envoy to the court of Samarcand. The reigning prince was Ameer Kurgan, a fierce old chief of the Zagatays, who had pulled the former sultan from the throne by force of arms. Timour's spirit and address completely won the heart of the old warrior. Kurgan had a grand-daughter, a princess of the name of Aljay Aga. He proposed that Timour should receive this damsel as his bride, and make his home at Samarcand. Aljay Aga was a maid of beauty and high spirit. Timour was enchanted;

and the wedding was celebrated with great splendour.

For three years Timour lived at Kurgan's court. His time was mostly spent in hunting, with now and then a burst of battle. More than once the thread of his career came very near to being cut off short. Once, while following a deer, his horse plunged head-first down a well, and he escaped as by a miracle. At another time, while hunting in the desert, a fierce snow-storm burst upon him; he lost his way, and after hours of wandering was perishing of cold, hunger, and fatigue, when he espied a gleam of firelight streaming from a cave. A group of shepherds who were sitting round their fire, over which a pot was boiling, received him as a guest, took off his hunting-boots and quiver, wrapped him in a horse-rug while his clothes were drying, and fed him back to life with steaming soup. At another time, he put in peril his own life to save the king's. Kurgan's son-in-law, a wretch named Kutlog, hired six desperadoes, with whom, during a hunting party, he lay in ambush, and sprang out upon the prince. Timour alone chanced to be at hand. He threw himself before the aged chief, and with his single sword beat off all seven assailants until help arrived.

Kutlog, with his men of blood, took flight into

the mountains. But a few weeks later, while Timour with his troop was absent in Khorassan, he heard with rage and horror that Kutlog had descended from the hills, had plunged a dagger into the king's heart, and had set himself upon the throne of Samarcand.

Timour instantly arrayed his men. Two other chieftains joined him—Hajy Berlass, his own uncle, and Byan Selduz, leader of the Oulus. These three chiefs marched straight to Samarcand, drove Kutlog and his crew into the wilderness, and shared among them the whole empire, as three equal kings.

But Timour's hour of fortune had not yet arrived. He was first to eat the bitter bread of tribulation.

Scarcely were the three kings settled on their thrones than Tugloc Khan, the fearful chief of Cashgar, marched from his illimitable wilds against them. Ere long the swarming tents of his fierce hosts blackened the banks of the Jaxartes. Resistance was a dream. Timour marched to meet the mighty despot, eager only to make terms. Tugloc at first received him as a vassal ; but Tugloc's son, a prince named Alyas Khwajeh, picked a quarrel with him ; and thereon Tugloc marched to Samarcand and set Alyas on the throne. The reign of the three kings was over. A price was set upon their heads. Hajy Berlass fled into Khorassan, where he was murdered by a robber. Byan Selduz had already drunk himself to death.

Timour, with his wife, her brother Hosein, and a band of about sixty followers, rode for their lives into the desert of Carisme. Their hope was to evade pursuit. But as they halted on an eminence, and looked behind them, a cloud of sand was seen on the horizon; and soon within the cloud appeared the flash of arms. Tugloc's captain, with at least a thousand men, was spurring hard and fast upon their track. To fugitives with women—for Hosein's wife was also with them—escape by flight was hopeless.

But it is not safe to press too hard a man of Timour's breed. He instantly drew up his little army, and wheeled round at bay. In the red light of sunset, the pursuers, confident in numbers, came sweeping forward in a flood of men and horses— and in an instant a fierce fight was raging. That fight was worthy of a minstrel's song. It was a fight all fire and daring. The loss was sore on both sides; but, when the sun sank, seven of the little band still kept the field against a hundred and twenty of their foes. An arrow wounded Hosein's horse; it plunged and threw him; and he was forced to take his wife's, who mounted behind Aljay Aga. In this order, as night fell, the seven surviving heroes, shooting their arrows as they went, drew slowly back into the gloom and vanished.

All that night they pushed into the wilderness. When day broke they were alone in the great waste. Hunger and fatigue had spent their strength; but by great good luck they found a desert well, and within its small oasis a goatherd with his flock. The wanderers bought a goat, roasted it between flat stones, ate and drank and rested till the evening. But they were not yet safe from danger of pursuit, and when the moon rose they pursued their flight. Next day, they fell in with a roving tribe, from whom, by payment of an armlet set with rubies which Timour wore upon his wrist, they bought three horses. Thence for two days they wandered through the wild. And now their plight grew yet more grievous. They discovered neither game nor desert wells. Nothing appeared except the mirage spreading its spectral waters, and the hot sand-pillars stalking giantlike before the wind.

At length, on the third day, they came upon a ruined village, in which they found a well. There they pitched their solitary camp, and for some weeks managed to subsist by trapping the wild beasts and birds that wandered to their spring.

In all this Timour had one consolation. Aljay Aga, his young wife, possessed a soul as fiery as his own. Amidst their bitterest afflictions she knew, like him, no drooping of the spirit. Such a companion on the road to empire was worth a squadron of armed men.

But their calamities were not yet ended. One night a tribe of savage Turcomans came by surprise upon the little camp. The fugitives were seized and bound, and dragged as prisoners to their captors' huts. Timour and his wife were thrust into a crazy hovel used for stabling camels; and there, for two long months, they were kept captives —half starved, half naked, and half devoured alive by swarms of vermin.

From such a depth of wretchedness—wretchedness by comparison with which a wild beast in a cage is happy—was the Shaker of the World to make his way.

The camel-house was kept by a strong guard. Timour strove at first to bribe his sentries; but he had only promises with which to tempt them, and he strove in vain. He then resolved upon a desperate venture. He watched his moment, hurled himself upon a sentinel, wrenched the weapon from his hand, and flew with such fury on the others that they raced before him. Ali Gurbany, as their chief was named, was lounging in his tent, when to his inexpressible amazement the rout of guards came flying panic-stricken into his presence, with the prisoner at their heels.

It was Timour's purpose to appeal to Ali Gurbany in person. But this feat of arms spoke for him. At that sight the savage chief was moved to admiration and to the magnanimity which awakens in the fiercest breasts at the sight of a brave deed. He sent for horses, placed the prisoners upon them, and bade them go in peace.

Once more Timour was a wanderer. But now the tide of destiny had turned. He gained in safety the margin of the Oxus; parties of his old companions joined him; and in a short time he was master of a hundred men. With this handful, he proclaimed himself the sovereign of Transoxania, the deliverer of the country from the hosts of Cashgar; and thenceforth his battle-standard, a crescent topped with a red horse-tail, was to be seen from far off shining in the wilderness, and calling every fugitive to arms.

The wandering warriors flocked in thick and fast. With a band of these, Timour stormed a fortress of a savage tribe of Beloochees in Seistan. In the rush along the rampart he was badly wounded. Two fingers of his right hand were lopped off; and he received a thrust in the left foot which crippled him for life.

It was from this mischance that he received the name by which he is best known. From Timour-lenc, the Arabic for Timour-lame, has sprung the form of Tamerlane; by which familiar title we shall henceforth call him.

While his wounds were slowly healing, crowds were swarming to the scarlet horse-tail. By the time he was himself again, six thousand warriors thronged round it. With this army he resolved to march against the fierce invaders. It was a desperate enterprise; for the enemy numbered at least thirty thousand. But the greatest victories of the world have been achieved in spite of numbers. And so it was to fall out here.

The armies met near Koondooz, on the Oxus. From noon till nightfall the fight raged; but at sunset the victory was still undecided. In the middle of that night, as Tamerlane was resting in his tent, a figure like an angel stood before him, and uttered in a clear voice, " Timour, victory is thine!" Tamerlane sprang up, formed his army for the charge, burst upon the camp of the invaders, and dispersed it to the winds.

Alyas Khwajeh tore his beard with rage and shame; but rage and shame were idle. Pressed by the conqueror at every step, he drew slowly back to the Jaxartes, and vanished into Cashgar.

A victory so splendid covered Tamerlane with glory. He was hailed as the saviour and the sovereign of the land. Rivals, of whom Hosein, the companion of his flight, turned out the fiercest, rose in vain against him. One by one he beat them down beneath his feet. In 1369, he was enthroned at Balkh. In the presence of a vast assembly of the chiefs, the fakirs, and the tribes, he bound about his waist the royal zone, and set the crown of empire on his brows. The princes, in the gorgeous custom of the East, showered over him a rain of gold and gems; and the great crowd, flinging up their hands, broke forth into a thunder, "Behold, behold the master of the world!"

Amidst the splendour of the installation, Tamerlane, as was his custom, sought an omen from the Koran. The page opened at these words: "God to whom he chooses gives the kingdom, and from whom he chooses takes away the realm."

The domains of Samarcand, a realm five hundred miles in length and breadth, might have appeased an ordinary ambition. But Tamerlane had taken as his motto the tremendous maxim, *There is one God of heaven—and there shall be one prince of earth.* He bent his eyes upon the neighbouring kingdoms, and he resolved to have them all.

And in truth he was marked out to be a conqueror.

The fame of his great exploits, his imperial aspect, his gigantic strength, his eyes of fire, his voice pealing like a battle-trumpet, all rendered him the idol of his soldiers and the terror of his foes.   His piety, his visions, his omens from the Koran, his custom of lying rapt in prayer all night before a battle, with his face against the ground of his pavilion, persuaded his believers that his projects were inspired by heaven, and certain of success. Fables of superstition soon crept in to magnify the terror of his name.   His suit of armour had been forged, in ancient days, by David, king of Israel. His finger-ring contained a wizard's opal, which turned colour when a lie was spoken.   In the hour of battle a celestial flame was wont to blaze upon his brows.

His camp, which had once consisted of a few black tents, began to grow into a gorgeous city. That camp was Tamerlane's true capital, and for thirty years his home.   His moving palace, an immense pavilion of red satin decked with arabesques of gems, together with his mosque, an edifice of gold and azure, with a turret and a flight of steps, went with him on his farthest marches; each dragged along by two-and-twenty oxen, on cars of which the wheels were twenty feet apart, and the axles like the mainmasts of a ship.   The aspect of the tented city, as it moved in warlike splendour on the march, exists before us in the tale that Prince Feramorz told to Lalla Rookh. Such was the aspect of the camp at which the Prophet of the White Veil trembled :

" Where are the gilded tents that crowd the way,
  Where all was waste and silent yesterday ?
  This City of War, which in a few short hours
  Hath sprung up here, as if the magic powers
  Of him who, in the twinkling of a star,
  Built the high-pillared walls of Chilminar,
  Had conjured up, far as the eye could see,
  This world of tents and domes and sun-bright armoury !—
  Princely pavilions, screened by many a fold
  Of crimson cloth, and topped with balls of gold ;—
  Steeds, with their housings of rich silver spun,
  Their chains and poitrels glittering in the sun ;
  And camels, tufted o'er with Yemen's shells,
  Shaking in every breeze their light-toned bells !

" But yestereve, so motionless around,
  So mute was this wild plain, that not a sound
  But the far torrent, or the locust-bird
  Hunting among the thickets, could be heard.
  Yet hark ! what discords now, of every kind,—
  Shouts, laughs, and screams are revelling in the wind !
  The neigh of cavalry, the tinkling throngs
  Of laden camels, and their drivers' songs ;
  Ringing of arms, and flapping in the breeze
  Of streamers from ten thousand canopies !—
  War-music, bursting out from time to time
  With gong and tymbalon's tremendous chime."

Such was the camp, and such the leader, that now set out to wander over Asia, and to gorge themselves with thirty years of victory.

The six books of Sheref-addin tell in full the story of those years. But here their endless scenes of siege and battle must sweep rapidly before our eyes. We see the camp go forth against the Kings of Persia; we see the fall of mighty cities, Ispahan and Shiraz, Ormuz, Bagdad, and Edessa; we see the enchanted shores of Tigris and Euphrates, from the ocean to the hills, brought under the dominion of the conqueror; we see army after army fly before him; we see great kings and sultans—Mansur, Ahmed, Ibrahim, Mozuffur—stoop their heads into the dust. The speed or tardiness with which they kissed his carpet saved or cost their lives. Ibrahim of Albania appeared before him with peace-offerings, robes, horses, gems, and slaves; the gifts, according to the Tartar custom, consisting of nine items of each kind. But Tamerlane observed that there were eight slaves only. "Where," he demanded, "is the ninth slave?" "I myself," replied the kneeling prince, "am he." The ingenuity of the surrender delighted Tamerlane; and he restored the kingly flatterer to his throne. Indeed, a flash of wit was certain of his favour. At Shiraz, Hafiz, the sweet singer of the rose and nightingale, appeared before him. " Are you," demanded Tamerlane, "the bold poet who presumed to offer my great city Samarcand for the beauty-mark upon your lady's cheek?" "I am," replied the minstrel, "and by such lavishness I have fallen on evil days, and am beholden to the bounty of great kings." Tamerlane laughed, took the hint, and gave the ready bard a bag of gold. But vastly different was the fate of those who ventured to defy him. Then his fury rose to madness; then appeared the true barbarian, brother of the wolf and tiger; then the terror of his vengeance shook the hearts of those who saw it. At Ispahan, when he received the keys, he spared the citizens from death or plunder. A party of them, notwithstanding, raised a riot in the night, and slew a number of his men. Tamerlane, in frenzy, gave the city to the sword, cut off the heads of sixty thousand of the people and built them into a monumental pile above the tomb of his slain soldiers. Spectators of that Tower of Warning found it hard to say whether by day or night it was most horrible ; by day, when swarms of vultures flapped about it, or sat sleepy and full-fed upon its summit ; or at nightfall, when the turret, with its grinning heads and ghastly birds, became apparent in the weird and fearful light of its own death-flames.

From the cities, the gardens, the palaces, and the treasure-towers of Persia, Tamerlane turned to the vast wilds of Kipchak. Tocatmish, ruler of the countless tribes that wandered in the *Steppes*, had, during his absence, harassed and put in fear his lands on the Jaxartes. Attended by a host that measured thirteen miles from wing to wing, Tamerlane set out towards the Caspian. Upon the crest of Ulog Toc, a lonely hill, from which the vast plains stretched on all sides to the sky, he reared a lofty pyramid, as a memorial of his march. Thence for five months he moved through a great solitude. The whole host lived by hunting; and at times the ration of each soldier fell to half a bowl of broth a day. At last the encampment of the khan appeared in sight—a force far vaster than their own. But Tamerlane relied on stratagem. He sent a spy into the hostile camp, with charge to bribe their standard-bearer. The man was gained, and, at the instant when the fight was fiercest, he turned his standard to the earth. At that sight, the signal of defeat, his comrades fled in panic, and Tamerlane was master of the field. The swarms of prisoners, the mighty herds of goats and cattle, which fell into his power, transformed the plains into a living sea. Before he turned his steps, he passed a month in hunting in the rich vales of the Volga, took the towns of Azof, Serai, and Astrachan, marched north so far that Moscow trembled, and saw, with infinite amazement, the strange gleam of the Aurora Borealis make the nights as bright as day.

For some time Tamerlane was occupied with the affairs of his vast empire. But soon his eyes were turned upon the tempting realms of India. In vain his chiefs and emirs murmured at his madness. In 1398 he marched with sixty thousand men towards the defiles of that mighty range of mountains which spring, barren and black, above the plains of Balkh. The ravines were haunted by fierce mountain-tribes; the precipices were a thousand feet in depth. But the army was let down the rocky walls by ropes from ledge to ledge, upon a stage of planks with iron rings; and the mountain-robbers, amazed at such a prodigy, raced in terror to their caves. The host crossed the Indus, marched to Delhi, and stood in arms before the gates. The sultan, at the head of fifty thousand soldiers and a herd of elephants whose tusks were armed with poisoned swords, rushed forth upon them. Tamerlane drew up a troop of camels, each loaded with a bunch of hay, which at the instant of attack was set on fire. The elephants, in terror at the flames, wheeled round and fled; and in a moment the whole army was in rout. The gates of Delhi were thrown open;

and Tamerlane, in triumph, took his seat upon the sultan's throne. The elephants, which fell into his power, served well to carry treasure; and a troop of ninety, loaded with the spoils of Delhi, were seen, a few months later, pacing through the streets of Samarcand.

While Tamerlane, who had advanced from Delhi towards the west, was hunting on the margin of the Ganges, Bajazet, Sultan of the Ottomans, was rising to a dazzling pitch of power. His fiery vigour, which had gained for him the name of Ildrim, or the Lightning, had been displayed on many a glorious field. The congregated hosts of Christian princes had come forth against him; and he had trailed their proudest banners in the dust. His career, for fourteen years, had been in Europe what that of Tamerlane had been in Asia. Such was the man who now aspired to match himself with the great conqueror.

From India Tamerlane marched back to Samarcand in triumph, advanced to Syria, sacked Aleppo and Damascus, and sat down before Angora. Bajazet marched to raise the siege; and on the 8th of June 1402 the two giants met. Then came one of the great battles of the world; but the star of Tamerlane maintained its splendour. Bajazet fell; and the only rival who might hope to smite the towering crest of Tamerlane was now a captive in his hands.

The fate of the fallen Ottoman is variously related ; it is certain that he died, a prisoner, within a year. According to the well-known story the great Turk was shut up in an iron cage and carried with the conquering army as a public spectacle. Nor is there in all history a more tragic picture of the mutability of earthly greatness than that of the fierce prince, whose nod had been the law of nations, and whose name the terror of vast armies, huddled in his narrow prison, gazed at by the gaping rabble, glaring like a wild beast through his bars, and eating out his heart in fury and despair.

Tamerlane marched slowly back to Samarcand. And now the man who once had been a desert wanderer had attained the height of earthly glory. One by one, his hand had grasped the crowns of seven-and-twenty kings. Asia, from the Volga to the Persian Gulf, and from Damascus to the Ganges, was under his dominion. In that vast region, which before his reign was torn in pieces among scores of petty princes, all was now tranquil and at peace. The camel-drivers, who once went in constant fear of desert robbers, now steered across the solitudes in perfect safety their caravans of pearls from Ormuz or of satins from Pekin. Samarcand, the royal city, gorged with the wealth of Persia, Syria, India, had grown into a splendour never seen in Cairo or Bagdad. But nothing could appease that fiery spirit. A new ambition seized him. He fixed his eyes upon the mighty Chinese empire—an exhaustless source of treasure. Nor was wealth its single object of temptation. A raid on the celestial land might be termed a holy war; and the victors, loaded with the spoils of hideous idols, might build the mosques of the true prophet upon the ruins of their shrines.

Preparations for the enterprise began. While they were going forward, Tamerlane decreed at Samarcand two months of triumph, revel, and repose.

Just at that time, an embassy from Spain arrived at court. One of the ambassadors, Ruy Gonzalez de Clavijo, has left a vivid picture of the scene. The Spanish knights, though reared in all the splendours of the West, gazed with amazement at the vast barbarian city—at the mosques and terraced palaces, at the gardens, rich as paradise, in which thousands upon thousands of pavilions, rosy, azure, and snow-white, stood glittering in the sun, at the festal tables of pure gold, the goblets rough with rubies, the silver dishes which three men could hardly carry, the showers of coins and golden rings which hailed upon the guests, the pyramids of meat, and the countless jars of precious wines. The king received them in the portal of a noble palace. At his side a fountain threw aloft its sparkling waters, in which red apples were kept dancing. He sat cross-legged upon a broidered carpet, strewed with silken cushions. His robe was of rich satin ; and he wore a lofty turban of snow-white, decked with a ruby and a ring of gems. His queen was not then with him ; but a few days afterwards the envoys saw her. How she looked and walked—how fifteen waiting-ladies bore her train of gold and crimson— how a spearman held her silken awning—how her face was plastered with white lead to shield it from the sun, until it looked like paper—how the crown upon her long black hair was like a castle made of gems, from which a white plume floated—all is depicted in Clavijo's record. Nothing struck the strangers with more wonder than the queen's pavilion, in which a golden table, with a top of solid emerald, was overshadowed by a tree exactly similar to those which charmed Aladdin in the Genie's garden—a tree of which the leaves and branches were of gold, the fruits of single rubies, pearls, and sapphires, and among the boughs of which sat golden birds expanding wings of gems.

Such is the true barbaric love of splendour. Yet

Gibbon's observation surely errs: " After devoting fifty years to the attainment of empire, the only happy period of his life was the two months in which he ceased to exercise his power." For the deep and true delight of Tamerlane was not in the magnificence of langour, but in the roving camp and the fierce splendour of great armies, in the fire of battle and the captured diadems of kings.

But now the standards were unfurled for his last march. On the 8th of January 1405, Tamerlane, attended by two hundred thousand fighting men, rode out of Samarcand towards the Chinese Wall. Thick snow was falling; and so bitter was the frost that the host passed over the Jaxartes on the ice. Three hundred miles from Samarcand the camp was pitched at Otrar; but it was fated to advance no farther. From Otrar, on February the 17th, a crowd of messengers flew forth with news that shook all Asia. The great conqueror was dead!

Exposure to the winter tempests had brought on a fit of ague. Draughts of icy water with which, in spite of his physicians, he assuaged his thirst, increased the evil. The fiery spirit which had been so long the terror of the earth was doomed to strive in vain with the Dark Angel. In a few hours all was over.

The body of the mighty emperor, embalmed, and

drenched in rose-water and musk, was placed in a casket of ebony, and laid, where it was fit that it should lie, within the walls of Samarcand. It was the city which his power had made the wonder of the world. It was the city under the walls of which, sixty years before, the boy had roamed among his father's tents, and dreamed his dreams of empire.

MARINO FALIERO

On the evening of the Thursday before Lent, in the year 1355, the Palace of the Doge of Venice was flaring with the lights of a masqued ball. A festival was in the ocean-city. The gondolas of all her proudest palaces shot everywhere across the glistening waters ; and every gondola set down a gorgeous company at the steps of St. Mark's Place. The grand hall, where the Doge received his guests, ablaze with lamps and torches, and humming with the strains of festal music, was thronged that night with all that was most gallant and most beautiful in Venice. All the sights and sounds of carnival were there ; cavaliers and lovely ladies, flowers and gems, magnificent attires, light feet whirling in the dances, bright eyes gleaming through the velvet masks. Venice,—night,—a masquerade !—who could dream that this was the first scene of a most dark and awful drama ? And yet so it was to be.

That drama is about to pass before us. But

without a clear conception of the Doge's character, it will be impossible to understand it. Thereupon the whole plot hangs. Fortunately that character, striking as it is, lies on the surface and requires no seer to read it.

Marino Faliero had been Doge of Venice hardly more than half a year; but he was already an old man. At the time of his election he was seventy-six; and the long life on which he could look back had been one brilliant course of triumphs. From the proud and ancient house of Faliero two Doges had, in former centuries, already sprung; but that house could show no name more splendid than his own. He had been a soldier—and had seen the King of Hungary with eighty thousand men fly like hares before his little army. He had been commander of the fleet; and had forced the haughty gonfalon of Capo d' Istria to stoop before his flag. He had been a senator, and had filled with high distinction all the loftiest offices of state. He had been ambassador at Genoa and at Rome. It was while on embassy at the latter city that he received intelligence of his election, during his absence, and without his solicitation, to the crowning dignity of Doge.

But, high-born, brave, and gifted as he was, Faliero was not one of those fine spirits who bear greatness with simplicity. His character, by nature quick and fiery, had become, by life-long habits of command, imperious, fierce and arrogant. Opposition, of whatever kind, aroused within him a tornado of vindictive passion which swept everything before it. No rival had been found of power enough to stand before him; no opponent was so small as to escape his anger. He resembled in courage, but not in magnanimity, the lion who flies with savage joy at the elephant or the tiger, but who disdains to crush the mouse that runs across his paw. Once, in a chapel at Treviso, where the bishop kept him waiting for the cup and wafer, he flew upon the holy man and boxed his ears. Hotspur was not more jealous in honour—Mercutio was not more quick in quarrel—than the grey-bearded Doge. And his jealous honour had one ever-vulnerable point. He was an old man married to a young and lovely wife.

Such was the man who stood, that night, amidst the bright assembly of his guests. It was, although he little dreamed it, the last scene on earth on which he was to look with peace of mind.

Among the masqueraders was a certain handsome youth, a patrician of high rank, named Michael Steno. Steno had selected as his partner one of the Dogessa's waiting-ladies, into whose ears he was now earnestly employed in breathing vows of everlasting adoration. At length, giddy with beauty, and perhaps with wine, he began to press his suit too ardently. The dame drew back, in real or feigned displeasure. The Doge beheld the little scene. With eyes of flame he strode up to the offender, and commanded him, in full view of the bystanders, instantly to quit the hall.

Michael Steno was one of the curled darlings of the nation. He left the chamber; but his blood boiled at the indignity which had so publicly been put upon him. His offence—a trifling indecorum—was one which the intoxication of the hour might have excused. Raging with resentment, he wandered aimlessly about the palace. At length, whether by design or accident, he found himself alone in the great senate-hall—a hall which our imagination peoples with immortal phantoms; the hall where Portia pleaded, where Shylock whetted his keen knife, and where Othello taught another Doge and senate the charms which had bewitched the heart of Desdemona.

The hall, when Steno entered it, was lonely and unlighted. Around the semicircle at the upper end were set the seats of honour of the senators, arrayed on each side of the Doge's throne. Steno, smitten with a thought of vengeance, went forward in the dusky light, and with a piece of chalk, such as the dancers used to prevent their shoes from slipping on the glassy floors, wrote up a dozen words, in staring characters, across the Doge's throne.

That done he stole away.

The masque broke up; the guests departed; and Steno's handiwork remained undiscovered. But early the next morning an official of the palace, on entering the senate-chamber, was stunned with horror and amazement at the sight of this inscription, chalked across the throne in letters a foot long :—

THE DOGE HAS A LOVELY WIFE—BUT SHE IS NOT FOR HIM.

The man, half-scared out of his senses, went instantly to seek his master. Faliero hastened to the council-chamber, and read with his own eyes the words of infamy. What truth there was in Steno's innuendo is not known; what glances, or what more than glances, may have passed between him and the young Dogessa is beyond our information. Faliero's wife, for aught we know, may have been as spotless as Othello's, and as foully wronged. But whether Steno spoke the truth, or whether he lied like an Iago, the poisoned arrow of his vengeance struck the mark. The effect of such an insult upon such a mind is not to be described. Shylock raging against Jessica—Lear cursing in the tempest—are but faint and feeble types of Faliero as he looked upon the writing on the throne.

It was not difficult to guess his enemy. An officer was instantly sent out, and Michael Steno was arrested. A tribunal of the Forty was convened with speed; and the culprit was brought up before his peers. Their task was easy. Steno instantly admitted his offence, left the facts to answer for themselves, and stood for judgment with a certain nonchalance which was not without an air of dignity.

The court passed sentence of two months' imprisonment, to be followed by a year of exile. The decree was certainly not too severe; for the fault was gross and glaring. Yet the case was not wholly without vindication. The act had been a freak of passing passion; the provocation had been cruel; and the avowal had been frank and open. Nor was the punishment a light one. A patrician locked up in a dungeon-cell suffered, in wounded honour, far more than in privation; and a year of exile was a bitter penance. On the whole, if fairly weighed, the sentence of the Signory will hardly seem to have erred grossly on the side of mercy.

But the Doge was blind with anger. He appears to have taken it for granted that his insulter would be doomed to lose his head. The verdict stung him to the quick. Instantly his rage was turned from

Steno to the Signory—to those false and wicked judges who had, in order to protect their fellow, flagrantly betrayed their trust. The white heat of his passion was of a kind of which the colder races of the north can hardly dream. In one moment the entire patrician order became transfigured, in his eyes, to the likeness of a single mighty foe.

No foe, however mighty, had ever yet opposed him with success. His motto should have been the fiery menace, *Nemo me impune lacessit.* But now, for the first time in his long life, he found himself confronted by an adversary more powerful than himself. The sense of impotence increased his frenzy. His rage became the image of Caligula's, when he wished that the Roman people had a single head, that he might cut it off. But with what weapon could he hope to strike that many-headed Hydra, the Signory of Venice?

In this temper he was brooding in his chamber, that same evening, gloomy and alone, when a man came panting to the palace gates, and desired to see him on a case of justice. The Doge bade him be shown in ; and speedily a startling figure stood before him. The man's dress was a plebeian's, torn and ruffled; the blood was streaming down his face; and the fierceness of his passion shook him like an aspen, as he burst into a flood of angry speech. His name was Israel Bertuccio; he was a workman in the arsenal; he had quarrelled with a certain noble of high rank, who had struck him in the face. And he appealed for justice.

"Justice!" said the Doge, with bitter emphasis, "Justice against a member of the Signory! I cannot gain it for myself."

"Then," said Bertuccio, fiercely, "We must avenge ourselves—as I will." And he turned to leave the chamber.

The man's implacable resentment struck in with the Doge's humour. He called him back, encouraged him to speak, and presently discovered, with a fierce delight, that chance had put a weapon in his hands. Bertuccio was a member of a secret brotherhood, which held the Signory in deadly hatred. A thousand fiery spirits of the lower class, stung to madness by a sense of wrongs, were ripe and ready for revolt. Faliero heard this news with glittering eyes. A gigantic scheme of vengeance rose before him. Bertuccio's horde of plotters might be used; and he resolved to use it.

Anger, like misery, acquaints a man with strange companions. Hours went by; and still the pair of strange associates sat together in the Doge's chamber, deep in consultation. When at length Bertuccio left the palace, it was late at night; and he was under an engagement to return in secret on the night succeeding.

Night came; and Bertuccio, bringing with him a companion, stole up the Doge's private stair. This companion was Filippo Calendaro, a sculptor employed upon the palace buildings. The Doge, attended by his nephew, Bertuce Faliero, was waiting for them. These four men sat down together, and drew up between them the details of the most tremendous scheme of vengeance that ever filled the brain of man.

Sixteen men, the fieriest spirits of the league, were first selected for the part of leaders. Each leader was to be assured of sixty followers, determined and well armed. At sunrise on the day appointed, the great bell of St. Mark's—the bell which never sounded except by order of the Doge —was to peal a loud alarm; and at that signal, the sixteen parties of conspirators, issuing from their posts in various quarters of the city, were to flock together to St. Mark's, crying aloud that the Genoese fleet had been descried at sea. Then, as the senators, roused by the tumult and summoned by the bell, came hastily to council, they were to be assailed in the Piazza, and cut down to the last man.

Such was the Doge's scheme; a scheme without

a parallel in history; a plot in which a gray patrician, crowned with age and honours, linked himself with desperadoes against the lives of his own peers, of men with whom for more than half a century he had lived in close and friendly intercourse, with whom he had drunk and feasted, sat in conference and bled in battle. Anger, said the wise Greeks, is a brief madness. The annals of the world contain no stranger instance than the plot of Faliero of the madness which is anger in excess.

Three days were judged sufficient to complete all preparations. It was then the 11th of April. The hour of sunrise, April the 15th, was appointed for the execution of the great design.

Bertuccio and Calendaro went instantly to work. During the next three days they toiled with speed and secrecy. All went well. The leaders were selected; the bands of myrmidons were drilled, and armed; the places of assembly were arranged. If all proved true, the hours of the proud Signory were numbered. And the hearts of the conspirators beat high.

But there was one exception. One of their number was tormented by a vexing spirit of compunction, which would not let him rest. This man was named Bertrando. By trade he was a furrier; and among the nobles who had bought his sable-skins and robes of ermine the chief was Niccolo Lioni, a member of the Senate. Lioni had not only bought Bertrando's furs, but had shown him many favours; and Bertrando at this crisis desired in gratitude to warn his patron of the deadly peril that hung over him. His position and his mood of mind closely resembled those of the conspirator whose letter warned Monteagle of the powder of Guy Fawkes. But Bertrando trembled to convey his warning. Eyes jealous of a sign of wavering were around him; the knives of a hundred desperadoes were ready, at an inkling of his purpose, to plunge into his heart. Fifty times a day he strove to screw his courage to the sticking-place, and to face the hazard of discovery. But time flew by; the day before the enterprise arrived; the sun set—the sun which at his next arising was to behold the stones of the Piazza heaped with corpses and crimson with the noblest blood in Venice. And still Bertrando quaked and vacillated.

Midnight came; and now in a few flying hours the deed would be accomplished. Bertuccio, Calendaro, and the other leaders, were at the waiting-places with their gangs. Bertuce Faliero, watching for the sun to peer above the grey lagoons, was ready in the turret of St. Mark's to wake the voice of the great bell. The Doge himself was in his own apartment—waiting in sleepless solitude for the signal which should sound the hour of his revenge.

Sed Dîs aliter visum. At last the waverer had fixed his purpose. At that very moment Bertrando, muffled in a cloak and a slouched hat, aghast lest a fellow-plotter should espy him, was slinking up the byways of the city to Lioni's door.

Lioni, when Bertrando reached his palace, had not yet retired to rest. A visit at that hour surprised him. He bade his men admit the visitor, but to linger within call in case of need; and Bertrando, slouched and muffled to the eyes, was accordingly ushered into the apartment. He paused till they were left alone; and then, with all the mystery of an oracle, gave forth his voice of warning. " My Lord," he said, " it is Bertrando come to warn you. Ask me no questions—I can answer none. But as you love your life, let nothing tempt you to go forth to-morrow."

If Bertrando expected his hearer to rest satisfied with such a warning, his ignorance of human nature must have been surprising. Lioni, as was to be expected, instantly poured forth a stream of questions. What was the threatened danger? Why was this need of mystery? Was there treason in the wind? Bertrando answered not a word, but turned away and would have left the room. But he mistook his patron's character in expecting to escape so easily. Lioni's suspicions were now wide awake. He raised his voice; his lackeys seized the conspirator as he made his exit, and brought him back a prisoner. "Come, Bertrando," said Lioni, "speak no riddles. I must know all the windings of this mystery before I let you go.'

Bertrando, thus finding himself taken, resolved to make a virtue of necessity. He bargained, not only for his safety, but to be well rewarded for his service. If he turned king's evidence to save the State, it was but just that he should have his recompense. Lioni gave his pledge; and Bertrando, throwing off his air of mystery, told everything he knew.

Lioni listened in amazement. There was not an instant to be lost. Leaving Bertrando still a prisoner, he threw his mantle round him, and hurried forth into the night. He first aroused another senator, named Gradenigo; and the pair then stole together to the house of Marc Conaro. These three nobles, creeping stealthily as thieves from house to house, rapidly roused all the members of the Council. They assembled, in the dead of night, in a chamber in the Convent of St. Saviour's. Bertrando was brought in; and the Signory of

Venice heard, with inexpressible amazement, of the sword that had been hanging by a thread above their heads.

All had been done so quietly that none of the conspirators had received the least alarm. It was now near morning; already a crimson tinge was glowing in the east. Two bands of guards were instantly sent out; one to the Doge's palace, the other to St. Mark's Tower.

The Doge was sitting, at that breathless hour, alone in his apartment, straining his ears for the expected bell. The signal of alarm delayed to sound; but as he vainly listened for its summons, another sound struck on his ear—a sound that checked the current of his blood. It was the tramp of men-at-arms along the corridor outside his chamber. In a moment more, the door flew open, and he was in the grasp of soldiers.

And all was lost; and hope had vanished in an instant; and all that now remained was to endure with lofty fortitude what was to follow. The plot had failed; the dream was over. He was in the hands of those whom he had plotted to destroy.

It was held fitting that an offender of such eminence should answer to his charge before a more august tribunal than the hasty council gathered at the Convent of St. Saviour's. His captors therefore left him, for the time, alone in his own chamber, the door of which was kept by a strong guard, there to experience, in the sense of failure, an expiation which, to such a spirit, must have been far bitterer than the bitterness of death.

Meantime, Bertuccio and Calendaro were brought in chains before the council. They had been seized among their gangs with weapons in their hands. At first, on being questioned, they refused to speak. But a rack was brought; the prisoners were stretched upon it; the rollers began to turn and the cords to tighten; and speedily, with gasps and groans, the details of the plot came out. When the council had learned everything they wished, the ropes were loosened, and the culprits carried to a cell. But their respite was of short duration. As soon as the day had dawned, a gibbet was erected in a gallery of the ducal palace over-looking the Piazza; and soon the whispering and excited crowd saw the conspirators brought forth to die. The bodies, left to hang like scarecrows, as a terror to all traitors, were long to be seen twirling in the wind.

More than four hundred of their companions were arrested; but the punishment of these was for awhile delayed. For now the great culprit was to come to judgment. The preparations for his trial at once began. A tribunal of peculiar dignity was formed. The Council of Ten, by whom all crimes against the State were tried, elected twenty of the Signory to sit in consultation with them. The court of thirty judges thus composed was known by the title of the Giunta.

By the time that all was ready, it was evening. The Doge's door was opened; he was conducted, in the midst of soldiers, to the hall of counsel; and the mighty traitor stood among the men whom he had schemed to massacre. It was a scene to put to proof the sternest spirit. The hall was crowded with familiar faces; among them many which, a week before, had worn the smiles of guests at his own festival. But every face was now morose and scowling. Eyes were glittering with the fire of hatred. Voices were muttering that he should be racked. There was not one among the thirty judges—there was, perhaps, not one in all the crowd of gazers—who, had the plot succeeded, would not at that hour have been a corpse.

But neither altered faces, nor the imminence of death itself, could shake the fiery spirit of the Doge. In truth, no penalty could now disturb him—and death the least of all. His care for life was over. From the instant when the soldiers of the Signory had burst into his chamber, life had no more to offer. He had staked everything upon the hazard of the die—and everything was lost. All this world and all the glory of it had vanished from him like an exhalation. He had fallen, like the Sons of the Morning, for ever from his high estate. He knew it well; and he looked round upon the faces of his foes with stern composure, as of one beyond the reach of hope or fear.

The President of the Council rose, and demanded of the prisoner whether he confessed the charge against him. Faliero answered, with contemptuous brevity, that the charge was true. The interrogation, and indeed the trial itself, was but the form and pageantry of justice. His guilt was manifest. One of his accomplices had turned informer; two others had confessed upon the rack. To all intents and purposes, his doom was sealed before the court assembled.

And nothing now remained but to proceed to judgment. The thirty judges were agreed upon their sentence. Every voice among the thirty was for death. The culprit was to be conducted to the landing of the Giants' Stairs, and there to be beheaded. The place of execution was not idly chosen. It was the spot on which succeeding Doges were, by ancient custom, invested, in the midst of pomp and splendour, with the robe and crown of state.

But the sentence of the Senators contained yet another count. The place of the prisoner's portrait in the Hall of Council was to be left void, and veiled with black. More than five hundred years have passed since that decree was spoken; but still the line of painted Doges in the council-hall of Venice contains not one of so profound and strange an interest as the veil of vacant black which fills, in place of portrait, the space of Marino Faliero, Doge and Traitor.

It was now late at night. The prisoner was conducted back to his apartment, where he was left alone with his confessor. The minutes of his life were numbered. At daybreak the next morning he must die.

At sunrise all the city was astir. The gates below the Giants' Stairs were closed and fastened; but a vast crowd thronged the Piazzetta, and fought for places at the grated bars. Thence could be plainly seen the landing of the topmost stair—the spot where, only a few months before, the head that now had stooped as low as death put on the Doge's crown. Now, all the place was draped and hung with black; and in the centre stood the block and sword.

And now the sun was rising, and the hour was come. The mournful train emerged from the interior of the palace, and came out upon the landing of the stair. First appeared the members of the Ten, the Senate, and the Forty; then came a guard of soldiers; and then the fallen Doge. His confessor, holding up the crucifix, walked at his right hand. At his left hand marched the headsman. It was observed that the prisoner still wore the ducal cap and robe. It had been ordered by the Council that he should carry to the scene of infamy these emblems of his lost supremacy. It was their purpose to afflict that haughty spirit with a last humiliation. As he reached the block, the headsman stripped the sovereign mantle from his shoulders and plucked the crown of empire from his brows. At the same moment, the great bell of St. Mark's— the bell designed to sound the doom of his opponents —began to toll the knell for his own death.

The Doge threw himself upon his knees and laid his head upon the block. As the headsman raised his sword, the gates below were thrown wide open. The crowd rushed in with tumult—and saw the grey head rolling down the Giants' Steps.

BAYARD

PIERRE DU TERRAIL was born in 1476, at Castle
Bayard, in Dauphiny. The house of Terrail belonged to the Scarlet of the ancient peers of France.
The Lords of Bayard, during many generations, had
died under the flags of battle. Poictiers, Agincourt,
and Montlehery had taken in succession the last
three; and in 1479, when Pierre was in his nurse's
arms, his father, Aymon du Terrail, was carried
from the field of Guinegate with a frightful wound,
from the effects of which, although he survived for
seventeen years to limp about his castle with the
help of sticks, he never again put on his shirt of
mail.

The old knight was thus debarred from bringing
up his son as his own squire. But the Bishop of
Grenoble, his wife's brother, was a close friend of
Charles the Warrior, the great Duke of Savoy.
When Pierre was in his fourteenth year, it was pro-
posed that he should begin his knightly education

among the pages of the Duke. The Bishop promised to present him. A little horse was bought; a tailor was set to work to make a gorgeous suit of silk and velvet; and Pierre was ready to set out. On the morning of his departure all the inmates of the castle were called together, and looked with wonder and delight on the little cavalier, his cap decked with a gay feather and his eyes bright with pride, making his small steed gallop and curvet about the castle court. The scene is one to be remembered. In after days, nothing so much delighted lords and ladies as the sight of little Bayard caracoling on his steed.

His father gave the boy his blessing; his mother put into his hand a little purse containing six gold crowns; and Pierre set off beside the Bishop to the Duke's palace at Chambery. Duke Charles, with a company of knights and ladies, had left the banquet-table and was sipping his tokay in an open gallery, when Pierre came prancing over the sward beneath them. The Duke was enchanted; the ladies fell in love with him instantly. The Bishop's proposal was eagerly accepted, and Pierre was at once enrolled in the list of the Duke's pages.

During six months the palace at Chambery became his home. The lovable and handsome boy soon won all hearts about him. The Duke

with delight saw him leap and wrestle, throw
the bar, and ride a horse, better than any page
about the court. The Duchess and her ladies
loved to send him on their dainty missions. His
temper was bright and joyous; his only fault, if
fault it can be called, was an over-generosity of
nature. His purse was always empty; and when
he had no money, any trifling service of a lackey or
a groom would be requited with a silver button, a
dagger, or a clasp of gold. And such was to be his
character through life. Time after time, in after
years, his share of treasure, after some great victory,
would have paid a prince's ransom; yet often he
could not lay his hand on five gold pieces.

When Pierre had lived at the palace about half a
year, the Duke made a visit to Lyons, to pay his
duty to the King. That king was Charles the
Eighth, then a boy of twenty, who was making his
days fly merrily with tilts and hawking-parties, and
his nights with dances and the whispers of fair
dames. The Duke desired to carry with him to
his sovereign a present worthy of a King's accept-
ance. A happy notion struck him. He resolved to
present the King with Bayard and his horse.

King Charles had a frequent custom of sailing,
after Vespers, up the Sâone to Ainay, to the
meadows where the tournaments were held. There

Pierre made his appearance—and there as ever his appearance was

> " As if an angel dropped down from the clouds
>   To turn and wind a fiery Pagasus
>   And witch the world with noble horsemanship."

The King, the moment he drew rein, cried out in ecstacy, " Piquez, piquez !—spur again ! " The crowd of knights and equerries caught up the words; and, amidst a storm of voices crying " piquez," the bold and graceful boy flew round the field. That day he gained a new name and a new master. Thenceforth, all his companions called him Piquez ; and his master was the King.

Charles placed his new page Piquez in the palace of Lord Ligny, a prince of the great house of Luxemburg ; and there for three years he continued to reside. During that time his training was the usual training of a page. But the child was the father of the man. Thoughts of great deeds, of tilts and battle-fields, of champions going down before his lance, of crowns of myrtle, and the smiles of lovely ladies — such already were the dreams which set his soul on fire.

At seventeen, Pierre received the rank of gentleman. Thenceforward he was free to follow his own fortune ; he was free to seek the glorious Dulcinea of his dreams—a fame as bright and sparkling as his sword. And thereupon begins to pass before us, brilliant as the long-drawn scenes of a dissolving-view, the strange and splendid series of his exploits. He had not ceased to be a page ten days before the court was ringing with his name.

Sir Claude de Vauldre, Lord of Burgundy, was regarded as the stoutest knight in France. He was then at Lyons, and was about to hold a tilt, with lance and battle-axe, before the ladies and the King. His shield was hanging in the Ainay meadows ; and beside it Montjoy, the King-at-arms, sat all day with his book open, taking down the names of those who struck the shield. Among these came Piquez. Montjoy laughed as he wrote down his name ; the King, Lord Ligny, and his own companions, heard with mingled trepidation and delight that Piquez had struck the blazon of Sir Claude. But no one had a thought of what was coming. The day arrived, the tilt was held, and Piquez, by the voice of all the ladies, bore off the prize above the head of every knight in Lyons.

The glory of this exploit was extreme. It quickly spread. Three days later, Bayard went to join the garrison at Ayre. He found, as he rode into the little town, that the fame of his achievement had arrived before him. Heads were everywhere thrust out of windows; and a band of fifty of his future comrades issued on horseback from the garrison to bid him welcome. A few days after his arrival, he held a tilt in his own person, after the example of Sir Claude. The palms were a diamond and a clasp of gold. Forty-eight of his companions struck his shield, and rode into the lists against him. Bayard overthrew the whole band one by one, and was once more hailed at sunset by the notes of trumpets as the champion of the Tourney.

It is not in tournaments and tilts, however, that a knight can win his spurs. Bayard burned for battle. For many months he burned in vain ; but at last the banners of the King were given to the wind, and Bayard, to his unspeakable delight, found himself marching under Lord Ligny against Naples.

The two armies faced each other at Fornova. The odds against the French were six to one, and the fight was long and bloody. When the great victory was at last decided, Bayard was among the first of those called up before the King. That day, two horses had dropped dead beneath him ; his cuirass and his sword were hacked and battered ; and a captured standard, blazing with the arms of Naples, was in his hand. At the King's order, he knelt down, and received upon the spot the rank of knight. At one bound he had achieved the height of glory—to be knighted by his sovereign on the field of battle.

Bayard was not yet nineteen. His figure at that age, was tall and slender; his hair and eyes were black; his complexion was a sunny brown; and his countenance had something of the eagle's.

He was now for some time idle. He was left in garrison in Lombardy; and at Carignan, in Piedmont, was the palace of the Duchess of Savoy, the widow of that Charles the Warrior who had been his former master. Bayard visited the Duchess, and discovered at her palace among other old acquaintances, a young lady with whom, when he had been a page, he had exchanged vows of everlasting love. Three years had passed since they had met; but the former lovers still found themselves fast friends. After supper, while the rest were dancing, they talked of old times together in a corner. The lady had heard of Bayard's feat of arms against Sir Claude de Vauldre; and Bayard vowed that before he left the palace he would hold a tourney of the same kind in her honour.

Next day, a trumpeter proclaimed his challenge through the neighbouring towns. The prize of victory was to be a lady's token, together with a ruby worth a hundred ducats. Fifteen knights took up the challenge; and four days later the event was held. Bayard, led by his lady in a golden chain, and wearing her ribbon flying from his crest, appeared, for the first time, in the noble vesture of a knight-at-arms — the figured armour, the white floating plume, the scarlet mantle, and the spurs of gold. A gorgeous company sat round the lists and watched the progress of the contest. The result was the counterpart of the tilt at Ayre. Bayard overthrew all his assailants, won the tournament, and kept his lady's token.

But fierier fields were soon to call him. Ludovico Sforza took Milan. At Binasco, Lord Bernardino Cazache, one of Sforza's captains, had three hundred horse ; and twenty miles from Milan was Bayard's place of garrison. With fifty of his comrades he rode out one morning, bent on assaulting Lord Bernardino's force. The latter, warned by a scout of their approach, armed his party, and rushed fiercely from the fort. The strife was fought with fury ; but the Lombards, slowly driven back towards Milan, at length wheeled round their horses, and galloped like the wind into the city.

Bayard, darting in his spurs, waving his bare blade, and shouting out his battle-cry of " France," was far ahead of his companions. Before he knew his danger, he had dashed in with the fugitives at the city gates, and reached the middle of the square in front of Sforza's palace. He found himself alone in the midst of the fierce enemy — with the White Crosses of France emblazoned on his shield!

Sforza, hearing a tremendous uproar in the square, came to a window of the palace, and looked down. The square was swarming with the soldiers of Binasco, savage, hacked, and bloody; and in the centre of the yelling tumult, Bayard, still on horseback, was slashing at those who strove to pull him from his seat.

Sforza, in a voice of thunder, bade the knight be brought before him. Bayard, seeing that resistance was mere madness, surrendered to Lord Bernardino, and was led, disarmed, into the palace. Sforza was a soldier more given to the ferocity than to the courtesies of war. But when the young knight stood before him, when he heard his story, when he looked upon his bold yet modest bearing, the fierce and moody prince was moved to admiration. "Lord Bayard," he said, "I will not treat you as a prisoner. I set you free; I will take no ransom; and I will grant you any favour in my power." "My Lord Prince," said Bayard, "I thank you for your courtesy with all my soul. I will ask you only for my horse and armour." The horse was brought; Bayard sprang into the saddle; and an hour later was received by his companions with raptures of surprise and joy, as one who had come alive out of the lion's den.

Milan fell; Sforza was taken; and Bayard went into garrison at Monervino. At Andri, some miles distant, was a Spanish garrison under the command of Don Alonzo de Sotomayor, one of the most famous knights in Spain. Bayard, with fifty men, rode out one morning, in the hope of falling in with some adventure. It happened that he came across Alonzo, with an equal party, abroad on the same quest. Their forces met; both sides flew joyously to battle; and for an hour the victory hung in the balance. But at last Bayard, with his own sword, forced Alonzo to surrender; and his party, carrying with them a large band of prisoners, rode back in triumph to the garrison.

The best apartments in the castle were assigned to Don Alonzo. No guard was put upon him; and Bayard demanded only his parole not to escape. Alonzo, thus put upon his word of honour, broke his pledge. He bribed a rogue named Theode, an Albanian, to be ready with a horse at sunrise at the castle gates, stole out in the grey morning, and was off before the garrison was stirring. He had been gone two hours when Bayard discovered his escape. Le Basque, a man of great trust, strength, and spirit, sprang on a swift horse, spurred after the fugitive, came up with him two miles from Andri, as he was stopping in the road to mend his horse's girths, and brought him back a prisoner. Bayard trusted no further to Alonzo's honour. The captive was locked up in a tower; and there, until his ransom, of a thousand crowns, arrived from Andri ten days later, he remained.

Sotomayor, on his release, beguiled his friends at Andri with a completely false account of his captivity. Bayard, he said, had used him badly—a statement which excited much surprise. A soldier of Bayard's garrison, who had been a prisoner at Andri, brought him the tidings of Alonzo's infamy. Bayard, though at that moment he was shaking with the ague, instantly despatched a herald, charging Alonzo to confess that he had lied, or to prepare to meet him in the lists of battle. Alonzo replied with insolence, and the combat was fixed to take place within twelve days.

The day came; the lists were set; and Bayard, dressed entirely in white velvet, and attended by a crowd of lords and knights, appeared upon the ground. The contest was to have been decided upon horseback; but Don Alonzo, at the last moment, declared that he would fight on foot. The antagonists, accordingly, armed with sword and dagger, and wearing no armour but a gorget and a cap of steel, advanced on foot into the lists.

The clarions sounded; both combatants threw themselves upon their knees and breathed a prayer to Heaven; then rose, made the sign of the cross, and advanced towards each other. At the distance of a dozen paces they stood still, and gave the question and reply: "Lord Bayard, what do you demand of me?" "I demand," responded Bayard, "to defend my honour." Then they met.

The partisans of each looked on in breathless silence. It was a combat to the death between two skilful swordsmen; and for some time the strife seemed equal. All at once, Alonzo made a pass which left his throat exposed. In an instant, Bayard's weapon struck him, went clean through his gorget, and stood out behind his neck. A cry of rage and consternation went up from the Spaniards. The fight was over. Don Alonzo, with the sword still in his throat, hurled himself upon the victor, dragged him to the ground, and fell upon him—dead.

The Spaniards, grim and scowling, carried off their champion. Bayard, who would willingly have spared his life, looked sorrowfully upon the body. But his companions, wild with triumph, set all their banners flying and their bugles singing, and bore him off the field in exultation.

A few days later, the Spaniards, panting for reprisal, proposed to meet a party of the French in combat, for the glory of their nations. Bayard received the challenge with delight. On the appointed day, thirteen knights of either side, glittering in full harness, armed with sword and battle-axe and prepared for a contest to the death, rode forth into the lists.

By the laws of such a tilt, a knight unhorsed, or forced across the boundary, became a prisoner, and could fight no longer. The Spaniards, with great cunning, set themselves to maim the horses; and by these tactics, eleven of the French were soon dismounted. Two alone were left to carry on the contest, Bayard and Lord Orose.

Then followed such a feat-of-arms as struck the gazers dumb. For four hours these two held good their ground against the whole thirteen. The Spaniards, stung with rage and shame, spurred till their heels dripped blood. In vain. Night fell; the bugles sounded; and still the unconquerable pair rode round the ring.

But great as this feat was, it was soon to be succeeded by a greater. A few weeks afterwards, the French and Spanish camps were posted on opposite sides of the river Gargliano. Between them was a bridge, in the possession of the French; and some way further down the river was a ford, known only to the Spanish general, Pedro de Paez. A stranger-looking knight than Pedro never sat a horse. He was a dwarf a yard in height, with a hump like a camel's on his back, and a frame so small and wizen that when he was hoisted up into his huge saddle nothing but his head appeared above it. But within this grotesque figure dwelt the cunning of the fox. Paez proposed to lure the French guards from the bridge, and then to seize it. And his stratagem was ready.

Early in the morning the French soldiers at the bridge were startled to perceive a party of the enemy, each horseman bearing a foot-soldier on his crupper, approach the river at the ford and begin to move across it. Instantly, as Paez had intended, they left the bridge and rushed towards the spot. Bayard, attended by Le Basque, was in the act of putting on his armour. He sprang into the saddle, and was about to spur after his companions, when he perceived, across the river, a party of two hundred Spaniards making for the bridge. The danger was extreme; for if the bridge were taken the camp itself would be in the most deadly peril. Bayard bade Le Basque gallop for his life to bring assistance. And he himself rode forward to the bridge, alone.

The Spaniards, on seeing a solitary knight advance against them, laughed loudly at his folly. Their foremost horsemen were already half-way over, when Bayard, with his lance in rest, came flying down upon them. His onset swept the first three off the bridge into the river; and instantly the rest, with cries of vengeance, rushed furiously upon him. Bayard, not to be surrounded, backed his horse against the railing of the bridge, rose up in his stirrups, swung his falchion with both hands above his head, and lashed out with such fury that with every blow a bloody Spaniard fell into the river, and the whole troop recoiled in wonder and dismay, as if before a demon. While they still stood, half-dazed, two hundred glaring at one man, a shout was heard, and Le Basque, with a band of horsemen was seen approaching like a whirlwind. In two minutes, the Spaniards were swept back upon the land in hopeless rout—and the French camp was saved.

Bayard received for this great feat the blazon of a porcupine, with this inscription, *Unus agminis vires habet*—" One man has the might of armies."

And still came exploit after exploit in succession —exploits of every kind of fiery daring. At Genoa, when the town revolted, Bayard stormed the fort of the insurgents, quelled the riot, forced the city to surrender, and hanged the leader on a pole. At Agnadello, against the troops of Venice, he waded with his men through fens and ditches, took the picked bands of Lord d'Alvicino on the flank, scattered them to the winds, and won the day. At Padua, during the long siege, he scoured the country with his band of horse, and frequently rode back to camp at nightfall with more prisoners than armed men. At Mirandola, where he faced the Papal armies, he laid a scheme to take the Pope himself. A snow-storm kept the fiery Julius in his tent, and Bayard lost him. A few days afterwards the pontiff's life was in his hands. A traitor offered, for a purse of gold, to poison the Pope's wine. But it is not the Bayards of the world who fight with pots of poison; and the slippery Judas had to fly in terror from the camp, or Bayard would infallibly have hanged him.

So far, amidst his life of perils, Bayard had escaped without a wound. But now his time had come.

Brescia was taken by the troops of Venice. Gaston de Foix, the Thunderbolt of Italy, marched with twelve thousand men to its relief. Bayard was among them. At the head of the storming-party he was first across the ramparts, and was turning round to cheer his men to victory when a pike struck him in the thigh. The shaft broke off, and the iron head remained imbedded in the wound.

Two of his archers caught him as he fell, bore him out of the rush of battle, and partly stanched the wound by stripping up the linen of their shirts. They then tore down a door, on which they laid him, and bore him to a mansion close at hand. The master of the house, who seems to have been a person of more wealth than valour, had disappeared, and was thought to be hiding somewhere in a convent, leaving his wife and his two daughters to themselves. The girls had fled into a hay-loft, and plunged themselves beneath the hay; but, on the thunderous knocking of the archers, the lady of the house came trembling to the door. Bayard was carried in, a surgeon was luckily discovered close at hand, and the pike-head was extracted. The wound was pronounced to be not dangerous. But Bayard, to his great vexation, found that he was doomed to lie in idleness for several weeks.

According to the laws of war, the house was his, and all the inmates were his prisoners. And the fact was well for them. Outside the house existed such a scene of horror as, even in that age, was rare. Ten thousand men lay dead in the great square; the city was given up to pillage; and it is said that the conquerors gorged themselves that day with booty worth three million crowns. The troops were drunk with victory and rapine. No man's life, no woman's honour, was in safety for an instant.

Bayard set his archers at the doorway. His name was a talisman against the boldest; and in the midst of the fierce tumult that raged all round it, the house in which he lay remained a sanctuary of peace.

The ladies of the house were soon reassured. Bayard refused to regard them as his prisoners or to take a coin of ransom. The daughters, two lovely and accomplished girls, were delighted to attend the wounded knight. They talked and sang to him, they touched the mandolin, they woke the music of the virginals. In such society the hours flew lightly by. The wound healed; and in six weeks Bayard was himself again.

On the day of his departure the lady of the house came into his apartment, and besought him, as their preserver, to accept a certain little box of steel. The box contained two thousand five hundred golden ducats. Bayard took it. "But five hundred ducats," he said, "I desire you to divide for me among the nuns whose convents have been pillaged." Then turning to her daughters, "Ladies," he said, "I owe you more than thanks for your kind care of me. Soldiers do not carry with them pretty things for ladies; but I pray each of you to accept from me a thousand ducats, to aid your marriage portions." And with that he poured the coins into their aprons.

His horse was brought, and he was about to mount, when the girls came stealing down the steps into the castle court, each with a little present, worked by their own hands, which they desired him to accept. One brought a pair of armlets, made of gold and silver thread; the other, a purse of crimson satin. And this was all the spoil that Bayard carried from the inestimable wealth of Brescia—the little keepsakes of two girls whom he had saved.

The scenes of Bayard's life at which we have been glancing have been chiefly those of his great feats of arms. And so it must be still; for it is these of which the details have survived in history. And yet it was such incidents as these at Brescia which made the fame of Bayard what it was, and what it is. To his foes, he was the flower of chivalry; but to his friends he was, besides, the most adored of men. It is said that in his native province of Dauphiny, at his death, more than a hundred ancient soldiers owed to him the roof that covered their old age; that more than a hundred orphan girls had received their marriage portions from his bounty. But of such acts the vast majority are unrecorded ; for these are not the deeds which shine in the world's eye.

Gaston de Foix was now before Ravenna. Bayard rode thither with all speed ; he was just in time. Two days after his arrival came the battle. Weak though he still was from his long illness, Bayard on that day was seen, as ever, "shining above his fellow-men." He turned the tide of victory ; he tore two standards from the foe with his own hand ; and he was first in the pursuit.

He emerged from the great strife unscathed ; but he nearly lost a friend. The horse which he was riding was an ancient favourite called Carmen —a steed almost as accomplished as the Bucephalos of Alexander, or as the speaking Xanthus of Achilles. In the thick of the battle he would fight with fury, would shake a foeman like a mastiff, and break swords and lances with his teeth. When the fight was over, he would stand before the surgeon to have his wounds dressed like a man. In this battle Carmen fell, and, with two pike wounds in his flank, and more than twenty sword-cuts on his head, was left for dead upon the field. Bayard's sorrow was extreme ; but the next morning, to his great delight, Carmen was found grazing, and began to neigh. The gifted creature was brought into his master's tent; his wounds were dressed, and he was soon as well as ever.

Two months after, Bayard was at Pavia. The little troop with which he was then serving had there sought refuge under Louis d'Ars. The armies of the Swiss burst in upon them. Bayard, with a handful of soldiers in the market-place, held, for two hours, their whole force at bay, while his companions were retreating from the town across a bridge of boats. As he himself was crossing, last of all, a shot struck him in the shoulder, and stripped it to the bone. No surgeon was at hand. The wound, roughly stanched with moss, brought on a fever, and for some time he lay in danger of his life.

When next he buckled on his battle-harness, it was to play a part in that renowned encounter which is known in English history as the Battle of the Spurs.

Henry the Eighth of England had laid siege to Therouane. Bayard was among the army sent to raise the siege. Lord Piennes, the commander of the expedition, weakly halted for some days in sight of the besieging camp. While he wavered and procrastinated, Bayard devised an expedition of his own. It happened that the English had a dozen cannons, which the King had christened by the names of the Apostles, from St. Matthew down to Judas. Bayard mustered a small band, darted out of camp, fell on the party which had charge of the Apostles, and dragged off St. John.

Meanwhile, the inmates of the town were starving. At last a party, having Bayard with them, was told off to force a passage to the city walls, and to throw meat into the fosse. The scheme leaked out; a spy flew with the tidings to the English camp; and when the party, each man with half a pig behind his saddle, pushed forward to the walls, an overwhelming force of the besiegers fell upon them. They fled. Bayard was left with only fifteen men. He took his stand upon a little bridge, and fought till all but three were killed or taken. Then, loth to sacrifice brave men in vain, he determined to surrender.

As he looked about him, in search of an officer to receive his sword, he descried at some distance an English captain, sitting alone beneath the shadow of a lime tree. The officer, panting with exertion, and thinking that the fight was over, had thrown himself upon the turf beside his horse, sheathed his sword, pulled off his helmet, and was enjoying the cool air. All at once, to his amazement, Bayard, bursting through the swords of his assailants, came spurring down upon him and bade him instantly surrender. The officer, having no alternative, gave up his weapon.

"And now," said Bayard, as he received it, "take my sword; I am your prisoner. But remember that you first were mine!"

By this bold and ready act he saved his ransom. The pair rode back together to the English camp. The case was laid before the King of England; and Henry decided, with kingly justice, that the officer was Bayard's prisoner, and that Bayard must go free.

And now Bayard was to follow a new master. Louis the Twelfth died; Francis the First received the crown; and Bayard, with the young King, marched to Milan, which the Swiss had seized and held.

On Thursday, the 13th of September, in the year 1515, King Francis pitched his camp at Marignano, before the City of the Spires. No danger of attack was apprehended; the King sat calmly down to supper in his tent; when all at once the Swiss, aroused to madness by the fiery eloquence of Cardinal de Sion, broke like a tempest from the city, and fell upon the camp. The French, by the red light of sunset, flew to arms, and fought with fury till night fell. Both armies sat all night on horseback, waiting for the dawn; and with the first streaks of morning, flew again to battle. It was noon before the bitter contest ended, and the Swiss, still fighting every inch of ground, drew slowly back towards the city. It had been indeed, as Trevulzio called it, a Battle of the Giants. And the greatest of the giants had been Bayard and the King.

That evening Francis held, before his tent, the ceremony of creating knights for valour. But before the ceremony began, a proclamation by the heralds startled and delighted all the camp. Francis had determined to receive the rank in his own person. Bayard was to knight the King!

In the days of the primæval chivalry, when even princes were compelled to win their spurs, such a spectacle was not uncommon. But not for ages had a king been knighted by a subject on the field of battle. Nor was any splendour wanting that could make the spectacle impressive. Nowhere in Ariosto is a picture of more gorgeous details than is presented by this scene of history; the great crimson silk pavilion, the seat spread with cloth of gold, the blazoned banners, the heralds with their silver trumpets, the multitude all hushed in wonder, the plumed and glittering company of knights and men-at-arms. Such were the surroundings among which Francis knelt, and Bayard, with his drawn sword, gave the accolade.

The sword with which he had performed the ceremony Bayard kept religiously until his death. It was then mislaid, and never rediscovered. The loss is a misfortune. For few relics could exist of more romantic interest than the sword with which the noblest of all knights did honour to the most magnificent of kings.

Bayard's glory had long been at such a height that hardly any exploit could increase it. And yet an exploit was at hand at which, even when Bayard was the actor of it, all France and Germany were to stand in wonder.

The German Emperor, marching with a mighty army on Champagne, took Monson by surprise, and advanced against Mézières. If Mézières were taken, the whole province would be in the most deadly peril. And yet defence seemed hopeless; the place had no artillery, and the ramparts were in ruins. At this crisis Bayard volunteered to hold the crazy city. "No walls are weak," he said, in his own noble style, "which are defended by brave men."

With a small but chosen band he hastened to Mézières. Two days after his arrival the Count of Nassau, with a vast array of men and cannon, appeared before the walls. The siege began—

a siege which seemed impossible to last twelve hours.

But day by day went by, and still the town was standing. Every day the ramparts gaped with cannon-shot; but every night, as if by miracle, they rose again. The defenders suffered from wounds, pestilence, and famine; but Bayard had put every man on oath to eat his horse, and then his boots, before he would surrender. Three weeks passed; and when at last the King arrived with forces to relieve the town, he found a few gaunt spectres still glaring defiance from their battered ramparts against a hundred cannon and more than forty thousand men.

Nothing can more strikingly describe the part of Bayard than the testimony of his enemies themselves. Some time after, Mary of Hungary asked the Count of Nassau in disdain how it came to pass that with a host of troops and guns he could not take a crazy pigeon-house. "Because," replied the Count, "there was an eagle in it."

It was Bayard's last great exploit. It had been his lifelong wish that he might fall upon the field of battle. And so it was to be.

Early in the spring of 1524, the French camp was posted at Biagrassa. Lord Bonnivet, who was in command, found himself, after a prolonged resistance, at last compelled by famine and sickness to retire before the Spaniards. It was Bayard's constant custom to be first in an advance and last in a retreat; and that day he was, as usual, in the post of danger. It was for the last time. Friends and enemies were to hear, before night fell, the thrilling tidings that Bayard was no more.

On both sides of the road which the retreating army had to traverse the Spaniards had placed in ambush a large force of arquebusiers. It was a weapon which Bayard held in detestation; for while skill and courage were required to wield a spear or sword, any skulking wretch could pull a trigger from behind a stone. From one of these hated weapons he received his death. As he was retreating slowly, with his face towards the foe, a stone from a cross-arquebus struck him on the side. He instantly sank forward on his saddle-bow, exclaiming in a faint voice, "Great God! I am killed."

His squire helped him from his horse, and he was laid beneath a tree. His spine was broken in two places; and he felt within himself that he was dying. He took his sword, and kissed the cross-hilt, murmuring aloud the Latin prayer, "*Miserere mei, Deus, secundum magnam misericordiam tuam.*"

The Spaniards were approaching. His friends made some attempt to raise him and to bear him from the field. But the least movement made him faint with agony ; and he felt that all was vain. He charged his companions, as they loved him, to turn his face towards the enemy, and to retire into a place of safety ; and he sent, with his last breath, his salutation to the King. With breaking hearts they did as he desired, and he was left alone.

When the Spaniards reached the spot, they found him still alive, but sinking fast. The conduct of Lord Pescara, the Spanish general, towards his dying foe, was worthy of a great and noble knight. He bade his own pavilion to be spread above him ; cushions were spread beneath his head ; and a friar was brought, to whom he breathed his last confession. As he was uttering the final words, his voice faltered, and his head fell. The friar looked upon his face—and saw that all was over.

It was the hour of sunset, April the 30th, in the year 1524.

The Spaniards raised the corpse, and bore it with deep reverence to a neighbouring church. There it rested till the morning, when a band of his companions, displaying a white flag, came from the French camp, and carried it away. It was determined that the bones of the dead knight should rest in his own land ; and a Convent of the Order of the Minims, founded by his uncle, the Bishop of

Grenoble, near that city, was appointed as the place of sepulture. The body, apparelled in white velvet, was placed in an oak coffin, and covered with a purple pall; a band of bearers was appointed; and the funeral train set forth across the mountains into France. By day, the bier advanced upon its journey; by night, it rested in the churches on the way. At length it reached the borders of his own Dauphiny; and thence it travelled through a land of lamentation. From the city of Grenoble, when the bier arrived within the distance of a league, a mourning multitude came forth to meet it. Bishops, knights, and nobles, mingled with the common people, walked before the coffin to the great cathedral, where it rested for a night, and where a solemn requiem was sung. On the morning after, the body was borne, in mournful splendour, to the church of the Minims, and there committed to the ground.

The grave lies just before the chancel steps, in front of the great altar. On the wall to the right hand, a graven stone records, in Latin characters, the deeds of the great knight; and above the stone his effigy, carved in white marble, and adorned with the collar of his order, looks down upon the grave.

WILLIAM LITHGOW

William Lithgow was, in the spring of the year
1609, a young Scot of six-and-twenty; the possessor
of a wiry frame, a slender patrimony, and a burning
eagerness to see the world. It came into his head
to make a pilgrimage on foot about the globe. At
a period when no traveller ever thought of crossing
Hampstead Heath without his pistols, it was certain
that a pilgrim journeying among the dens of Cretan
bandits, or steering with a caravan across the deserts
to Jerusalem, would not fail to meet adventures.
Nor was Lithgow at all the man to pass in peace
through lands of Infidels and Papists. He was a
burning Protestant, with his creed at his tongue's
end, and ready—to his credit be it said—to be its
martyr. For the rest, he was a man of generous
heart and daring courage, but with a head as rash
as Harry Hotspur's.

He took his life into his hand, and started. He
got as far as Rome without disaster; but there he

began the series of his perils by coming very near to being burnt alive. The brazen image of St. Peter in the great cathedral moved him to proclaim his indignation at what he called idolatry. The Inquisition sent to seize him, and would assuredly have doomed him to the stake and faggot, but for a brother Scot named Robert Moggat. This man, a servant in the palace of the aged Earl of Tyrone, smuggled Lithgow to a garret in the palace roof, and there for three days kept him hidden, while the hue and cry went up and down the streets. On the fourth night, at midnight, the two stole out together to the city walls, where Lithgow, with the help of his companion, dropped in safety to the ground, and escaped into the darkness, laughing at his baffled foes.

Alas! though he little dreamt it, there was a day to come, though yet far distant, when the Holy Office was to turn the laugh terrifically against him.

He made his way to Venice, stepped aboard a ship for Corfu, and thence set sail for Zante. Off Cape St. Maura a sail was spied; it was a pirate Turk in hot pursuit. The captain put it to the vote among the passengers whether he should fight the ship or strike his colours. Every voice but Lithgow's was for pulling down the flag and buying off the Turk with ransoms. But Lithgow had no money for the purpose, and nothing was before him but the prospect that the Turk would sell him as a slave. He therefore gave his vote for fighting; he called upon the company to pluck up spirit, to quit themselves like men, "and the Lord would deliver them from the thraldom of the Infidels." Captain, crew, and passengers took fire together at his words; they rushed upon the pikes and muskets, loaded their two cannon to the muzzle, and received the pirate with such fury that he durst not try to board. When, however, darkness parted them from their assailants, their plight was evil; seven men were killed, a dozen more were wounded, Lithgow had a bullet in his arm, the ship was leaking through the shot-holes, and a tempest was beginning to howl fiercely. It seemed as if he had escaped from slavery only to be drowned by shipwreck. But, by great good luck, the tempest drove them safely into Largastolo Bay.

At Zante a Greek surgeon took the bullet from his arm, and he resumed his wanderings. But he was soon in new disaster. As he was walking through a solitary region on the way to Canea in Crete, four bandits, armed with cudgels, sprang upon him from a thicket. In spite of Juvenal's authority, the empty pilgrim does not always sing before the thief. It was not till after they had stripped and cudgelled him that the rogues discovered that his whole possessions consisted of two groats. With the good-nature of contempt they let him go; and, penniless and smarting, he dragged his way for thirty-seven miles to the next village. There he endeavoured, by the help of signs (for he knew nothing of the language), to beg a supper and a lodging of the natives. But among the simple villagers of Pichehorno, a stranger was a sheep among the wolves. They were preparing, without more ado, to plant a dagger in his heart, when a woman, more friendly than the rest, informed him of their purpose by a signal. He took to flight, and racing for his life into the darkness, gained the shore, and plunged into a cave among the rocks. There, famished, aching, and in peril of his life, he lay concealed till daybreak.

In the grey of morning he crept out, and made his way in safety to Canea. Again adventures were before him. While he was in the town, six convict-galleys put into the bay from Venice. One of the prisoners got leave to come on shore, attended for precaution by a keeper, and shackled with a heavy ankle-ring. Lithgow, who was as curious as a monkey, entered into conversation with the culprit, and soon learnt his story. He was one of four

young Frenchmen who had been present at a duel
between a friend of theirs and a Venetian signor for
the love of some fair lady. The signor fell; the
guards came down upon the duellists, who fled for
refuge to the French ambassador's. Except himself, they all escaped; he stumbled in the street,
was seized, was dragged before the signory, and
was condemned to pull a galley-oar for life.

The Frenchman chanced to be a Protestant.
Lithgow's soul took fire with sympathy. He began
to scheme to set the prisoner free. He borrowed
from his laundress, who was an old Greek woman, a
gown and a black veil. Then he treated the keeper
to strong drink until he rolled upon the ground,
struck off the captive's irons, dressed him in the gown
and veil, and sent him with the old Greek woman
past the sentries at the gate. Lithgow, with the
prisoner's garments, met them in an olive-grove outside the city; and thence the Frenchman fled to a
Greek monastery across the mountains, which was
appointed as a place of sanctuary for all fugitives
from justice, and where a man-of-war from Malta
touched at intervals to take away the refugees.

The Frenchman was secure; but not so his
deliverer. As Lithgow was re-entering the city,
he met two English soldiers of his acquaintance,
who were rushing out to warn him. The captain

of the galleys, with a band of soldiers, was seeking for him up and down the streets. The danger was extreme ; but by good fortune it so happened that the smallest of the city gates was guarded by three other English soldiers. These five men, who presently were joined by eight French soldiers, formed a little troop, and with Lithgow in their midst marched up the streets towards the monastery of San Salvator. The galley-soldiers, who were on the watch, rushed furiously upon the party ; but too late. While the swords were flashing in the hurly-burly Lithgow slipped into the monastery, and was secure.

Here he stayed until the galleys sailed. He shared the lodging of four monks as jolly as Friar Tuck. Wine was flowing all day long ; and every evening after supper Lithgow was compelled to dance with one or other of his boon companions, while all four drank until they dropped upon the floor, and snored till morning. During the five-and-twenty days that he remained there, Lithgow never once saw these gay brothers sober.

The galleys sailing, he was able also to make merry with his English friends. While in their company, he one day made acquaintance with another Englishman, named Wolson, who had just arrived from Tunis. This man was a strange character, and was bound by a strange vow. His elder brother, a ship's captain, had been murdered at Burnt Isle, in Scotland. Wolson, in reprisal, had sworn to have the blood of the next Scotchman he should meet; and this happened to be Lithgow.

Wolson resolved to lie in wait for him that very night; but luckily, in screwing up his courage for the act, he drank too much, and blabbed his secret. John Smith, who heard him, ran in search of Lithgow, whom he found just sitting down to supper at a tavern. The host, together with four soldiers who were drinking there, resolved to see him home. The assassin, a true Bobadil, espied the party, and his heart forsook him. Finding that he could not take his victim by surprise, he slunk away to bide a better time.

Before he found his chance, however, Lithgow had set sail from Crete, to cruise among the islands of the Cyclades, on board a vessel which was little better than a fishing-smack, and carried only eighteen souls. At Eolida a storm swept off the mast and sails, and drove the boat upon the rocks. Seven of the crew, insane with terror, leapt into the boiling surf, and were never seen again ; the others with great labour worked the boat into a cavern, the back of which sloped upwards from the sea. Lithgow was the last to disembark ; for the sailors swore to put a bullet through his skull if he should dare to step before them. Scarcely had he landed when the boat went down.

The cave was cut off by the waters, and the wrecked men had no food. Three days passed, and the spectres in the cavern were beginning to regard each other with the eyes of wolves, when a fishing-boat came by, and heard their hail. A little later, and Lithgow, who had so narrowly escaped already from the stake, the pirates, the banditti, the galleys, the assassin, and the shipwreck, would probably have furnished forth a meal for his companions.

He made his way at leisure across Turkey, and joined a caravan of pilgrims bound through Syria to Jerusalem. His dress was now a Turk's, with turban, robe, and staff; and while all the others rode on camels, horses, or asses, he walked on foot, according to his constant custom, beside his baggage-mule.

The caravan had hired a guide named Joab, who called himself a Christian, but who proved to be a traitor. This rascal planned to lead the caravan into an ambush of three hundred murderous Arabs of Mount Carmel, with whom he was in league, who were to butcher every man among them, and to gorge themselves with plunder. The plot was excellent; it seemed certain of success; but fortunately Joab feared to reach the place of ambush before the time appointed, and by lingering up and down through rugged spots and pools of water, he awoke suspicion. A Turkish soldier of the party then remembered having seen him send a Moor from Nazareth on some mysterious errand. At this, the guide was seized, was lashed upon a horse, and, under threats of death, confessed his treachery.

And now all was panic; every face was white with terror; for while to trust the guide was madness, night was falling, the ambush was in waiting, and they might walk into the trap. In the midst of the confusion Lithgow noticed that the polar star hung low, and judged that they had been conducted too far south. He cried out to the caravan to turn north-west, lest they should fall into the snare. But not a soul except himself could read the mystery of the star, and he was called upon to take the place of guide. And thus there came to pass a spectacle strange even to grotesqueness—the spectacle of thirteen hundred terror-stricken Turkish and Armenian pilgrims following a Scotchman all night long across a moon-lit desert in the heart of Syria.

When day broke, the caravan was half a mile from Tyre; the ambush was escaped. Another guide was taken, the journey was resumed, and in due course Lithgow found himself before Jerusalem.

There was, within the city, a monastery of Cordeliers, whose duty was to welcome Christian pilgrims. The Prior came out to ask if any such were in the caravan. The only one was Lithgow. A pilgrim from so far a country was held a kind of saint; and the Prior, with twelve monks, walked before him through the streets, each carrying a huge wax candle, and chanting a *Te Deum*. Within the monastery, the Abbot washed his feet and the monks knelt down to kiss them. But in the middle of the ceremony Lithgow happened to observe that he was not a Catholic. In an instant the monks' faces grew a yard in length. They had lavished all this glory on a heretic!

Lithgow, however, could not well be ousted; he remained—a saint descended to a guest. One day a party from the convent under the Abbot and a guard of soldiers set out to view the Jordan. Before the pilgrims turned, they stripped to bathe, and Lithgow, before dressing, took a whim to climb a tree upon the margin and to cut a hunting-rod, which he designed to take to England as a present to King James. As he sat concealed among the leaves, trimming "a fair rod, three yards long, wondrous straight, full of small knots, and of a yellow colour," a strange sound struck his ears. He peered out through the leaves; his companions had gone off without him, and were now waging a fierce battle with a band of Arabs a quarter of a mile away. He was caught between the devil and the deep sea; for while to venture forth was deadly peril, to be left behind was certain death. Lithgow tumbled from his tree, and rod in hand, but without a stitch of clothing, darted towards the place of combat. The thorns and sharp grass gashed his feet; a pikeman of his own side charged him as an enemy; but at last, to the amazement of the pilgrims, who scarcely recognised this light-armed warrior, he came rushing in among them, panting to aid the battle with his rod. But the fight was over, and the beaten pilgrims were discussing terms of ransom. The Abbot, scandalised at his appearance, gave him his own gown; and Lithgow, who had started as a turbaned Turk, returned as a grey friar.

From Jerusalem he wandered up and down the earth until he chanced to meet, at Algiers, a French jewel-merchant named Chatteline, who was on his way to Fez to purchase diamonds. Lithgow joined him. The pair reached Fez in safety, and thence resolved to strike across the desert to Arracon. With a tent, a mule, a dragoman, and two Moorish slaves, the bold adventurers set out on foot. Lithgow was a man who never seemed to know fatigue; but in eight days Chatteline was so exhausted that his companions were compelled to add him to the baggage on the mule, and to carry him to Ahezto, where he fell into a fever and refused to stir. Lithgow, with a guide, the dragoman, and one of the two slaves, went on without him. When the guide had led them four days' march, he missed the track, stole off in terror in the night, and left them helpless in the middle of the desert.

Nothing seemed before them but a lingering death. In four days their food was gone, and for four days more they were reduced to chew tobacco. All night the wolves and jackals were heard howling, which, as soon as weakness forced them to let out their little fire of sticks, would pick them to the bone. On the eighth day a foe more terrible than wolves or jackals came suddenly upon them—a horde of naked savages, driving before them a vast flock of sheep and goats, and bloody with the slaughter of a neighbouring tribe.

The wanderers were dragged before the savage prince — a potentate apparelled, to the awe and admiration of his subjects, in a veil of crimson satin and a pair of yellow shoes. To him Lithgow, through the dragoman, related his adventures.

The effect was marvellous. His dusky majesty was so delighted with the story, that he not only spared the prisoners' lives, but granted them a guide to Tunis, and presented Lithgow, as a kind of keepsake, with his own bow and arrows.

This memento inspired him with a project. The rod from Jordan was designed for James I.; he would present the bow and arrows to Prince Charles.

But would he get these treasures—or himself—to England safely? It was his plan to traverse Poland. For a time he made his way without disaster; but one day, while passing, lonely and on foot, through one of the vast solitary forests of Moldavia, six robbers sprang upon him from a thicket, seized his money, stripped him naked, tied him to an oak-tree, and left him to the wolves.

Nothing seemed more certain than that the end of his adventures was at last at hand. But Lithgow, like the heroes of romance, who come unscathed from perils which to the villains would be certain death, seemed charmed against destruction. All that night the voices of the wild beasts filled the forest; but not one approached to rend him. At break of day a band of shepherds found him. They cut his bonds, wrapped him in an old long coat, and bore him to the castle of their lord, a certain

Baron Starholds, fifteen miles away. The Baron was a Protestant; he received the pilgrim with great hospitality, kept him for a fortnight in the castle, gave him a fat purse, and sent him with a guide to Poland.

Lithgow reached Dantzic; fell so ill of fever that the sexton dug his grave; recovered as by miracle; and thence took ship for London. His curiosities, which the robbers had contemptuously discarded, were still in his possession; and Lithgow, who in that age was himself a greater curiosity, was presented to King James at Greenwich Gardens, and made to King and Prince his offerings of the rod from Jordan and the bow and arrows of the savage chief.

He stayed some time in London, where he wrote and printed an account of his adventures. But Ulysses was not worse adapted for a settled life. Ere long the ache for roving became irresistible, and he determined to set forth on pilgrimage once more. He had better, had he known it, have cut off his right foot; for now there lay before him an adventure to which all his previous perils were as nursery games—an adventure strange and terrible as ever mortal man escaped alive to tell of.

King James supplied him with safe-conducts, and with letters to the courts of foreign sovereigns. He wandered for a time in Ireland ; then he crossed the Straits, and made his way into the south of Spain. On reaching Malaga he struck a bargain with the skipper of a French ship bound next day for Alexandria.   But he was fated never to set sail.

That night the town was thrown into a tumult ; a cloud of strange ships, vague as phantoms in the darkness, were seen to sail into the harbour and cast anchor.   A rumour ran abroad like wild-fire that the ships were Turkish pirates ; and forthwith the town went wild with terror.   Women and children fled into the fortress ; the castle bells rang backwards ; the drums thundered an alarm.   But when day broke, the English colours were seen flying at the top-masts ; it was a squadron which had been despatched against the corsairs of Algiers.

The panic seemingly subsided.   Lithgow took a boat and went on board the *Lion* to salute the Admiral, Sir Robert Mainsell.   Sir Robert invited him to join the fleet, with which were many of his old acquaintances from London ; but time pressed, and Lithgow's clothes and papers were on shore. Accordingly, as soon as the sails spread, he stepped into a fishing-boat and put to land.

But jealous eyes had been upon him.   As he was passing up a narrow street to gain his lodging, a band of soldiers burst upon him, seized him by the throat, muffled him in a black frieze mantle, and bore him to the governor's house, where he was locked up in a parlour. He could not guess the charge against him; but he was soon to learn. The governor, the captain of the guards, and the town-clerk entered, the latter armed with pen and ink to take down his confession. Lithgow, of course, had nothing to confess; but the captain, Don Francesco, "clapping him on the cheek with a Judas smile," bade him acknowledge that he had just arrived from Seville. On his denying this, the governor burst into a storm of curses. "Villain!" he cried, "you are a spy. You have been a month at Seville, keeping a watch upon the Spanish navy, and have just visited the English fleet with your intelligence." Lithgow offered to call witnesses to prove that he was nothing but a simple pilgrim; but in vain. He produced his papers with King James's seal; but these the judges held to be a blind. It was resolved to force him to confession.

A sergeant was called in to search him. In his purse were found eleven ducats; a hundred and thirty-seven gold pieces were sewn into the collar of his doublet. This treasure-trove the governor put into his pocket. The sergeant and two Turkish slaves then seized him, bore him to a cell above the governor's kitchen, threw him down upon his back, and chained him immovably to the stone floor. One of the two slaves, whose name was Hazior, lay down before the door by way of guard; and he was left to pass the first night of his misery.

Next day the governor came to him alone. He urged the prisoner, as he hoped for pardon, to confess that he had been a spy. At his denial the governor roared out furiously that he should feel the rack. He then gave orders that the captive should receive three ounces of dry bread and a pint of water every second day—fare just sufficient to keep body and soul together, while his strength wasted to the lowest ebb. He also ordered that the window should be walled up, and the grating in the door stopped up with mats. The cell was turned into a tomb; and here, in pitchy darkness, gnawed by undying hunger, and in daily expectation of the rack, Lithgow wore away seven weeks of horror, chained motionless on the bare stones.

It was five days before Christmas; the time was two o'clock at night; when he was awakened from his feverish slumber by the sound of a coach drawn up outside his prison. The cell-door opened, and nine sergeants entered, who bore him, chains and all, into the coach. Two took their seats beside him, while the others ran on foot; and the coach, of which the driver was a negro, rolled swiftly from the city westward. At the distance of a league it pulled up at a lonely vineyard; the prisoner was lifted from the coach, was carried to a room within the building of the winepress, and was left, still chained, until the morning. He could only guess what was before him. He had been brought there to be tortured.

Late in the afternoon the three inquisitors came in; the victim, for the last time, was exhorted to confess that he had been a spy, and of course again denied it. He was then carried to another room. Against the wall was a thick frame of wood, shaped like a triangle, in the sides of which were holes, with ropes and turning-pins. This was the rack.

The tormentor stripped him, and struck off his ankle-rings; one with such violence as to tear his heel. Then he was lashed upon the rack.

It was about five o'clock. From that time till ten he lay there "in a hell of agony." As if the torture of the cords, which cut the flesh into the sinews, was not fierce enough, at intervals his jaws were forced apart, and a stream of water from a jar impelled into his throat, so that he was kept half-drowning. When he fainted in his agony, a little wine was given him, to bring him round. At last, when it seemed likely that the victim, who was weaker than a child with famine, would escape their hands by giving up the ghost, he was taken from the rack, his gashed and broken limbs were loaded with his irons, he was driven back to his old dungeon, and once more bolted to the stones.

As before, he was left to starve on bread and water; but now, by order of his persecutors, baskets of vermin were emptied on his mangled body, from whose maddening irritation he could do nothing to relieve himself; for, even had he been unchained, his arms were broken and incapable. His misery was such as moved the pity even of the Turkish slave. Hazior, at the risk of his own safety, sometimes swept the vermin into heaps with oil, and set them in a blaze. Occasionally he also brought the starving prisoner a bunch of raisins or a handful of dry figs in his shirt-sleeves. It is probable that, meagre as it was, this addition to the captive's pittance saved his life.

In the meantime the governor had discovered that he was no spy. Unluckily he had, at the same time, been looking over Lithgow's papers. The latter had, when at Loretto, been shown the cottage of the Virgin Mary, which is said to have miraculously flown from Palestine, and had dubbed the story "a vain toy." To the governor the case was clear; the Virgin Mary, in permitting Lithgow to be tortured as a spy, had wrought a miracle against a scoffer.

Two days after Candlemas he went to Lithgow's cell, and told him bluntly that, unless he wished to burn alive, he must within a week turn Papist.

But the governor knew nothing of his man. Lithgow, roused like a wounded war-horse who smells battle, instantly poured forth an argument to prove that the Pope was an impostor. The governor retired in anger. Next day he brought two Jesuits to assist him ; but in a little while he lost his temper, kicked his opponent in the face as he lay upon the floor, and, but for the two Jesuits, would have stabbed him with a knife. On the last day of the week he changed his tactics. Lithgow was assured that, at a single word, he should be taken from his cell to a luxurious chamber, to be nursed and fed on dainties—that he should regain his property, be sent to England, and receive a yearly pension of three hundred ducats. If, on the other hand, he still held out, he should that night be tortured in his cell ; after which he should, at Easter, be removed to Granada, to be burnt alive at midnight, and his ashes cast into the air.

Up to this moment Lithgow, though a victim, had not been a martyr—his escape had not depended on himself. But now a syllable would set him free —and he disdained to speak it.

That night the torturer was brought into his cell.

At first the water-torment was applied. When he had suffered all the agony of drowning, he was strung up to the cell-roof by his toes until he fainted. Then, having been restored with wine, he was once more bolted to the floor. His enemies had left him just sufficient strength to lift up his weak voice and sing defiance in a psalm.

And now nothing was before him but the martyr's fire. It was Mid-Lent; in a fortnight he must mount the faggot. Nor is there any kind of doubt that Lithgow would, at the appointed time, have sung his psalm amidst the flames, but for the strange and striking freak of fate about to be described.

One night it happened that a Spanish cavalier from Granada was taking supper with the governor, who, for the amusement of his guest, related Lithgow's story. The servant of the cavalier, a Fleming, listened from behind his master's chair. The tale of terror chilled his blood; all night it robbed him of his rest. At dawn he stole off to the English Consul and told him all he knew. The Consul went to work with speed. The case was laid before the King of Spain. On Easter Saturday, at midnight, the governor received a mandate which made him tear his beard. His victim was to be instantly set free.

The cell-door was thrown open; but the captive

could as soon have flown out of his prison as have walked out on his feet. Hazior took him on his shoulders and conveyed him to the dwelling of an English merchant near at hand, whence he was carried in a swinging blanket to a British man-of-war, the *Vanguard*, which lay at anchor in the bay. Three days later he was bound for England.

Lithgow was wavering between life and death. Every care that pity could devise was lavished on him; but when the ship reached Deptford seven weeks later, he had not risen from his couch. The fame of his adventure spread before him. King James himself desired to see him; and Lithgow, borne upon a feather bed, was carried to the private gallery at Theobalds. There the King, together with the lords and ladies of the Court, flocked eagerly about his mattress, and broke into cries of horror and compassion at the sight of the scarred, shrunk body, and the visage like a corpse's, which they had seen a few months earlier so full of life. The King himself was so much moved with pity that he ordered Lithgow, at his own expense, to be conveyed to Bath, and nursed back into strength.

In that pleasant city Lithgow passed six months. By slow degrees his health returned to him; but there were tokens of the wild beasts' den which he would carry to his grave. The fingers of one hand were drawn into the palm by the contraction of the sinews; the crushed bones of one arm remained ill-set; and his right foot was lamed for life.

By the King's agency, the Spanish Envoy, Don Drego Sarmento de Gardamore, had undertaken that he should receive his property from Malaga, together with a thousand pounds as a solatium for his wrongs. When, however, Lithgow came from Bath to London, the Envoy seemed inclined to shuffle from the bond. Lithgow, never the most patient of mankind, waited and fretted, and at last went mad with passion. In the presence-chamber of the palace he flew at the astounded Don, and beat him with his fists. The lords-in-waiting pulled him off; but not before the Don had suffered woefully.

The public sympathy was all with Lithgow; but the offence to the decorum of a Court was gross, and he was sentenced to be kept for nine weeks in the Marshalsea. The punishment was light enough; but he had made a deadly enemy of Don Drego, and of his thousand pounds he never got a shilling.

This was his last adventure and misfortune. He retired to Scotland, and from that time forth, until his death in 1640, he roamed abroad no more.

During his life he was, by those who knew his story, regarded as a hero and a martyr. Fame has treated him unkindly, and in our days he is more than half forgotten. But to those who know his story he is a hero and a martyr still.

JACQUELINE DE LAGUETTE

At Mandres, not far from Paris, stood, in the year
1612, a little house like a toy castle, with turrets and
a moat.   Its owner was a retired officer named
Meurdrac, a soldier who had fought in more than
twenty battles under Henri Quatre, but who had
become lame with rheumatism and compelled to
leave the army.   He was now a man of forty-five,
with a red beard, a huge moustache, a face tanned
to parchment, and keen sparkling eyes.   He wore,
summer and winter, a buff coat, top-boots, and a
rapier.   His character was quick and fiery.   His
cane was the terror of his groom and lacquey ; and
he would rather have laid his head upon the block
than have changed the least of his opinions.

Monsieur Meurdrac had built himself a house at
Mandres in order to be near the Castle of the Duc
of Angoulême, his oldest friend.   When his house
was finished, he looked about him for a wife.   He
chanced to meet at Paris a bewitching demoiselle

of twenty-five, good, lovely, and sweet-tempered. They married: and in the month of February 1613 a little girl was born, whom they called Jacqueline.

This child's life was destined to be distinguished from the common lot by three particular events—a love-story, an adventure, and a tragic death. And these three scenes are the romance of history which we now intend to tell.

The girl combined her mother's beauty with her father's fiery spirit. As she grew up, Jacqueline, like other maidens, stitched and spun, worked pictures on her tambour-frame, and woke the strings of her guitar; but her heart's delight was to fire off her father's musket, to practise with her fencing-master, to swim across the river Yères, or to mount her palfrey and scour the country like the wind. At eighteen she had grown into a girl of dazzling beauty —the Dulcinea of rival cavaliers for ten miles round. On Sundays, when she went to Mass, the little churchyard glittered like a palace court, with the horses and white plumes of her adorers. But Jacqueline was a Diana. Her eyes were never lifted from her missal to shoot back a speaking glance. Admirers came in crowds to seek her hand of Monsieur Meurdrac; but Jacqueline declared that she would never marry, and the suitors were sent sighing away. At length she became known throughout the province as the Maid of Mandres—the fair one who had vowed to live and die a vestal. But here the gossips were in error. These candidates were merely what the Prince of Morocco and the Prince of Arragon were to Lady Portia. Bassanio had not yet appeared.

But it so happened that one day the Meurdracs visited the Duc of Angoulême at the Castle of Gros-Bois. Among the company was an officer whom Jacqueline had never before seen. His name was Marius de Laguette, a cavalier of eight-and-twenty, tall and handsome, who had just returned with glory from fighting in Lorraine. He looked at Jacqueline as Romeo looked at Juliet in the ball-room at Verona. For the first time in her life she blushed and trembled. They did not speak a word together; but when she left the Castle the Maid of Mandres was no longer fancy-free.

Some days later she was sitting at her window, when she saw her father returning from the chase of a wild boar. To her surprise and joy, Laguette was with him; the pair had made acquaintance at the hunting-party, and old Meurdrac had invited his companion home. The young man stayed two hours, gazing at Jacqueline with glistening eyes and talking to her father. For three or four days after, he came every morning; and at last, as they were walking in the garden, he found a chance to speak to Jacqueline alone.

"Mademoiselle," he said, "I am a plain man, and cannot beat about the bush. I am here to tell you that I love you. I have often vowed that I would never marry; but the moment I beheld you I felt the folly of my vows."

"I also," replied Jacqueline, "have made such vows;" and in a lower tone she added, "and I also have repented."

There was no need for a word more; what followed was a love-scene, brief and sweet. It was hastily arranged, before they parted, that Laguette should speak to Monsieur Meurdrac the next day.

But their course of true love was not destined to run smooth. The next day came; Jacqueline sat watching at her window; but no Laguette appeared. Hours passed, and she was trembling with a thousand vague misgivings, when a farmer's boy brought her a billet from her lover. She tore it open; it told her in despair that he was ordered to rejoin his regiment, and had the sorrow of departing without bidding her farewell.

Jacqueline at first burst into tears; but her lover was a soldier, and his honour was her own. To kill time till his return she fenced and swam, she shot the deer in the Duc's park, she galloped her courser over fence and field. Three months went slowly by; the campaign ended gloriously; Laguette flew home; and Jacqueline, with inexpressible delight, beheld her hero at her feet once more.

In the meantime, she had told her mother all. Madame Meurdrac gave the pair her warm approval; but her husband's humour was by no means certain. It was determined by the three in council that Laguette should speak to him without delay.

Both ladies urged upon the suitor the need of deference and soft speech in dealing with the choleric old man. Laguette promised to obey; but in truth, though gallant and frank-hearted, he was himself as fiery-tempered as a weasel. Hotspur would not have made a worse ambassador. And in this lay their chief peril.

Monsieur Meurdrac was in his study, engaged in casting up some figures with his agent, when Laguette knocked and entered, and, signing to the old man not to interrupt himself, took his seat in a corner till the business should be over. His visit was unfortunately timed. Monsieur Meurdrac hated to be disturbed at business. He continued his employment; but his attention was distracted, and his figures soon began to go astray. At length he flung his pen into the agent's face, bade him return later, and, turning with ill-concealed impatience to Laguette, desired to know how he could serve him.

"Monsieur Meurdrac," said the young man ; "I have come to ask for your advice. I wish to marry —if my income justifies my doing so." And he thereupon explained his prospects, which were good, but not magnificent.

"Well," said the old man, "you should explain all this to the young lady's father."

"Monsieur," replied the suitor, "you are he."

The delicacy with which this news was broken did not gain its object. The old man answered, with forced courtesy, that his family were greatly honoured, but that Laguette was there a week too late ; he had promised his daughter to another suitor, and would not break his word. Laguette argued ; but in vain. The tempers of both dis-putants began to rise.

"No doubt," said Laguette bitterly, "my rival is a richer man than I am."

"You are insulting, sir," said Meurdrac. "But let this suffice you—you shall never have my daughter."

"If another has her," said the young man hotly, "I will run my rapier through him."

"Leave the house, sir!" roared the other ; and he thundered down his fist upon the table.

Then all was uproar; the swords of both flew out like lightning; Jacqueline and Madame Meurdrac rushed in screaming. While the old lady seized her husband round the neck, Jacqueline hustled her lover from the room. Laguette, with her reproaches ringing in his ears, rode off, cursing his own folly; old Meurdrac was left raging like a madman; and the hopes of the two lovers seemed destroyed for ever.

Some days passed, and affairs were still in this position when Laguette was once more summoned to his flag. This time the lovers made a scheme to correspond—a friend of Jacqueline engaging to receive their letters. All further steps toward their marriage had to be suspended till Laguette's return.

But in the meantime her father had no thought of resting idle. Laguette had not been gone a week when a letter came for Monsieur Meurdrac from his friend the Abbess of the Convent of Brie-Comte-Robert. He sent word aloud that he would call, together with his daughter, the next day. Jacqueline heard this message with a beating heart. A convent! Did they mean to force her to become a nun? She plagued her father with inquiries; but he would tell her nothing. Early the next morning a carriage took them to the convent. The Abbess welcomed them in her apartment, in which dinner was laid out for several guests. Among the company were three or four young cavaliers, one of whom her father greeted with surprising heartiness. A sudden light broke in on Jacqueline. She had been brought to take a husband, not the veil!

At table the young man sat beside her, and pressed her with polite attentions. After dinner, as the guests were strolling in the convent-garden, Monsieur Meurdrac whispered that his name was Voisenon, that he was rich, and that he loved her. Among the roses and the hollyhocks the cavalier renewed his gallantries; but at night, as they were waiting for the carriage, she seized a moment, while her father was intent upon the horses, to inform him of the truth. She was, she told him, already plighted to another. He might trouble her by his attentions, but he could never win her hand; and she appealed to his forbearance. Voisenon replied, with great good sense, that he was not the man to urge a girl against her will, however greatly he admired her. Jacqueline responded gratefully; and the two parted on the best of terms, as friends, but nothing more.

Laguette was at that moment at the siege of Lamotte. Jacqueline, in her next letter, told him what had happened. She added that she ran no danger. But lovers' fears are keen; Laguette, in much disturbance, hurried to the Marshal's tent, gained leave of absence for a month, and hastened home. He dared not visit Jacqueline by daylight; but when night came—a night in which the moonrise "tipped with silver all the fruit-tree tops"—he climbed into her garden by a ladder. Jacqueline stole out to meet him; and Laguette, with all a lover's eloquence, urged her to marry him at once in secret. At last she yielded, but on one condition— she would not leave her father's house until Laguette and he were reconciled.

Next day Laguette took counsel with the Duc of Angoulême, with whom Jacqueline had always been a favourite. The old Duc was ready, then as ever, to spoil his little pet. He gave Laguette a letter to the Archbishop of Paris, who granted him a licence to be married without the consent of the bride's father. Armed with this document, and with a purse of gold, he gained the vicar of the village. The good man mumbled out the banns at a Low Mass, before some half a dozen deaf old wives. The nine days of rigour passed. It was arranged that the marriage should take place, before six witnesses, at two hours after midnight.

The secret was well kept; but something in his daughter's manner touched old Meurdrac with suspicion. At night he set a watch upon her chamber-door, and turned his hounds into the garden. But Love laughs at locksmiths, and at cruel fathers. The sentry slumbered; Jacqueline, attended by her maid, escaped through a low window; the hounds, who knew her, made no sound; and she gained the village church in safety. The priest, the bridegroom, and the six witnesses were already waiting. And there, at dead of night, by the red glare of torches, the two adventurous lovers took their bridal vows.

At the church door they parted. Laguette rode back to his château at Suilly, six miles off; Jacqueline, together with her maid, stole home and crept in at the window. And thus it came to pass that Monsieur Meurdrac woke up next day provided with a son-in-law, without having the least idea that he was so well off.

A fortnight passed, and Monsieur Meurdrac showed no sign of cooling. The very name of the offender was the signal for a burst of rage. Laguette began to wax impatient. It was only by plotting like a couple of conspirators that he could ever see his wife. He desired to take her home; and Jacqueline at last consented that the Duc of Angoulême should be asked to break the tidings to her father, and to endeavour to appease his anger.

The Duc agreed. A messenger was despatched to invite the old man to step up to the castle. He came, suspecting nothing. Laguette was posted in an antechamber of the Duc's apartment, where he could overhear what passed. The Duc began by asking Monsieur Meurdrac for what reason he objected to Laguette.

"For no reason," replied the choleric old gentleman, "except that I detest him."

"Come," said the Duc, "be reasonable. He is your son-in-law; your daughter is married."

The old man reeled back as if he had been shot. Then he burst into such a storm of fury that Laguette, fearing that Jacqueline herself would not be safe, rushed out of the castle, took a couple of horses from the stables, rode at full gallop to her father's house, bade her leap into the saddle, and carried her out of danger to his own château.

Scarcely were they out of sight, when the indignant father came galloping to the door, inquiring for his daughter. A trembling lacquey stammered out that she had ridden away with Monsieur de Laguette. The old man knocked him down upon the spot. Then, locking himself up in his own chamber, he gave way to an access of fierce resentment which for a long time nothing could appease.

But time is a great reconciler. Some months passed; and still, to Jacqueline's extreme distress, her father steadfastly refused to see her. Madame

Meurdrac and the Duc assailed him with entreaties
—with reproaches; but in vain. But, although the
obstinate old man held out firmly in appearance, in
spirit he began to waver; and at last he wanted
nothing but a fair pretext for yielding with good
grace. In this position of affairs the Duchesse of
Angoulême fell ill. She sent for Monsieur Meurdrac, and besought him, as a last request, to see his
daughter and forgive her. He replied that there
was nothing which he could refuse her Grace.
Jacqueline was in the next apartment. She burst
into the room, and in a moment more was sobbing
in his arms.

Laguette then entered, with the Duc. The two
disputants shook hands; but the interview passed
off so stiffly that they were evidently far from being
reconciled. It was left for a freak of fortune, as
laughable as a scene of Molière, to render them fast
friends when every other means had failed.

As Laguette, after the interview, was passing
through the castle-court, he observed a group of
gentlemen belonging to the Duc, who seemed to be
exceedingly amused. He demanded what diverted
them so highly. "Your reconciliation," answered
one of them, who had been present; "to see you
and Monsieur Meurdrac shaking hands! you were
like the couple in the comedy: 'we were reconciled,

we fell into each other's arms—and from that time forth we have been deadly foes!'" And they laughed more boisterously than ever.

Their laughter stung Laguette to frenzy. "What!" he cried, "am I and Monsieur Meurdrac hypocrites? Are we to be insulted by a pack of jack-a-dandies? I will teach you better manners. I tell you that I honour Monsieur Meurdrac; I respect him — I esteem him." And in an instant he was rushing, sword in hand, against the whole fifteen.

Monsieur Meurdrac and the Duc came running to the spot—and the old man heard, to his infinite amazement, his son-in-law proclaiming at the sword's point that he honoured and esteemed him. He whipped out his rapier in an instant, and darted to his side.

The Duc was forced to throw himself between the combatants. His authority at length appeased the tumult. The cavaliers apologised; but the insulted pair walked off together arm in arm, breathing forth execrations against the coxcombs who had dared to turn them into ridicule. At Mandres they agreed to dine together; and, by dint of storming in company at the tom-fools who had compared them to a pair of actors in a comedy, they ended by drinking to their eternal friendship in a bumper of tokay.

Such was the wooing and wedding of Jacqueline Meurdrac. Two centuries and a half have passed away; Jacqueline and all her little world have long been dust; but here are the joys and sorrows of her love-story still vividly surviving. "The unfathomable sea whose waves are years" has swallowed in its depths much mightier things; and this glimpse into the darkness of the past would never, in all probability, have been open to us, but for the adventure which was to make the name of Jacqueline familiar far beyond the village of her birth.

And this brings us to the second of our scenes.

Over the happy but uneventful days which succeeded to the marriage of the lovers we pass to the year 1648—the year of the rebellion of the Fronde. All the great names of France took sides in the contending ranks of royalists and rebels. Laguette threw in his portion with the latter, and rode away to battle under the banners of Prince Condé.

Jacqueline was left alone in the château at Suilly. The vivacity of her spirit loved excitement; and excitement, even in the village, was not wanting. Sometimes she was awakened at the dead of night by the noise of drums and trumpets, or by the church-bells pealing an alarm. Sometimes she was compelled to arm her servants, to turn her house into a fortress against a party of besiegers, or to dash upon a band of foragers who were busy with their sacks and sickles in her cornfield. But, in spite of these diversions, she found the separation from her husband more than she could bear. One day she took into her head a wild resolve. She determined to ride off in search of him, and to tell him simply, when they met, that she had come to share all perils at his side.

She immediately made ready for the venture. Without adopting, like the Maid of Arc, a helmet and a coat-of-mail, she presented none the less a gallant figure. She kept her woman's dress; but she wore, besides, long boots and gauntlets, a belt, sword, and pistols, a grass-green scarf, and a hat with three green plumes. Thus arrayed, and mounted on a fiery horse, with two armed servants riding at her heels, she cantered out of Suilly on the road to Paris.

Although she was about to join her husband in the army of the rebels, Jacqueline, like most women, was a Royalist at heart. She burned to exert her influence — the influence of love, eloquence, and beauty—to convert her husband to the royal cause. Nay, more. She and Prince Condé were already friends. Some time before, the Prince, while on the march through Mandres, had stopped for a few minutes at her husband's house, and had, on his departure, laughingly invited Jacqueline to become his aide-de-camp. What if she could win the Prince himself?

But as yet her husband and the Prince were far away. And before she could be with them many things were to befall.

As she now rode forward on the road to Brie, there appeared before her the advanced guard of a band of rebels. The Duke of Lorraine was at their head. The men were loosening their swords and looking to their firelocks; for the scouts had brought intelligence of a troop of Royalists who were endeavouring to retreat across the river near at hand, and the Duke, having twice their strength of numbers, made sure of cutting them to pieces. From the summit of a limekiln Jacqueline could plainly see the standards of the King. A sudden impulse set her blood on fire. She resolved to save the royal army by a stroke of woman's wit.

She rode up to a captain of the rebel force.

"Monsieur," she said, "I come from Gros-Bois, and can give you tidings of importance. A band of Royalists is lurking in the forest; this force is only a decoy. Beware how you advance too quickly, or you will run your head into a trap.

The captain bade her follow him at once into the presence of the Duke. Lorraine listened, and was much disturbed. The order of attack was countermanded ; and scouts were instantly sent out to scour the forests. While these were prying into brakes and dingles, the royal army gained the time they needed, crossed the river, and were saved.

Jacqueline attempted to ride forward ; but she soon found out that she was watched. With a bold appearance, though with a fluttering heart, she pushed her horse towards a bridge which crossed the river. An officer commanded her to halt. " Advance no further, Madam," he said, "or I must bid my soldiers fire upon you." " Fire, then," said Jacqueline. " Heaven will defend me. I have served my country and my King." At the same instant she drove the spurs into her horse, and dashed across the bridge. A storm of bullets whistled round her ; but by a miracle of fortune she escaped scot free.

An hour afterwards she galloped into Paris.

She learnt that Prince Condé and her husband were at that moment in Guienne. She prepared to follow them ; but she had friends at Paris whom she wished to visit ; and before she started all the town was talking of the trick by which the band of rebels had been cheated of their prey. Soon her part in the affair leaked out ; she was recognised as she was walking in the street, was carried off to the

Palais Royal by some gentlemen belonging to the court, and ushered into the presence-chamber of the Queen. Anne of Austria received her with the most signal marks of favour, and not only thanked her publicly for her service to the royal cause, but invited her to spend a week at court. Jacqueline, as was to be expected from a loyal subject, accepted with delight, and was welcomed into all the pleasures of the court. She feasted in the palace-gardens under the shadow of the lime-trees, she angled for gold-carp in the Queen's fish-ponds, she danced from dusk to daylight beneath the lamps of the arcade. But all her experiences were not so pleasant; and once a little scene occurred which is of curious interest both as an illustration of her character and as a picture of the times.

One evening, in the Queen's Saloon, an officer of her acquaintance, one of those idle busybodies who are never so delighted as when making mischief, drew her attention to a certain pretty woman lying in a chair, by the side of which a cavalier was standing. "That is the coquette," observed the gossip, "who used to make us die of laughing by her designs upon your husband, when he was at Paris."

The effect of this piece of tittle-tattle must have surprised the speaker. Jacqueline was more

a country girl than a court lady.   Of all the
heroines of France, the one she most admired,
and, indeed, the one she most resembled, was
Barbe St. Belmont—a modest, pious, but high-
spirited girl, who, having been insulted by a captain
of the guard, put on a man's dress, challenged her
insulter, fought a duel with him, and made him
yield his sword.   Jacqueline walked up to the lady
and her cavalier.

"You flourish your fan charmingly," she said,
with eyes of fire.   "Can you handle a sword
also?"

"No, indeed," replied the other, laughing.   "I
am no Amazon as you are; I confess I am afraid
of swords."

"Then beware," said Jacqueline, "how you venture on my lands.   But you have here a cavalier to
represent you; I challenge him to draw his rapier
with me."

"Not I," replied the young man, laughing.   "I
would not hurt so beautiful a woman for the
world!"

This condescending gallantry poured oil upon
the fire.   By this time several persons had collected round them.   The Queen demanded what
was going forward.   Jacqueline poured forth the
story of her wrongs, and desired permission to

appeal to arms. The Queen, who could with difficulty keep from laughing, peremptorily forbade it; but the opponents might, she said, decide the matter, in a friendly fashion, with a pair of buttoned foils. They both agreed; the foils were brought, the eager company stood round, and the cavalier stepped forward, smiling with disdainful confidence. But his discomfiture was great; for, at the first encounter, Jacqueline, amidst a tempest of applause, broke through his guard with such a thrust as would, with pointed foils, assuredly have run him through the body and left him dead upon the field.

Before she left the palace, Jacqueline became aware that she had no cause for jealousy; and she and her fair rival parted on the best of terms.

The week went by; and Jacqueline, attended by a guide, rode out of Paris on the road to Guienne. And then began a journey of adventures. The country, troubled by the civil war, was in no pleasant state for travellers; and so Jacqueline was soon to find. On one occasion she was seized by a party of Royalists, who took her for Count Marsin escaping in disguise; at another, while riding on a lonely road, eight brigands started from a coppice, and bade her stand and deliver. These rascals went off with her horse, her valise, and every piece of money she possessed. Her guide had fled in terror; and thence she was obliged to make her way alone—as poor a pilgrim as a begging friar. But nothing could subdue her resolution. Sometimes she was able to obtain a ride for a few miles in a charcoal-burner's cart, or on a gipsy's donkey; but for the most part she was forced to trudge on foot. Sometimes she begged a bed at night at the cottage of some friendly rustic; but often she was glad to lie down, after a supper of black bread, to sleep in a granary among the straw.

At last, one morning, after all her misadventures, she had reached the margin of a river, and was about to cross the water by a ferry, when suddenly the sound of trumpets and the roll of drums struck on her ear. A troop of cavaliers appeared, approaching at a gallop; and first among them was Prince Condé.

"What, Madame de Laguette!" he cried, in wonder and delight. "Are you looking for your husband?—he is behind us—or have you come, as I desired, to be my aide-de-camp!"

"Both, Prince," said Jacqueline, "if you will provide me with a horse."

A horse was brought, Jacqueline mounted, and the band rode forward. A quarter of a league

before them a party of the enemy were lying in a
gorge among the hills. A sharp skirmish followed,
in which the Royalists were put to flight. A bullet
cut off one of Jacqueline's green plumes; and in
return, although she could not bring herself to
shoot a Royalist, she shot the horse of their commander with her pistol. Before the rider could
shake off his stirrups, she rode up and bade him
yield.

"Yield," said Condé, riding up. "And yield
your heart together with your sword, for your
victor is a woman."

The affair was over; the Prince's officers came
crowding round her with congratulations; and the
Prince himself declared that he would knight her.
But amidst this storm of compliment she heard, in
a familiar voice, an exclamation of surprise. She
turned, and saw her husband, who had just ridden
to the spot.

Laguette's astonishment may be imagined. But
he was a man to feel a proud delight in the possession of a wife of so much spirit. The day passed
off in feasting and rejoicing for the victory; and it
is safe to guess that, among the toasts proposed
that evening in the Prince's tent, that of the health
of Madame de Laguette was drunk with thunders
of applause.

But half her project still remained to be achieved; it was her dream to win the Prince to his allegiance. Next day, she seized a chance to touch upon the subject. To her surprise and joy, she found her eloquence work wonders. The truth was, although she did not know it, that at the time of her arrival, Condé, owing to desertions from the rebel ranks, had already determined to throw up the contest, and submit to the Queen's grace. But it pleased the gallant Prince to give his fair acquaintance the delight of thinking that her power had won him over; and he succeeded perfectly. He made a show of holding out, but pledged himself at last to send in his submission. And Jacqueline had the pleasure of believing—a belief which lasted to her dying day—that she alone had softened the great rebel leader, and furled the flags of battle of the Fronde.

A few days later she set out, together with her husband, on the return to Suilly. The journey was not quite without adventures: at one place, her horse slipped and threw her, and she put her shoulder out of socket; at another, she was nearly drowned by falling from a boat into a river. At last the towers of Gros-Bois came in sight; and she found herself a public character. All the village had heard with pride and wonder how she had tricked the army of Lorraine. When, some time after, the report began to spread that it was she who had recalled Prince Condé, the admiration of her circle knew no bounds. The fame of Barbe St. Belmont was eclipsed, and even Joan of Arc had found a rival.

Such was the second of the scenes—the scene of her adventures—by which the tenor of her life diverged into romance.

And now we pass again a space of many uneventful years. · Children were born in the château at Suilly — two boys and then a girl. While her children were growing into men and women, the life of Jacqueline was happy, calm, and undisturbed beyond the common lot. Then suddenly there came a time of tribulation—a time in which disasters rained as heavily upon their wretched house as when the great wind of the wilderness smote the mansion of Job's sons. Almost at the same time she lost her husband by a fever, her daughter died while on a visit to a friend, and her eldest son was killed in battle by a cannon-shot. Her second son, a brave and handsome youth, alone was left to her. And through this son, on whom was settled all the strength of her affections, it was destined that she should meet with her own death.

And this brings us to the last of our three scenes.

The young man was the favoured suitor of a celebrated beauty of the town of Gand. His fiery and impetuous temper—the temper of his race—made him an object of hatred and terror to a score of jealous rivals. Linked by a common enmity, they combined together to destroy him.

The young man was passionately fond of hunting, and was often to be found alone in the most solitary recesses of the forests.

One morning, while her son as usual was out hunting, Jacqueline was awakened before daybreak by a strange alarm. A peasant, panting with the speed with which he had been running, was hammering at the door of the château. The man turned out to be the keeper of the village tavern; and his story was a strange one. Late the night before, three ruffians had slouched into his hostel, and had called for liquor. Over their tankards he had heard them muttering together of a person whom they had been hired to murder in the morning at a certain corner of the forest. To his amazement, he had caught the name of the intended victim. He knew it well; it was the son of Madame de Laguette. He had dared not, for his life, detain the villains, or awaken their suspicions; but as soon as they had left the tavern he had rushed off with the tidings. Help still might be in time; but there was not an instant to be lost.

Jacqueline, though struck with terror, did not lose her sense or spirit. She seized a sword and pistols, called her lacqueys to bring horses, and sprang into the saddle. In five minutes the whole troup, with the tavern-keeper at their head, were racing over fields and hedges towards the bandits' place of ambush.

When they reached the spot, however, to their amazement not a living thing was to be seen. Yet clearly they were not too late : the earth was nowhere trampled, the grass and bushes showed no traces of a struggle. The peasant stared about him, scratched his skull, and began to stammer that he must have blundered. But Jacqueline was seized with a new terror—the brigands might have changed their lurking-place ; at that very instant, when help was close at hand, her son might be in peril of his life. She bade the party separate in haste, and scour the neighbourhood in all directions ; and she herself rode forward into the woods, alone.

Presently her eye was caught by hoof-prints marked upon a piece of boggy ground. Galloping at full speed along this track she came upon a group of horses fastened to a tree. Close by them, the three brigands were seated on the turf. It was apparent at a glance that she was yet in time.

Prudence was a virtue of which Jacqueline knew nothing. She instantly rode up to the assassins, and demanded what they did there. They stared at her in wonder.

"Pass on your way," said one of them, "and do not meddle with us. We have a piece of work to do this morning."

"I know it, villains," she said fiercely, "you are here for murder; but, by Heaven, I will prevent it!" And, driving the spurs into her horse, she dashed among them, firing her pistol as she went. The shot struck one of them in the right hand; her horse knocked down another, and left him rolling on the ground; but in another moment all three were upon her, sword in hand, and mad with fury. The skill with which she wheeled her horse prevented them from striking; but, before she could present another pistol, one of them threw down his weapon, and running to the tree where they had left their horses, snatched up a musketoon, and fired upon her. The piece was loaded with twelve balls. One of the shots struck her. Her arms dropped; and she sank out of the saddle to the ground.

The villains, struck with consternation at their handiwork, and fearful of the consequences, fled into the forest. An hour later, Jacqueline was found where she had fallen—shot through the heart. She had died, of all deaths possible, the death by which she would have wished to die. She had saved her son's life with her own.

VIDOCQ

Vidocq's father kept a baker's shop in the Place d'Armes at Arras; and there in July 1775 he came into the world. Eugene François, as the boy was called, grew up astonishingly tall and strong; but a more good-for-nothing little scapegrace never hopped a gutter. At eight years old he was the terror of all the cats and urchins in the square, and was commonly remarkable for two black eyes and a jacket rent in tatters. At thirteen he was sent out with the baker's basket, and began to pick up friends among the thieves and trollops of the slums. In this society he quickly learnt how to provide himself with pocket-money. He fished up coins from the shop-till with a feather dipped in glue; he sold the loaves and rolls out of his baskets; he pawned the coffee-spoons; he robbed the hen-roost. In this last exploit he was once detected by a pair of chickens in his breeches' pockets thrusting out their heads below his apron. At length his father,

weary of drubbing him without avail, had him
locked up for a fortnight in the city prison. But all
was useless. No sooner was he taken home and
pardoned, than he broke the money-coffer with a
crowbar, helped himself to forty pounds, and ran
away to sea.

He reached Ostend with just a shilling. But he
was not fated to become a sailor. As he was looking
for a skipper who would let him work his passage to
America, he chanced to hear a Merry-Andrew blow
his trumpet on the platform of his show. A Merry-
Andrew's was the life for Vidocq! He spent his
shilling on a pint of gin, treated the trumpet-player
to a bumper, was by him presented to Cotte-Comus,
the director of the show, and was accepted as a
learner. But Vidocq's joy was brief. The show
combined a troop of acrobats with a collection of
wild beasts; but Vidocq as a tumbler proved an
utter failure—the grand fling nearly killed him, and
the chair-leap broke his nose. He was reduced to
scour the lamps and sweep the cages, to be kicked
and beaten, to make his dinner of a crust, and to
sleep with the Jack-pudding. In a month his aspect
grew so wretched that his master, looking at his
scare-crow garments, drenched with lamp-grease
and tattered by the monkeys, his hair in tangle, and
his bones peeping through the skin, cried out in

ecstacy that he would make a splendid cannibal. In order to rehearse the character, he brought a bludgeon and a tiger-skin, and bade him glare and gibber, bound like an ourang-outang, and gnaw the flesh of a live cock. But raw cocks were not to Vidocq's liking. He refused; the master cuffed his ears; and Vidocq, snatching up his bludgeon, was about to knock the master on the head, when the whole troop rushed upon him, and kicked him out of doors.

Then he joined the keeper of a Punch-and-Judy; but he neglected the puppets to kiss the keeper's wife, and was speedily obliged to fly. Then he decided to return to Arras. In return for food and lodging by the way, he undertook to carry the pack of an old pedlar, who was waxing weak with age. The pedlar, who sold drugs, cut corns, and sometimes pulled out teeth, turned out to be a skinflint, who kept him starved on mutton-broth and turnips, and lodged him for the night in barns, in one of which he shared his pile of fodder with a camel and a pair of dancing bears. When at last he sneaked into the shop at Arras, his own mother scarcely recognised him. He was welcomed like the Prodigal. But as to making him a baker, they might as well have tried to make a baker of Cotte-Comus's ourang-outang.

For now he took a whim to be a soldier. His family consented, and he joined a troop of Chasseurs. Vidocq, at fifteen, was six feet high, an admirable fencer, and as ready for a quarrel as Mercutio. In a short time he was known to all the regiment by the name of Reckless. Within six months he fought in fifteen duels, in two of which he killed his man. When he was neither lying in the hospital with a rapier-thrust received in an affair of honour, nor in the dungeon of the citadel for a breach of discipline, he was engaged in making love to half the pretty girls in Arras. In this pursuit, his dashing air and handsome figure, his ruddy cheeks, brown curls, and grey-blue glittering eyes, were aided by a tongue as glib and wits as subtle as Satan's at the ear of Eve.

At length his troop was ordered into action ; but Vidocq, in a skirmish with the Austrians, received a bullet in his leg, and was sent home to recover. When he re-entered Arras, he found the Reign of Terror there before him. A guillotine stood in the fish-market ; a white old man was fastened to the plank ; and, as directing spirit, on a platform raised above the terror-stricken crowd, stood that filthy grinning devil, Joseph Lebon, supported on his sabre. Vidocq saw the knife fall, and the old man's head drop off. His blood ran cold, and doubtless would have run still colder, had he foreseen how soon that knife would threaten his own neck.

He had scarcely been a week in Arras, when, on stealing out one morning to fight a duel with a trumpet-major, a band of gendarmes rushed upon him ; his rival, a rank poltroon, had denounced him to Lebon. Vidocq, accused of having spoken evil of the Jacobins, was shut up in a garret, in which a crowd of captives of the noblest families were kept half-starving, with the guillotine before their eyes. That he did not mount the scaffold in the fish-market—that he did not, in the pleasant phrase then popular, look through the little window and sneeze into the sack—was owing to a lady. A certain Mademoiselle Chevalier, whose brother was Lebon's assistant, interceded for him, and obtained his liberty.

Mademoiselle Chevalier was lean and ugly, and also, as it turned out, fickle. But she set her cap at Vidocq, and inveigled him to marry her. Unluckily, the honeymoon was scarcely over, when, on coming home one evening unexpectedly, he heard the clatter of a sabre, and espied a soldier jumping out of his wife's window. Vidocq pursued and caught the fugitive. A duel was instantly arranged. But Madame Vidocq played him a new trick. Before the time appointed for the meeting, he was seized by the police, was dragged before Lebon, was accused by his wife's friends of treating her with cruelty, and was expelled from Arras.

He was now a wanderer on the earth. At first he joined a gang of sharpers. Then, armed with forged credentials, he set up as a captain—Captain Rousseau of Hussars. Under this character he made acquaintance with a rich old baroness of Brussels, and became engaged to marry her. But, vagabond, deserter, and forger as he was, he lacked audacity to become a bigamist. At the last moment he revealed so much of his true story that the baroness recoiled from him in horror. Next day she sent him a rich casket with six hundred louis-d'ors. But he never saw her face again.

He tossed away his money with such speed that he was soon without a shilling. He then joined a troop of gipsies, whose chief employment was to creep by night into the farmers' cattle-sheds and put poison in the mangers, in order to obtain a fee next day for curing the sick beasts. This strange profession did not suit his tastes, and he was looking round him for a new one, when an event occurred which altered his whole life.

At Lille he fell in love with a frail beauty by the name of Francine, of whom he was as jealous as Othello. One night he found his goddess supping at a tavern with a rival. He rushed upon the pair in fury, was arrested for assault, and was sent for three months to St. Peter's Tower. There he was put into a solitary chamber called the Bull's-eye ; but the common room, where near a score of dirty scoundrels roared and squabbled all day long, was also open to him. Three of these gaol-birds, who had conspired to forge an order of release, requested him to let them use his room "to draw up a memorial." He did so. The order of release was forged ; the forgery was detected ; and Vidocq, though quite innocent, was held guilty with the rest.

And now, instead of a few weeks of light captivity, his prospect was the galleys for a term of years. At first his anger and despair brought on a fever. Then, as he recovered, he began to rack his wits. Schemes of deliverance arose before him. As yet he did not know his own capacity. But he was soon to show that in the art of making an escape he was the cleverest rascal in the world.

Francine had made all speed to jilt his rival, and now came to see him daily. By degrees she brought him in her muff the uniform of an inspector. Vidocq's power of mimicry resembled that of Garrick or the elder Mathews. He put on the disguise, and with a face which his own mother would have failed to recognise, walked boldly to the prison-gate. The gate-keeper, an ancient galley-slave, and as sharp-eyed as an lynx, pulled off his cap and threw the barrier open. In a moment Vidocq was at liberty.

He hastened to the lodging of a friend of Francine, where, as long as he kept quiet, he was perfectly secure. But Vidocq's name was Reckless. Next morning, when the hue-and-cry was ringing after him, he walked abroad in his disguise. He was sitting down to dinner at a tavern, when a sergeant by the name of Jacquard, attended by four men, came in to look for him. Vidocq went up to Jacquard, and led him to a pantry with a window in the door. "If you are looking for that rascal Vidocq," he said, "hide here, and you will see him. I will make a sign to you when he comes in." The sergeant led his men into the pantry, and Vidocq turned the key. Then, crying to his prisoners, "It is Vidocq who has locked you in; farewell!"—he went off at his leisure, leaving the sergeant, mad with fury, trying to kick down the door.

But such bravado could not long escape scot-free. A few days later he was caught, was taken to the Tower, and was locked up in a dungeon with a culprit named Calendrin. Calendrin had already worked a secret hole half through his wall ; and with Vidocq's help the task went forward gaily. The third night all was ready ; the moment of escape arrived; and Vidocq, stripped stark naked, thrust himself into the hole. To his horror and dismay, the passage held him like a trap. He could not stir; his agony became unbearable; and he was forced to call the sentry. The guards rushed up with torches. He was tugged out, flayed and bleeding, and dragged off to another cell, where he was vigilantly guarded.

But soon his trial came on. With eighteen other culprits he was taken to the court. The entrance of the ante-room, in which they waited, was guarded by a corporal with a troop of soldiers. The prisoners were attended by two gendarmes. One of these put down his hat and cloak to go into the court. In an instant Vidocq slipped them on, took a prisoner by the arm, and led him to the door. The corporal threw it open, and the pair walked out into the street. An escape so prompt, so simple, so audacious, is sufficient of itself to mark a master-mind.

Vidocq went off to hide with Francine. They resolved to fly to Belgium. But on the eve of their departure Vidocq stole abroad, and chanced upon a girl of his acquaintance, who took him home with her to supper. Francine, at this neglect, went mad with jealousy. She vowed to call the guards and hand him over to the retribution which his infidelity deserved. Willing to let the storm blow over,

Vidocq left her, and lay for five days hidden in a suburb of the city. Then, dressed as a country bumpkin, he returned to make his peace. But instead of finding Francine, as he expected, he was seized by the police, was dragged to prison, and was accused, to his amazement, of attempted murder. As he stood before the magistrate a door flew open, and a girl, supported by two gendarmes, staggered, white as death, into the court, cast her eyes upon him, broke into a shriek, and fainted. The girl was Francine! A few hours after his departure she had been discovered lying senseless in a pool of blood, stabbed in five places, and with Vidocq's knife beside her. As soon as she could speak, she had declared that in a fit of jealous passion she had stabbed herself. But her story was suspected; for their quarrel had been overheard, and it was thought that she desired to screen him. Vidocq's narrative confirmed her story. But he had had a near escape. Had Francine's hand but struck a little surer, he must infallibly have ended his career by an assassin's doom.

His life was safe; but he was once again in prison, with the galleys waiting to receive him. A few days afterwards a strange thing happened. The gaoler left his door unfastened. In the grey dawn, while all the prison was asleep, he walked out of his cell.

The gatekeeper had that moment slipped into a tavern opposite; but as Vidocq issued from the gate, he rushed out bawling in pursuit. Vidocq escaped by speed of foot; but the city-gates were guarded, and he could not leave the town. At dusk he gained the ramparts, glided down a rope, fell fifteen feet into the fosse, and sprained his ankle. He was discovered by a carter, who, with striking kindness, drove him to his hut in the next village, rubbed his sprain with soap and brandy, and kept him hidden for some days.

Thence Vidocq made his way to Ostend. He wished to sail for India; but he had no papers, and no skipper would convey him. In this predicament, he joined a gang of smugglers, with whom he helped to run ashore by starlight some kegs of muslin and tobacco. But the custom-officers attacked the party; two smugglers were shot dead; and Vidocq, though the bullets missed him, caught a chill, and fell into a fever. One night's experience was sufficient for him. He decided that he did not care to be a smuggler.

Moreover, he was dying to see Francine. He resolved to venture back to Lille. On the road, two gendarmes who were drinking at a wine-shop asked him for his papers, and, on finding that he had none, took him to the guard-house. A brigadier of

Lille, who had seen him at the prison, happened to come in, and recognised him. He was conveyed to Lille, and thence to Douai, where he was locked up once more.

He shared the dungeon of a pair of desperados who were already scheming an escape by burrowing beneath the pavement, and thence through the prison-wall. The three now worked by turns. One man was always in the hole; while, in case the guards should enter unexpectedly, a shirt and vest, stuffed out with straw, lay on the bed to represent him. The rubbish from the hole was thrown into the river Scarpe, which ran below the window. The work was slow, for the walls were five feet thick; but after two months' labour the last stone was reached. At dead of night the captives knocked it out. But they had, in error, made the hole too low. To their horror and dismay, the river rushed in like a mill-race. The turnkeys heard them bawl, ran up with lights, and found them splashing in the flood. Dripping and crestfallen, they were hoisted out, and lodged in separate cells.

A little after, Vidocq was conducted to a den in the town-hall, a narrow, wet, and pitchy dungeon, in which he passed eight days cramped up among the sodden straw, with both hands fettered to his ankle-rings. His very misery inspired him with a scheme.

On being put into a coach to be conducted to his former prison, he, with a handkerchief across his eyes, as if the daylight dazzled them, sat feebly huddled in a corner. His guards, contemptuous of so weak a captive, soon relaxed their vigilance. All at once he dropped the handkerchief, threw open the coach-door, bounded out upon the road, and was off like the wind. Almost before the gaping guards, impeded by their sabres and jack-boots, had struggled from the coach, the fugitive was out of sight and danger.

But, in truth, a fugitive of Vidocq's character was never out of danger. He reached Dunkirk, and there struck up a friendship with the supercargo of a Swedish brig, who promised him a berth. But before the brig set sail, Vidocq, in his sailor's dress, was taken up for brawling at a pot-house, was suspected, from his lack of papers, to have escaped from prison, was taken back to Douai, and locked up once more.

And now his trial, repeatedly postponed by his escapes, at last came on. Of the forgery of the order of release he was entirely innocent; for the conspirators who had used his cell had told him nothing of their purpose. Appearances, however, damned him. He was condemned to eight years at the galleys.

The chain of galley-slaves, linked two by two, set out upon the march for Brest. By day they toiled on foot, dragging a weight of fifteen pounds at either ankle, or rode upon long waggons, while their irons, white with hoar-frost, struck cold into their bones. At night they huddled like foul beasts in cattle-stalls or stables, and munched a crust of mouldy bread. Yet the march was paradise beside the Bagne at Brest. The first appearance of that home of woe—of the vast grim dens, in each of which six hundred cut-throats, thieves, and rake-hells, dressed in the red frocks, the sail-cloth trousers, and the green caps of galley-felons, sat in endless rows—in which no sound was audible amidst the ceaseless clank of bolts and ankle-rings, except some curse or filthy jest—in which no sight was visible but haggard eyes, shorn heads, and faces of despair—these things awoke the horror of the boldest. Such was the place, and such the company, in which the luckless Vidocq was condemned to wear away eight years.

But the prison was not built that could hold Vidocq for eight years. His wits went instantly to work. Some of the galley-slaves possessed more freedom than the rest, and were wont to smuggle articles into the prison. Vidocq obtained from one of these a file, a sailor's shirt and trousers, and a wig. That night he cut his fetters nearly through, and, with a dexterity which gulled the sentries, put on the sailor's dress beneath his convict's frock. Next day, his gang was sent to work the pumps. He watched his moment, slipped behind a stack of timber, stripped off his galley-frock and trousers, popped on his wig, snapped his nearly severed fetters, and before the guards had missed him was off into the town.

But to pass the city gate was thought impossible for fugitives. It was watched by an old galley-slave, Lachique by name, who was celebrated for the eagle eye with which he could distinguish a cropped head beneath the closest cap, or the almost imperceptible dragging of a leg accustomed to the fetter. But Lachique that day had met his match. Vidocq, in his wig and sailor's suit, came gaily up, and asked him for a pipe-light. The old man gave it with the utmost courtesy ; and Vidocq walked off, puffing, through the gate.

He took the road for Cannes. For two days all went well ; but on the third he met two gendarmes, who asked him for his papers. Vidocq was ready with a story :—his name was Duval, born at l'Orient, a deserter from the frigate *Cocarde*. Duval was no imaginary being ; such was the name of a real sailor, of whom he had heard spoken at the

Bagne. In accordance with this story, he was led to l'Orient, and was lodged, as a deserter, in the naval prison. There, among other captives, was a sailor who looked at him with a mysterious smile. "My boy," said he, " I do not know you, but you are not Augustus Duval, for he died two years ago at Martinico." Then, as Vidocq stood dumbfounded, he continued, "But no one knows that he has hopped the twig; you can pass for him with ease; he ran away to sea when very young; and I can tell you all about his family. But you must have his mark upon your arm—a tattooed altar with a garland." Then the new friends laid their heads together. They pelted a sentinel with crusts of bread, for which they were locked up for punishment in a solitary cell. There, with a bunch of needles dipped in Indian ink, the sailor pricked on Vidocq's arm the altar and the garland. A fortnight later he was taken from his cell to be confronted with his family. He fell upon his father's neck; and his father, his mother, his uncle, and his cousin, all recognised with joy their lost Augustus.

His kinsfolk filled his purse with louis, and he was sent off, still in custody, to join his ship, which was in harbour at St. Malo. His fate now hung upon his chances of escaping by the way; but when the party entered Quimper he had found no means to dupe his guards. Then he resolved to try his chance as a sick man. He munched tobacco for two days, until he gave himself a gastric fever, and was ordered to be sent to the infirmary. There he soon found out that one of the attendants, who had been a convict, could be prevailed upon, for lucre, to procure him a disguise, and to show him where to scale the garden wall. A disguise was not so easily obtained; but Vidocq hit upon a scheme of strange and ludicrous audacity. When Sister Frances, the tallest and the stoutest nurse in the infirmary, had gone to early matins, Vidocq's confederate stole into her cell, and helped himself to a nun's robe and bonnet with a veil. Vidocq put them on. The two conspirators crept out, before the dawn, into the garden, where Vidocq, with the help of his companion's shoulders, scaled the wall with ease.

Before the sun rose he had walked two leagues. At ten o'clock he reached a little hamlet with a church. The sexton of the church, a little busy village gossip, besought the weary nun to rest and take refreshment at the vicar's house. The vicar, a kindly grey old man, was on the point of celebrating mass. Vidocq was pressed to join the service, and consented; but the awkward style in which he made the signs and genuflexions, very nearly let his secret slip. Then, with the vicar and the sexton, he sat down to breakfast, where, although he was so starved that he could easily have cleared the table, he was forced to nibble like a mouse. He announced that he was bound upon a pilgrimage of penance. " For what sin, dear sister?" inquired the busy little sexton. "Alas, dear brother," replied the simple nun, "for the sin of curiosity." And the sexton, at that answer, held his peace.

With the vicar's blessing he resumed his journey. A week later he reached Nantes. In that city was a robbers' tavern, of which a fellow-convict had informed him. He sought the house, knocked, gave the watchword, and was ushered by the landlady through a sliding panel into a low room, in which eight men and women were engaged in playing cards and drinking brandy. At the sudden entrance of a nun they stared in stark amazement. But in an instant, to their wonder and delight, he dropped his robe and veil, and appeared before them as the famed escaper.

Next day, he discovered on his bed a parcel of new clothes and linen. In return for this good fellowship he found himself expected to assist to break into a house. But Vidocq had by this time seen enough of crime and criminals, and had resolved to lead henceforth an honest life. He secretly exchanged his clothes for a smock-frock, and, with a stick and bundle, started off again upon his wanderings.

Two days later he reached Cholet, in La Vendée, a town of battle-battered ruins, black with fire, in which nothing was left standing but the steeple. Soldiers were watering their horses in the holy vessels of the church, and getting up a dance among the wreckage. A cattle-fair was being held among the ruins of the market. Vidocq, in his yokel's frock, addressed a farmer, and was hired to drive a herd of beasts as far as Sceaux. It was the custom of the cattle-drovers to sell the forage of the oxen committed to their charge, and to turn the profits into brandy. But Vidocq was a model drover. At Sceaux his bullocks were worth twenty francs a head above the price of any others. His master, in an ecstasy, offered to engage him as his foreman. But Vidocq had resolved to make his way to Arras; and he accordingly declined.

He started, and the third day reached the town. His friends received him as one risen from the dead. But, even in disguise, the danger of discovery was great, and he resolved to hide himself in Holland. At Rotterdam he fell in with a Frenchman who was pressing sailors for the Dutch. The knave invited him to dinner, and put a drug into his wine. When

Vidocq woke up from his stupor he found himself on board of a Dutch brig-of-war.

The crew, two hundred landsmen, pressed by force or trickery, were a lamentable herd of lubbers. One was a book-keeper; another was a gardener; another, like Vidocq, was a soldier. Not one in ten could keep his legs, or knew the difference between port and starboard. But every man of them was perfectly acquainted with the boatswain's rope's-end, which at the slightest provocation descended on their backs. Resistance seemed a dream; for a guard of five-and-twenty soldiers watched them with cocked muskets. But no guard was close enough for Vidocq. He hatched a plot among his fellow-slaves. A hundred and twenty of them watched their moment, and when half the guards were sitting down to dinner, seized the whole troop, and locked them in the hold. One of the mutineers, a sailor, was set to steer the vessel. But unluckily this man turned out to be a traitor. He ran the ship beneath the cannon of a fort, to which he made a secret signal. A boat of officers and men put off from shore. Escape was hopeless; for at a sign the fortress could have blown them all out of the water. The party came on board. Vidocq, as the ring-leader, was seized, and would probably have ended his career by swinging at a yard-arm, had not his companions sworn, with one accord, that if he suffered the least injury, they would throw a torch into the magazine and blow the ship into the air. The officials thought it best to gain the service of a man so powerful. The mutineers were pardoned; the hardships of their life were mitigated; and Vidocq rose to be an officer, with the rank of bombardier.

And now for a short time his lot was useful, quiet, and contented. But fate was not to let him be so long. The French authorities were on the watch for Frenchmen pressed on board the vessels of the Dutch. Vidocq sought refuge on a pirate-ship; but even here misfortune dogged him. A band of gendarmes came suddenly on board one morning, to look for an escaped assassin. They failed to find the man they wanted—but they found Augustus Duval the deserter, with whose escape in a nun's dress the ears of the police were ringing. To Vidocq's infinite disgust, he found himself led off in custody, and turned into a galley-slave once more.

At Douai, his old quarters, the turnkeys who had previously had charge of him discovered his identity. He was sent to Toulon with the chain-gang, and placed in the department of the dangerous captives. He was now worse off than at the Bagne at Brest.

There, as a working convict, he was sent out daily with his gang ; but now he sat by day, and stretched his limbs at night, among the riff-raff of the galleys, upon the same eternal bench to which his chains secured him. The sentry's eye was never off him. Escape from this department was impossible. But how could he contrive to get himself removed? At last, one night, as he was lying half asleep upon his bench, a project flashed upon his mind.

Next day, when the inspector came his round, he burst into a prayer for mercy. He was, he said, the victim of a fatal likeness to his brother, who was the Vidocq so renowned for his escapes. He was an injured innocent. Yet he did not ask for freedom. All that he begged was to be saved from the society of villains, though he should pass his life in fetters at the bottom of a loathsome dungeon. He played his part with such reality that the inspector listened with belief and pity. His first step was gained. He was ordered to be placed among the working convicts.

His state was now the same as it had been at Brest ; and he proceeded to escape in the same manner. As before, he put on a disguise beneath his convict's frock ; as before, he slipped away without discovery ; as before, he reached the city gate. But here he found, to his dismay, that no one was allowed to pass without a green card given by a magistrate. As he stood in great perplexity, he heard the cannon of the fortress fire three shots, which told that his escape had been discovered. He trembled; but at the moment of despair, he saw a coffin, with a train of followers, proceeding to the burial-ground outside the city. Vidocq mingled with the sad procession, burst into a flood of tears, and passed in safety through the gateway as a wailing mourner.

He walked till five o'clock that evening, when he fell in with a stranger with a gun and game-bag, whom at first he took to be a sportsman, and with whom he struck up an acquaintance. This new friend asked him to his cottage, and set him down to supper on a kid and onions. Then the stranger told his story. He was one of sixty honest citizens who had refused to serve the press-gangs, and had retreated to the woods in self-defence. If Vidocq chose to join the brotherhood, he was willing to present him. Vidocq jumped at the proposal. Next day they journeyed to a solitary hut among the mountains, where he was welcomed by his new companions and by their leader, Captain Roman. But he soon discovered that his friend had duped him. The next night he was sent out with a party to waylay a diligence. The honest citizens were a gang of highway robbers!

Vidocq was now in a predicament. If he attempted to escape, he ran the risk of being shot; if he became a bandit, he ran the risk of being hanged. A curious freak of chance delivered him. One night he was awakened by a bandit screaming out that he had lost his purse. Vidocq, as the last recruit, was the first to be suspected. In an instant, he was seized and stripped, and the brand of the galley-slave was discovered on his shoulder. A roar of rage went up. A galley-slave!—a rogue!—perhaps a spy! It was resolved to shoot him on the spot. A firing-party was told off. Vidocq heard the muskets click; but even in that peril he preserved his readiness. He drew the captain of the gang apart, and proposed to him a stratagem to discover the true thief. The captain listened, and consented. He prepared a bunch of straws, and bade the superstitious brigands each to draw one. "The guilty man," he said, "will draw the longest." All drew; the straws were re-examined; and one, held by Joseph d'Osiolles, was found shorter than the rest. The captain turned upon him furiously. "You are the thief," he said. "The straws were all of equal length. A guilty terror made you shorten yours." D'Osiolles was seized and searched, and the purse, fat with ill-got booty, was found hidden in his belt.

Vidocq was saved. But the captain told him

that, with all regret, he could not keep a galley-slave among his band. As he spoke, he slipped into his hand fifteen gold pieces, and bade him go in peace, and hold his tongue.

Vidocq went with a glad heart. He put on a smock-frock, scraped acquaintance with some waggoners, and drove a team as far as Lyons. Thence he made his way to Arras. His father was now dead; but he took refuge with his mother, who placed him in a safe concealment. But Vidocq's recklessness was still his failing. On Shrove Tuesday he was fool enough to go to a masked ball, apparelled as a marquis. A girl of his acquaintance guessed his secret, and whispered it among the company. The rumour reached the hearing of two sergeants, who were there on duty. They stepped up to the pretended marquis, and bade him follow them into the court. He did so; but as they were proceeding to untie his mask, he knocked them down like lightning, and raced into the street. The sergeants darted after him. Vidocq soon outstripped them; but presently he found, to his dismay, that he had run into a *cul-de-sac*. As the sergeants rushed up to secure him, he snatched a house-key from a door, and pointing it, in the dim light, as if it were a pistol, swore to blow out the brains of the first man who touched him. The guards recoiled ; he darted past them, and in a moment was beyond pursuit.

The sergeants, returning chopfallen from the chase, gave out that he had fired two bullets at their heads. Nor was this lie by any means the most ridiculous which the discomfited police invented to maintain their credit with the simple. One gendarme swore that Vidocq was a were-wolf. Another gravely related that one day, when he himself had seized his collar, the fugitive had turned himself into a truss of hay, of which, in just displeasure, he had made a bonfire.

But, wizard or no wizard, Vidocq found that Arras was too hot to hold him. He left the town ; but he had only jumped out of the frying-pan to fall into the fire. He was trudging, as a pedlar, from the fair of Nantes, when he was recognised and seized, placed among a chain-gang, and set out upon the march to Douai.

While on the road he was secured one night within the citadel at Bapaume. Next morning, while the prisoners were being counted in the barrack-yard, and while the notice of the guards was taken by the sudden entrance of another gang, Vidocq spied a baggage-waggon just about to leave the yard. In an instant he had slipped in at the back. The waggon jogged out of the city ; and

Vidocq, while the driver was stopping for a tankard at a tavern, glided from his hiding-place, and concealed himself till nightfall in a field of maize.

He wandered to Boulogne, where he fell in at a tavern with a crew of pirates, who, having just put into harbour with a prize, were roaring songs in chorus, filching kisses from the pretty women, and getting all as drunk as pipers. Vidocq joined these merry buccaneers. A few days afterwards they put to sea. At first they were unlucky; but one midnight, off Dunkirk, a sail was seen to glitter in the moonlight. The pirates boarded with such fury that within ten minutes the black flag was flying from the masthead of the prize. But they had lost twelve men. One of these, Lebel, who formerly had been a corporal, so curiously resembled Vidocq, that they were constantly mistaken. Vidocq hit upon a lucky thought. Before the corpse was stitched into the sack of sand in order to be thrown into the sea, he took possession of the dead man's pocket-book and passport. He resolved to be no longer Vidocq, the escaping galley-slave, but Lebel the corporal.

At Boulogne, to which the ship returned, he joined a company of gunners. As Lebel, he took at first the rank of corporal; but his zeal and steadiness soon marked him for promotion. One night, when he was on his rounds, he spied the twinkle of a light within the powder-magazine. He darted in. A lamp was set beneath a powder-cask; the wood was taking fire; another instant, and the building would be blown into the air. Vidocq rushed up, seized the lamp, stamped out the sparks, and saved the magazine. The keeper of the stores, who had contrived this scheme in order to conceal his thieveries, had disappeared. Six weeks afterwards he was discovered lying in a wheat-field, with a pistol by his side, and a bullet through his head.

Vidocq, for this act of promptitude, was made a sergeant. And now at last his path seemed clear before him. Lebel, the sergeant, was a rising soldier. Vidocq, the galley-slave, was at the bottom of the sea.

But how long was this to last? Not long. Fate made him quarrel with a certain quartermaster. They drew, and Vidocq wounded his opponent in the breast. On stripping off the quartermaster's shirt to staunch the hurt, Vidocq perceived a serpent's head tattooed upon his chest, the tail of which went round one arm and coiled about an anchor. Vidocq recognised the serpent; he had seen it at the galleys. The quartermaster, like himself, was an escaper; and what was worse, at the same instant he looked eagerly at Vidocq, and recalled his face to mind.

The pair of galley-slaves, thus strangely met, struck up a show of friendship. Each swore to keep the other's secret; but the quartermaster proved a traitor, and conveyed a hint to the police. At five o'clock one morning Vidocq was arrested, bound with ropes, and once more started on the march to Douai. His dream was over. Lebel was dead in earnest, and the old Vidocq was alive once more.

At Douai, where he was detained some months, he sometimes ate his dinner in the gaoler's room, of which the window, opening at a dizzy height above the river Scarpe, had been left without a grating. One evening, after dinner, Vidocq watched his moment, bounded through the window, and made the giddy plunge into the river. The window was so far aloft that the astounded gaoler failed to spy him swimming in the twilight down the stream. The banks were searched; his hat was found; but unhappily for the pursuers his head was not inside it. By that time, he had reached the watergate beneath the city-walls, dived under it, and found himself outside the town. Then, gasping and exhausted, he dragged himself to land.

He dried his dripping garments at the oven of a friendly baker, and again made off across the country. For some days he hid himself at Duisans in the cottage of a captain's widow, an old friend.

Thence, in a disguise, he made his way to Paris, where, buried in the heart of the great city, he conceived a hope of living unobserved. His mother joined him, and with her assistance he acquired the shop and business of a master-tailor. Ludicrous as the idea appears to those who know his character, for eight months Vidocq handled patterns, measured customers, and, what is more, grew prosperous and contented. But his disasters were not over. One day he chanced to come across Chevalier, his wife's brother, whom the world had used so basely that instead of sending lords and ladies to the guillotine he had just come out of gaol for stealing spoons. This reptile worked on Vidocq's trepidation, drained him of his money, and as soon as he had sucked him dry, betrayed him to the guards, with whom it was his aim to curry favour.

A few days afterwards, at daybreak, a band of gendarmes knocked at Vidocq's door. He rushed into a neighbour's attic and concealed himself beneath a mattress, where the searchers, though they shook the mattress, failed to find him. Then he took lodgings with a coiner by the name of Bouhin. But Bouhin also turned against him. At three o'clock one night a party came to seize him. Vidocq, in his shirt, jumped out of bed, dashed up the stairs, and crept out of a window on the tiles.

But the pursuers were behind him; there was no escaping from the roof; and he was seized among the chimneys.

Vidocq was weary of escapes and captures. He took a vital resolution, a resolution which affected his whole future life. He wrote to M. Henry, the chief of the police, and offered him his service as a spy.

M. Henry wavered. There were points in Vidocq's favour—and there were points against him. His power was great and might be of enormous value. The very qualities—the strength and courage, the ready-wittedness, the cunning in disguises—which had rendered him the dread of the police, might render him in turn the scourge of evil-doers. He could venture into slums and hells in which no officer durst show his face; for in these slums and hells he was a paragon—a hero—to whom the sharpest and the boldest reprobate looked up as a disciple to a master. His skill in making an escape was regarded as unearthly; there was thought to be no turnkey at whom he could not snap his fingers, no fetters that he could not break in sunder, no wall through which he could not pierce his way. His advice was sought as if he were an oracle. Secrets of which the revelation would have hanged a dozen men were whispered eagerly into his ears. The lives of scores of gallows-birds were at his mercy. Turned loose among them, in appearance their confederate, but in secret their betrayer, he might well be of more profit to the cause of law than a battalion of armed men.

But was he to be trusted? M. Henry thought he might be trusted. He had committed no great crime—and he had lately done his best, when he was free, to lead an honest life. These things argued in his favour. It was decided to accept his offer, though not without a stringent guarantee. He was required to bring to justice every month a certain minimum of culprits; and it was understood that if he failed to reach the stipulated number, he was to be delivered to the hulks once more.

The compact was concluded on these terms. Vidocq was taken, handcuffed, from the prison, was put into a wicker car, was driven from the city, and was suffered to escape. The same evening he was loose among the cut-throats and the ring-droppers; in appearance, still a fugitive—in reality, a spy.

This act, the turning-point of his career, has given rise to very opposite opinions. In the eyes of his admirers, Vidocq was a penitent, who, turning resolutely from the paths of crime, gave up his varied talents to the service of the State. In the eyes of his detractors, he was a miscreant who turned sneak to save his skin. The truth lies between the two extremes. Vidocq was not a beau-ideal of virtue; but, wild and graceless as his youth had been, he was a bird of very different feather from the rabble of the hulks. His only proper cause of quarrel with the law had been the punching of a rival's head. His prison-glory was not of his own seeking. With the Yahoos of the galleys, among whom he had been forced to live, he considered that he broke no faith, because he owed none. Moreover, the word spy is apt to be misleading; for, at least to English ears, spy, sneak, and coward are all tarred with the same brush. But Vidocq's undertaking was not merely that of an approver; it was also that of an arrester; and how far that task was fitted for a coward or a fool may easily be judged by the examples of his captures— a few among a thousand—which it has now become our business to describe.

His first achievement was the capture of a coiner by the name of Watrin—a fierce and cunning desperado, who had completely baffled the police. Vidocq tracked him to his lair above a certain cobbler's shop. At midnight he went, single-handed, to the spot, met, by chance, the coiner at the doorway, and rushed instantly upon him. Watrin dealt him a tremendous blow, and darting back into the building through a window, snatched up the cobbler's knife. To follow was to rush on certain death; for the ruffian, armed with such a weapon, was as dangerous as a wounded beast of prey. But Vidocq used his wits. He made a sound like that of steps retreating; Watrin put his head out of the window to make sure that he was gone; and in an instant Vidocq seized him by the hair. The bravo struggled furiously; but gradually Vidocq, by sheer strength of muscle, dragged him through the window, and the pair fell, locked together, to the ground. Before his enemy could use his weapon, Vidocq wrenched it from his grasp, bound his arms, and dragged him single-handed to the guard-house. M. Henry and the officers on duty could scarcely trust their eyes when they beheld the pair come in.

Watrin (who was hanged) was a mere savage. St. Germain was a rascal of a different dye. This rogue, a clerk turned felon, was a dandy and a wit, and so great a master of the graces, that in spite of his pig-eyes, his pock-marked cheeks, and his mouth like a hyæna's, the ladies of his circle thought him charming. St. Germain had conceived a spirited design—to climb one night into a banker's garden, to break into the house, to knock the inmates on the head, and to go off with the cash-box. He had already two confederates, but he required a third; and he invited Vidocq. Vidocq, who thought he saw his way to take the rogues red-handed, readily consented. But he soon found that he had been too hasty. The scheme was to come off that very night, at midnight. As yet it was not noon; but St. Germain, who, like Sampson Brass's father Foxey, suspected every one on principle, whether friends or foes, required that they should spend the interval together in his lodgings. The other two assented willingly; and Vidocq was compelled to do the same. But while his three companions were employed in cleaning pistols, and in putting a keen edge on murderous knives which, at the least suspicion of his falsity, would have plunged into his heart, he racked his brains for a device to send a line to the police. At last he found one. He remarked that at his lodgings he had some bottles of choice burgundy, which, if they could be fetched, would make the time fly gaily. The robbers roared in approbation. St. Germain's porter went off with the message; and Vidocq's mistress, Annette, brought the wine. Vidocq meantime had stretched himself upon the bed, and traced a few words secretly upon a scrap of paper, which, under the pretext of kissing Annette as she left them, he slipped into her hand. The scrawl instructed her to watch them in disguise, and to pick up anything he might let fall. He next proposed that, for precaution, he should be taken to inspect the place of action, which as yet he had not seen. The rest agreed. Locking their two companions in the room, St. Germain took him to the banker's garden, and showed him where they were to scale the wall. Vidocq had now learnt all he wanted. While St. Germain, on returning, stepped into a shop to purchase some black crape to use for masks, he scribbled his directions, and let fall the missive in the street. Annette, who was behind them in disguise, picked up the twist of paper and carried it to the police.

Midnight came. The confederates stole forth upon their deed of darkness, scaled the wall, and dropped into the garden. Vidocq was still astride upon the coping, when a party of police, who had been lurking in the shrubbery, sprang out upon the robbers. The latter fired their pistols; several officers were injured; but at last the rogues were struck down, seized and bound. Vidocq, to play his part to the conclusion, tumbled from the wall, as if shot dead, and was carried off before the eyes of his companions under a white sheet.

Father Moiselet, whose story we have next to tell, was sexton, bell-ringer, and chorister at the church of Livry. He was by trade a cooper, and though commonly regarded as a saint in humble life, was in reality an oily hypocrite. His vicar, frightened at the rumoured coming of the Cossacks at the first invasion, resolved to bury the church vessels in a barn. A friend of his, a wealthy jeweller, determined to conceal his diamonds in the same receptacle; and honest Father Moiselet was employed to dig the hole. The treasure was regarded as secure; but one day Moiselet came rushing to the vicar, just able to gasp out, "The hole!—the hole!" The vicar, nearly dead with terror, hurried to the barn. The hole was empty.

Vidocq was employed to trace the thief. He first had Moiselet arrested on suspicion. While the sexton was in prison he disguised himself as a Jew hawker, and called on Madame Moiselet, in the hope that she might offer him for sale a golden chalice, or a rope of diamonds. But, for reasons to be seen, the hope was idle. Then, as a German valet, he got himself arrested, and shut up with Moiselet in prison. He and the worthy sexton soon became the best of friends. The latter loved a glass of wine. In each of Vidocq's buttons a gold piece was sewn. He cut them off, a button at a time, called for bottle after bottle, and when his boon companion was in a merry vein, he told his story. His name was Fritz; his master was an Austrian officer; and he had stolen his havresac and buried it among the woods of Bondy. Moiselet was at first too wary to return this confidence; but he confessed that he was tired of Madame Moiselet, and that nothing would delight him better than to fly with his new friend to Germany, and to lead a merry life. That he could not lead a merry life on nothing was self-evident; and Vidocq now felt certain that he had the treasure. It was ageed that they should take the earliest chance of making an escape; and a chance was soon discovered. Vidocq secretly directed the police to take them to another prison, bound together by a slender cord. At a lonely corner of the road they snapped the cord, and plunged into the woods of Vaujours. No spot for their escape could have been better chosen. Presently the sexton looked about him, thrust his arm into a thicket, drew forth a spade, stripped off his coat, began to dig beneath a certain birch-tree, and speedily turned up the box of treasure. But as he gazed upon the spoil with glistening eyes, to his inexpressible dismay his colleague seized the spade, threatened to knock him on the head if he resisted, and marched him off to meet his doom. The luckless sexton walked as if in stupefaction; but on the road he muttered over to himself a thousand times,

"Who could have believed it! And he looked so green!"

These exploits, and a thousand of which these are merely typical examples, raised Vidocq's fame to a prodigious height. As a felon, he had been the prince of prison-breakers. He was now regarded, and with justice, as the greatest felon-catcher ever seen. Soon he rose to be chief agent of the Guard of Safety. For eighteen years the mingled skill and daring of his captures were without a parallel. It is said that, in that time, he cleared the slums of Paris of more than twenty thousand rogues. Yet the man who was the scourge of criminals was himself a galley-slave, for whom, if the authorities so willed, the fetters and the bench were still in waiting. At length, in 1827, he was considered to have earned his pardon. He had made sufficient money for his wants; and he resigned.

But the vicissitudes of fate were still before him. He started, with his little fortune, a card and paper factory at St. Mandé, in which all the workmen were old criminals. But his capital ran short; the neighbours grumbled at this colony of rogues among them; and the business had to be wound up. He then set up, at Paris, a Secret Information office, which was, at first, a great success. But before long he was charged with wringing money from the fears of those whose secrets he acquired. He was arrested, tried, and though at last acquitted, was brought down to the verge of ruin.

He then resolved to try his fortune as a public entertainer. In 1845, he crossed to London, and produced his exhibition at the Cosmorama. His exploits were on every tongue; and thousands of spectators flocked into his show. Vidocq, at seventy, was a striking figure. No spectator could forget the tall form, now grown portly, in drab breeches, white silk stockings, and shoes with silver buckles, the bull-neck, the strange face sloping upwards like a pear, the ears pierced with slender golden rings, the grizzled hair, and the bushy brows above the steel-grey eyes which glittered like a lynx's. His performance must have been immensely entertaining. He told the story of his life; he donned his chains, his galley-dress, and the huge iron balls which he had worn at Brest; he brought forth relics of great malefactors—Fieschi's coat, Paparonie's cap, the crucifix which Raoul had used in the last cell; he related his escapes, and his most famous captures—and as he told his stories, he changed his face and decked himself in the disguise which he had worn on each occasion, and appeared successively before the eyes of the spectators as a pick-pocket, a coal-heaver, a galley-slave, a Jew, a scullion, and a nun.

By this performance, Vidocq cleared enough to buy himself a small annuity. He retired to Paris, and there lived quietly in lodgings until 1857, when, at the great age of eighty-two, he was struck down with paralysis. On finding his end near, he sent for a confessor, and—so whimsical a thing is human nature—he greatly edified the holy man by dying like a saint. One trifling peccadillo he perhaps forgot to mention. The breath had scarcely left his body, when ten lovely damsels, each provided with a copy of his will which left her all his property, arrived upon the scene. Alas for all the ten! Vidocq had always loved the smiles of beauty, and had obtained them by a gift which cost him nothing. He had left his whole possessions to his landlady.

LOCHIEL.

THE romance of the ancient Highland kingdoms has a colour of its own. Its themes are not, like those of the romance of chivalry, of love and love's adventures ; its tales are not of vows and tokens, of soft lutes sighing in the bowers of ladies, of knights in golden armour glittering in the lists. Its scenes are, like its own deep forests and dark mountain gorges, full of Gothic gloom and savage splendour. The fiery cross wandering like a meteor over hills and valleys, the gathering of the warlike clans, the glowing tartans, the badges, the terrific slogan, the glitter of the dirks and battle-axes—all its sights and sounds have in them something wild and eerie, from the fierce shriek of the pibroch in the front of battle, to the mournful wailing of the coronach above the dead man in his shroud — from the minstrel touching his rude harp to music of bar-baric sweetness, to the wild-eyed wizard girding on his robe of raw bull's-hide and lying down to catch prophetic voices in the roaring of the lone cascade.

Among such sights and sounds a boy was born, in February 1629, at Kulchorn Castle, a pile of grey towers rising under the shadow of Ben Cruachan, on an island of Loch Awe. His mother was a Campbell. His father, who died before the boy was old enough to recollect him, was the eldest son of Cameron of Lochiel, one of the most famous of the Gaelic kings, a shrewd and fierce old chief, who for seventy years had lived amidst a whirl of wild adventures, and who had been long regarded with a double terror, partly as a warrior and partly as a seer. His ancestry went back, through times of history, into times of fable—from a chief who fought for Mary at Corrichy, to a chief who fought for James at Flodden Field; from John of Ochtry, who bore at Halidon the Bloody Heart of Douglas, to that Angus who, three hundred years before, is said to have rescued Fleance from the vengeance of Macbeth. The old man desired to give his grandson a more courtly education than he had himself received; and Ewen, as the boy was called, was brought up by the Marquis of Argyle, who placed him, at the age of twelve, under a tutor of his own choice at Inverary. But Ewen had no taste for books; and too often his preceptor saw, in agony of spirit, his pupil rush away from spelling-books and grammars, to hunt foxes and red hares among the neighbouring glens, to fill his creel with fish out of Loch Fyne, or to listen, for half a summer's day together, to some tattered pilgrim, the Homer of the villages, who could pour forth endless stories of the ancient heroes — of Wallace at the Brig of Stirling, of Bruce swimming from the blood-hound, of Black Donald's exploits over the Lords of the Isles, or of the vengeance of Allan-a-Sop. In spite, however, of his tutor's lamentations, at sixteen Ewen was, in mind and body, worthy of his race; tall, well-built, fresh-coloured, eagle-eyed; of that high temper to which dishonour is more terrible than death; and of the same innate sagacity which had so often made the enemies of his grandfather, who saw their plans outwitted, mutter that the old chief must have sold his soul to Satan.

While he was still at Inverary the old warrior died. Ewen, at sixteen, found himself the chieftain of his clan. He did not, for some months, however, put on the eagle's feather, or take command of his wild tribe among the hills. Argyle desired that he should go to Oxford. The Marquis was about to make a journey into England. Donald Cameron, Ewen's uncle, took, for the time, his nephew's place as leader of the clan; and Lochiel, as he must now be called, set out among the men-at-arms who rode with Argyle's carriage. The party never saw the oriels and quadrangles of the ancient city; but Lochiel, within the space of a few months, saw much stirring life, and gained a kind of knowledge which is very little to be learnt from deans and doctors. One of the first of his adventures might, however, very well have proved to be the last. At Stirling, where the party halted, the pestilence was raging. The utmost care was necessary. Argyle himself, with a prudence quite his own, refused to stir outside his coach. But when the party was about to start, Lochiel had disappeared. The Marquis was in terror; squires and pages ran wildly up and down the city; and presently the object of their agitation was discovered affably conversing with the inmates of a hovel, every one of whom was struck with the plague. At Berwick, where the party made a longer stay, Lochiel cheered the time by fighting duels in the streets with the gay youths of the city. But this amusement was soon interrupted. Montrose was marching into Fife, and Argyle was compelled to mount in haste and gallop at full speed to Castle Campbell. That ancient pile, which stood in a wild glen among the Ochil hills, had once been known, together with its stream, by names of strange romantic sound. The castle had

been Castle Gloom, and the waters which rolled
past its walls, the waters of the stream of Grief.
Within this ominous tower Lochiel had some experience of a siege. A fierce band of the Macleans attacked the fort. It was not taken ; but the
defenders showed themselves so little lion-hearted
that Lochiel bluntly told the governor that his
quaking poltroons deserved hanging, and himself
among them. Then came, as in Othello's story,
battles, fortunes, and disastrous chances. At Kil-
syth, Lochiel saw Argyle's trim troops fly like hares
before the clansmen of Montrose. A month later,
by a turn of fate, he formed part of that soft-footed
band who stole upon Montrose at Philiphaugh, and
started like ghosts out of the morning mist upon his
sleepy camp.

Among the prisoners taken at that action was Sir
Robert Spottiswood, an ancient friend of Lochiel's
father, and of his grandfather before him. The old
man was brought up for judgment at St. Andrews,
and condemned to be beheaded. Lochiel, who was
present at the trial, watched the proceedings with
the keenest interest, and was, like all the rest of the
spectators, struck with wonder and admiration at the
calm and noble bearing of the prisoner, and by the
moving eloquence of his defence. On the night
before the execution he made his way to the cell-

door. The jailer had strict orders to admit no visitor. But Lochiel was the favourite of Argyle. The door opened, and he entered.

Before he left the cell Lochiel's whole destiny was altered. Sir Robert, finding him the son of his old friend, spoke with him long and earnestly about the cause for which he was condemned to suffer. He found a willing hearer. Lochiel was by natural bent a cavalier. In secret, Montrose had long been his hero. And his own sagacity had taught him that Argyle was false, cunning, and cold-hearted. These things he now heard solemnly impressed upon him by a voice which was no longer of this world. He left the cell at midnight, his heart beating, and the tears streaming from his eyes. The next morning, from a window opposite the scaffold, he saw the prisoner, with cheek still ruddy, and with eagle eyes that looked proudly on the crowd, mount the steps, and lay his grey head on the block. The death of a brave man confirmed his words. From that moment Lochiel determined to follow his own course, to cast off Argyle's authority, and to take, without delay, command of his wild kingdom on the uplands of Ben Nevis, and along the rocky ranges of Glen Roy.

Indeed, there were reasons why he should not linger. His uncle Donald had turned out a sluggard ; and his clan, which had received some tidings of his character, were already looking for him eagerly. Argyle, finding his mind fixed, made no attempt to thwart him ; and in December 1646 Lochiel started for the Highlands. At the news of his approach his tribesmen mustered and marched out to meet him ; and thus, with colours flying and pipes playing, he came to his ancestral residence, Torr Castle, on Loch Lochy. He was not yet quite eighteen.

And now the eyes of friends and of enemies were bent alike upon him. A chief, at the beginning of his reign, was virtually on his probation. His empire over his wild clansmen had to be established by his own capacity. A coward or a fool, set over that fierce host, was not regarded simply with contempt, but was fortunate if he escaped, to use Dalgetty's phrase, "a dirk-thrust in his wame." On the other hand, a great chief was the idol of his tribe. The minstrels were never weary of singing, nor the people weary of hearing, of the splendour of his rush to victory, or of the craft and skill with which he could stalk the wariest mountain-stag, or thrust his spear into the fiercest wolf. But first his powers as a warrior and a hunter had to be set clear before all eyes. Lochiel had now to show what blood ran in his veins.

An opportunity was not likely to be wanting.

The little kingdom of the clan Cameron was girdled on all sides by the estates of rival princes, Campbells, Stewarts, Gordons, Macintoshes, Macphersons, Macdonalds, and Macleans. Every one of these sovereigns was either at daggers drawn with all the rest, or ready at any moment to become so. No reader of the *Legend of Montrose* will have forgotten the gathering of the clans at the Castle of Darnlinvarach : the assembly of the chiefs, the fire glittering in their eyes, the dirks ready at every instant to fly out of the scabbards, the rival pipers strutting up and down, each piping for his life to drown the rest, the sleeping-quarters settled jealously apart in the barn and the stables, the malt-kiln and the loft. Some of the feuds between the clans were as old as the quarrel on which, two centuries and a half before, Lochiel's ancestors and the ancestors of Macintosh had fought their immortal fight at Perth, in the days of the Fair Maid. Others were disputes of yesterday ; and one of these Lochiel found ready to his hands.

Macdonald of Keppoch owed him a sum of money for a piece of moorland which he rented in Glen Roy. This was the same Keppoch who once, it is related, gained a curious wager from an English lord, as to which of them possessed the finest candlesticks. The Englishman's candlesticks were of massive silver; Keppoch's turned out to be two brawny Highlanders, each grasping in his fist a blazing torch. This wily potentate had speedily discovered that, against Lochiel's uncle, it was an easier policy to bluster than to pay; and, on Lochiel's arrival, he soothed his soul with the reflection, that against so young a leader that policy would certainly prove easier still. He soon found out his error. Before he knew it, Lochiel, with five hundred men behind him, was marching down on his domain. Keppoch, who began with his old policy of bluster, wavered, put his claymore back into its scabbard, and sent a herald with the money.

Lochiel, burning for battle, regarded such a victory with disgust. But he was soon to have his heart's desire. The Earl of Glencairn, after the defeat of Worcester, summoned the clans, as volunteers, to fight for their Uncrowned King. Lochiel, with seven hundred claymores, was the first to join him. Then came adventures thick and fast. Wherever the thickest of the fighting fell, there was Lochiel with his seven hundred.

Glencairn had one evening pitched his camp at Tulluch, a village approached only by a steep and narrow pass, in which Lochiel was posted. A large force of the enemy was known to be at hand; but an immediate attack was not expected. On a sudden, in the twilight of the morning, the scouts came running in. The enemy were approaching in great numbers, evidently resolved to force their way through the ravine.

Lochiel, who had lain down on the heather, wrapped up in his plaid, was instantly aroused. The night was frosty, and a thin veil of mist hung above the valley. He climbed a lofty pinnacle of rock, from which he could plainly see the horses, the red coats, the glittering mail, and the dancing colours of the English soldiers. Lilburn himself was at their head. The peril was extreme; for their mere numbers were, in open ground, sufficient to cut Glencairn's entire force to pieces. Lochiel sent off a messenger to warn the general to retire into a place of safety. Then he prepared to hold the way to his last man.

Scarcely had he set his force in order, when the enemy dashed gaily forward, confident of victory. They found themselves confronted by a grim array of targets, behind each of which a savage soldier, armed with a glittering claymore, was quivering like a greyhound in the leash. Twenty times the horsemen charged that wall of warriors — and twenty times went reeling back, stabbed, hacked, and broken. Lochiel himself fought in front of his array; and at every charge his voice was heard,

above the clash of battle, sending forth the slogan.
Four hours passed in desperate conflict; and still
the little band held fast the gorge against the most
furious efforts of the English.

At last, when the men were weary, drenched in
blood, and weak with wounds and bruises, a herald
came from Glencairn. He had retired into a
swamp, some two miles distant, where it was impossible that a horse could follow, and was now in
perfect safety.

Lochiel instantly drew off his men. But he retreated, not towards the village, but up the sides of
the ravine, where nothing but a cat-o'-mountain or
a Highlander could cling. Lilburn, to his amazement, found the enemy suddenly above his head,
and the passage through the gorge left open. He
pushed forward at full speed; but Glencairn was
now safe beyond his reach, and he was compelled
at last, to his extreme vexation, to drag his horses
from the quag, and to march back through the pass.
There, as his tormented troopers made their way,
every boulder, every heather-tuft, along the walls
of the ravine, seemed to have turned itself into an
enemy shooting an arrow, or hurling down a stone;
and with every stone and arrow came the notes of
a terrific chorus :

"Wolves and ravens, come to me, and I will give you flesh!"

It was the war-song of Lochiel.

This exploit raised his glory to a great height. For every man he lost, the enemy lost six. Glencairn welcomed him as a deliverer; and not long afterwards the King himself sent him a letter, which acknowledged in the warmest terms the signal service which his valour had rendered to the royal cause. But as yet his fame was only in its dawn.

Monk marched into Scotland. It was that general's policy to fight with gold as often as with steel. He tried to bribe Lochiel; but on the young chief's blunt refusal, he resolved to plant a fortress in the heart of his domains. Lochiel received intelligence that five ships, carrying three thousand soldiers and a colony of workmen, were sailing up Loch Eil towards Ben Nevis.

He instantly marched homewards along the mountain ranges, and looked down on Inverlochy. The ships were riding off the shore, the troops were landed, the garrison was already fortified against all danger, and the fort was rising fast. To attack them would have been mere madness, and Lochiel was forced to lie in watch for an opportunity of avenging their presumption. With thirty-five picked men he posted himself upon the woody heights above Achdalew, having the lake and the garrison beneath his eye. His men were grievously in want of forage; and he was compelled to send out the remainder of his party to drive in cattle from some distance round.

The men were scarcely gone, when a boat belonging to the garrison put forth upon the lake, and stood over the water to the shore beneath him. A hundred and fifty soldiers were on board. Their purpose was to strip the village and to cut down wood. Lochiel resolved that they should not touch a girdle-cake or break a twig. His men were ready to follow him through any peril. But the risk of an attack was fearful; the enemy were more than four to one against them; and they besought him not to expose his life to such a hazard. Lochiel replied that if he fell, his brother Allan, who was with them, would take his place as chief. But the lives of both must not be jeopardised; and Allan positively refused to be left out of the adventure. It was found necessary, for his own security, to lash him to a tree, where he was left under the guard of a young boy. And then the little band prepared for the attack.

By this time the English soldiers had landed, and were busy in the village, stripping the hovels of eatables and putting the ducks and the hens into their sacks. While they were thus employed, a scout dashed in among them. They had scarcely time to draw up in rough order on the shore, when Lochiel at the head of his party came rushing out of the wood upon their ranks.

A desperate fight ensued. The English had a vast superiority of numbers. But the first fire of their muskets did no injury; and before they could reload, the enemy were among them. The clansmen, after their manner, caught the sword-cuts and the bayonets on their targets, and stabbed upwards from beneath them; and the English, thus fighting at great disadvantage, were slowly driven down the strand into the water.

Lochiel himself had driven three or four assailants into the wood, where after a sharp contest he had left them lying in a heap. He was returning at full speed towards the shore, eager to rejoin his men, when a gigantic officer, who had concealed himself in a thicket, sprang out upon him with a cry of vengeance. Their blades were instantly opposed. And then came a combat which, under a slight disguise, was destined to become famous over all the world. It was the fight between Fitz-James and Roderick Dhu.

The parts of the Gael and the Saxon are, however, interchanged. Lochiel is the Fitz-James; the officer is Roderick Dhu. With this fact borne in mind, the words of the Great Wizard set the fight before our eyes :—

> " Three times in closing strife they stood,
>   And thrice the Saxon blade drank blood.
>
> " Fierce Roderick felt the fatal drain,
>   And showered his blows like winter rain—
>   And as firm rock or castle-roof
>   Against the winter shower is proof
>   The foe, invulnerable still,
>   Foiled his wild rage by steady skill—
>   Till, at advantage ta'en, his brand
>   Forced Roderick's weapon from his hand,
>   And, backward borne upon the lea,
>   Brought the proud chieftain to his knee.
>
> " ' Now yield thee, or by Him that made
>   The world, thy heart's blood dyes my blade !'—
>   ' Thy threats, thy mercy, I defy !
>   Let recreant yield, who fears to die !'—
>   Like adder darting from his coil,
>   Like wolf that dashes through the toil,
>   Like mountain-cat who guards her young,
>   Full at Fitz-James's throat he sprung ;
>   Received, but recked not of a wound,
>   And locked his arms his foeman round.—
>   Now, gallant Saxon, hold thine own !
>   No maiden's hand is round thee thrown !
>   That desperate grasp thy frame might feel
>   Through bars of brass and triple steel !—
>   They tug, they strain !—down, down they go,
>   The Gael above, Fitz-James below."

Lochiel and his antagonist, however, fell not on soft heather. Locked in the deadly conflict, they tottered, wavered, and rolled together down a steep bank into the dry gulley of a brook. Lochiel, who was undermost, wedged between rocks, and crushed against the pebbles by the weight of his huge foe, was unable to stir hand or foot. But as his enemy stretched forth his hand to reach his dagger, which had fallen out of his belt, Lochiel, with a last effort, darted his head upwards and fixed his teeth in his opponent's throat. He fell back, writhing, and Lochiel stabbed him with his dirk.

> " Unwounded from the dreadful close,
>   But breathless all, Fitz-James arose."

But his adventures were not ended.

As he was issuing from the wood, a soldier, who was skulking in the thicket, levelled his musket at him through the branches, and in another instant would have shot him dead. A true *deus ex machinâ* saved him. While he had been engaged with his opponent, his brother Allan, who had been left lashed, in fancied safety, to the tree, had bribed the boy who attended him to cut his cords. At this instant he came running up, and espying the musket-barrel peeping from the bush, instantly fired his own piece in that direction. The soldier tumbled dead into the thicket, and the brothers hurried down the shore together.

The combatants, who were now of almost equal numbers, were fighting in the water. Lochiel, in a loud voice, offered quarter to all who would throw down their arms. The offer was accepted; and both parties began to wade ashore. Among the first to surrender was an Irishman, who must have been a fellow of delightful humour. As soon as this worthy felt himself on land, he cast down his weapon, seized Lochiel's hand in a friendly grasp, bade him adieu, and was off like the wind. Before the victors had done staring at one another he was half way back to Inverlochy.

He reached the fort in safety, with the tidings of the fray. His escape was narrower than he imagined. While he was turning his hearers into stone with horror, his late companions were in evil plight. Lochiel's offer of quarter had been accepted; the men were laying down their arms; when one of their party, who had swam out to the boat, found there a loaded firelock. He rested the barrel on the gunwale, and aimed deliberately at Lochiel. Lochiel's foster-brother, who stood beside him, saw the action. He threw himself before his chief, and the next instant was shot through the heart.

His blood was instantly and bitterly avenged. Lochiel himself, with his sword between his teeth, dashed through the water to the boat, and drove his blade into the assassin's heart. There was no more thought of mercy. The English soldiers snatched up their arms and fought with desperation for their lives. But the mountaineers, breathing forth vengeance, cut them down to the last man.

That night Lochiel himself bore in his arms the body of his preserver, over three miles of crags and moorlands, to the dead man's home among the hills; and there the coronach which was wailed above his bier, ere he was laid among the graves of his own people, doubtless had in it as much of pride as of sorrow, as for one who had died for his chief.

And now the fight was over—a fight of which the incidents of self-devotion, of single combat, of hair's-breadth escapes, of victory achieved against appalling odds, resemble some wild fable of romantic story rather than events of history. The whole of the English force, except a single fugitive, lay dead upon the shore or in the wood. Lochiel, though nearly all his band were bruised and wounded, had only lost five men.

Some of his wild warriors had that day set eyes for the first time on Saxon soldiers. There was a singular superstition in the Highlands, often muttered by the ancient wives, that an Englishman in one respect was like a monkey; and it is recorded that, after the battle, the conquerors were to be seen inspecting the dead bodies with lively curiosity, and breaking forth into cries of disappointment because they had no tails.

Next morning Colonel Bryan, the governor of the garrison, marched out two thousand soldiers, thirsting for revenge. In vain. He could see the Camerons on the lofty crags, their colours flying and their bagpipes yelling in triumph; but he could no more reach them than if they had had wings. On the other hand, wherever parties of his men were to be seen, the mountaineers came swooping from the hills, attacked them, slew them, and rose again, uninjured, like a flight of eagles, into their wild heights and inaccessible ravines. For some days this war went on. But Lochiel, who could no longer absent himself from the main army, at last drew off his men. The Colonel instantly told off a strong troop to pursue him. The man who took Lochiel, alive or dead, was to receive promotion and a bag of gold.

Lochiel marched by day over the mountain-ranges, and slept by night upon the heather, or in the little shealings, made of turf and branches,

which the mountain shepherds build on the bare
moors. In one of these he lay one night among
the hills of Braemar. No enemy was known to be
at hand, and the watch was kept with negligence.
In the dead of night an apparition stood beside him.
It was the figure of a small red-bearded man, with
troubled features and wild eyes, who struck the
sleeper on the breast, and bade him instantly arise.
Lochiel awoke, and gazed about him ; but he could
see nothing, and soon fell asleep once more. Immediately the figure reappeared, and awoke him with
the same alarming cry. Lochiel, in some amazement, roused his henchman, who lay beside him.
The man had seen no visitor ; and Lochiel, for the
third time, sunk to slumber. But now the ghost,
appearing with an angry aspect, struck him more
sharply than before, and cried in a compelling voice,
"Arise, arise, Lochiel!" With the accents ringing
in his ears, Lochiel sprang up and looked forth at
the doorway of the cabin. To his unspeakable
surprise, the moor was covered with the red coats
of English soldiers. His pursuers had stolen between his outposts, and were creeping up to seize
him in his sleep.

Whoever the red-bearded ghost might be, he
certainly came through the Gate of Horn. His
warning was delivered just in time. Lochiel in-

stantly dashed out of the hut, and favoured by the dusky light of morning, got clear away among the trackless hills.   His men soon gathered round him ; but two or three were missing ; and Lochiel, moreover, had lost all his baggage, in which were some unset diamonds, and a dozen silver spoons engraven with the ten commandments.

He joined his allies without misadventure.   But the campaign was nearly over ; and he was soon at liberty to revisit his old foes.   He marched back in deep secrecy to Inverlochy.   It chanced that on the day of his arrival about a hundred of the officers were celebrating his absence by holding a hunting-party in his forests, and killing his red deer.   They were destined to enjoy, that day, the excitement both of the hunter and of the game.   In the midst of their amusement Lochiel came suddenly upon them, hunted them out of the forest, and left only ten of them alive.

Nor did he confine himself to Inverlochy.   Some days later three colonels, with their guards and servants, who had been sent out to survey the country, were drinking their wine at evening in their inn at Portuchrekine.   The door was well guarded ; no danger was thought possible ; when suddenly the party were electrified to perceive a hole appear among the rafters of the roof.   Through the hole Lochiel, with a string of men behind him, came tumbling into the room. In a moment he had made every man of them a prisoner. They were conducted, under the darkness of the night, to the shores of Loch Ortuigg, where a boat was waiting, and lodged in a crazy cabin on an island in the middle of the lake. Except for their lodgings, however, they had little to complain of. Their servants were permitted to attend them ; and every day, as long as they were prisoners, their table was loaded with venison and wild-fowl. Lochiel, though an appalling enemy, was, after the ancient Highland manner, a host of the most lofty courtesy ; and he chose to consider his captives as his guests.

His enemies were, by this time, eager to buy peace. Every chief in Scotland, himself excepted, had now submitted to the Protector, and had been compelled to take an oath of fealty to the State. Lochiel alone received an intimation, that on passing his bare word to fight no longer for Prince Charles, he should receive full compensation for all injuries, and be left, for the future, in undisturbed possession of his lands. These conditions—as glorious to his fame as any feat of arms—Lochiel accepted. At the head of his clan, he marched to the garrison at Inverlochy. The treaty was ratified ; and Lochiel found himself at peace.

His name was now renowned all over Scotland. And his appearance was worthy of his name. He had now attained to his full growth. His figure was six feet high, slender, yet of amazing strength. His face was eminently handsome. His swarthy skin, and his dark and piercing eyes, caused him to be known throughout the country by the title of Black Ewen. In nobility of bearing he was said, in after years, to present a striking likeness to Louis the Fourteenth. The resemblance, however, must have been rather in impression than in reality; for the majestic Frenchman, in spite of a towering periwig, and shoes with heels like stilts, would hardly have come up to Lochiel's shoulder.

And now, for a time, the claymore was put back into the scabbard. The war-pipes were to warble the gay strains of peace. The wild pibroch was to change to wedding reels. Lochiel was to be married.

His bride was a beautiful Macdonald—a daughter of the lofty house whose chieftains had, for many ages, been known by the proud title of the Lords of the Isles. The wedding was long remembered for its splendour, for the brilliance of the company who gathered to the feast, and who danced from night to morning to the joyous skirling of the pipes. Among the merry-makers was one ancient minstrel, who had made a pilgrimage of many miles, that he might add to the festivities the humble tribute of his song. A version of the Gaelic ditty which he sang before the guests is still extant. It is an amusing specimen of the simplicity of art. The singer, having extolled the virtues of the chief, leads, by a deft transition, to the loss of three cows which had befallen himself, and for lack of which, he sings, he fears that he shall be reduced to feed on grass. Lochiel presented the performer, who in point of poverty, at least, seems to have been the equal of most poets, from Homer downwards, with three fresh cows from his own stock; the company filled his sporran with silver pieces; and hills and valleys echoed with thanksgivings, as the joyful bard departed.

Up to this point we have traced Lochiel's career with some minuteness. The course of events between his marriage and the battle of Killiecrankie may pass more rapidly before us.

In times of peace, among the ancient Highlands, vast hunting-parties took the place of war. The wolves, that once had prowled in mighty packs among the mountains, were by no means yet extinct. Twenty years later, Lochiel himself drove his spear into the ribs of the last wolf that howled in Scotland; but at this time numbers of the fierce beasts were to be found, and provided a dangerous and exciting

sport. Lochiel's hunting-parties soon grew famous.
They were varied by occasional campaigns against
the neighbouring clans. He marched against
Macintosh. He fought with the Macleans against
the Campbells. In 1660, when Monk declared his
pleasure that the King should enjoy his own again,
Lochiel marched with Monk to London, rode at his
side on the day of the triumphal entry, was presented, kissed the King's hand, and might, as it
appears, have had the bliss of holding the King's
stirrup, had he not lacked grievously the courtier's
art of thrusting himself forward. It was not, however, from the Merry Monarch that Lochiel was
destined to receive the most distinguished marks of
favour, but from James, then Duke of York.

In 1682 some villagers of Lochiel were seized
and brought for trial to Edinburgh, on the charge of
having killed two soldiers, who had attempted to
drive off cattle from the village, and who had caused
the death of an old woman, to whom the herd belonged. ' Thither Lochiel repaired to answer for his
men. The Duke happened to be visiting the city;
and Lochiel, who waited on him, was most graciously
received. The Duke talked long with him about
his exploits in the royal cause, and finally demanded
Lochiel's sword. Lochiel chanced to be wearing,
at the time, an ornamental rapier, such as he never

used in actual fighting. He handed his weapon to James, who attempted to draw it; but the blade, which had grown rusty, would not stir. "Lochiel's weapon," said the Duke, with a smile, "has not often stuck in its scabbard when the royal cause required it." Then, as Lochiel, with a slight effort, drew the blade himself, "See, my lords," he continued, turning to the crowd of courtiers who stood round, "the sword of Lochiel obeys no hand except his own!" And with this graceful speech he took the rapier, made Lochiel kneel down, struck him on the shoulder with the blade, and bade him rise up Sir Ewen.

The courtiers who were present at this ceremony smiled so affably that Lochiel believed himself to be among a host of friends. No sooner, however, had the Duke departed than some of these, bursting with envy, pushed on the case against his villagers with the most bitter vigour. The culprits would certainly have been doomed to dangle in a row, had not Lochiel, who had no mind to see his clansmen hanged to spite himself, set his own wits against his enemies. He hired a band of pot-companions to pick acquaintance with the most dangerous of the witnesses against him. These genial spirits earned their pay. On the morning of the trial the witnesses were discovered, after a long search, snoring under a table covered with bottles. No effort could erect them on their legs. The case was dismissed for want of evidence, and Lochiel returned in triumph to Lochaber.

Strategy was, indeed, as native to his character as a feat of arms. In 1685 the Sheriff of Inverness was charged by the Council to hold assizes in the Highlands. In the course of his circuit he came into Lochaber, attended by a guard of six or seven hundred men. Lochiel, incensed that any but himself should dare to exercise authority in his domains, marched to the Court with five hundred of his followers. These he professed were intended as a band of honour to the judge; but he had dropped a broad hint in the ears of two or three of his most turbulent spirits: "This judge will ruin us all. Is there none of my lads so clever as to get up a tumult, and send him packing? I have seen them raise mischief at less need." His listeners, eager to seize the least sign of his pleasure, caught up the words in a moment.

The Sheriff was sitting; the Court was crowded to the doors; when on a sudden, no one could say where, a blow was struck, a scuffle arose, and in two minutes the place was ringing with uproar and dazzling with the gleam of swords. The Sheriff, frightened out of his wits, threw himself on the protection of Lochiel; and Lochiel, with much loyal parade, escorted him out of the country, into which he never ventured to set his foot again. To add the last touch to the comedy, the Sheriff regarded Lochiel as the preserver of his life, and commended his name to the Council, who sent him a letter of thanks.

But although Lochiel permitted no rival — not even the King's representative — to usurp his authority, he was ready at all times to fight for the King. When Dundee summoned the clans for his last venture, it was from Lochiel's castle that the fiery crosses took their flight. His part in the campaign that followed is one of the well-known events of history. No reader of Scott or of Macaulay will have forgotten how his voice induced the Council to give battle; how, before the fight, he drew from every Cameron an oath to conquer or to perish; and how his onset whirled the red-coats in a torrent down the gorge of Killiecrankie.

He had never led his men except to victory— and such a victory was the fitting crown of his career. And at this point we must leave him. After the battle he retired into his kingdom, where he lived, taking no further active part in public matters, till 1719, when he died of fever. But, with the exception of a few vague glimpses, we have no record of his later years.   In truth, in this point, as in others, he resembles the ancient hero to whom he has been likened.   We know little more of the old age of Lochiel than of the last years of Ulysses.

Nevertheless, his character, his picturesque and striking figure, are as distinct to us as those of any hero of history or romance.   " The Ulysses of the Highlands "—the title is no freak of fancy.   There is no act, no exploit, of the Ithacan, which will not perfectly well suit the character of Lochiel.   Nothing is easier than to picture him among the scenes of Homer; to see him, in the mind's eye, rising in the hushed assembly of the Grecian kings—whirling in his chariot along the banks of the Scamander— emerging like a phantom from the wooden horse— plunging the burning brand into the eye of the Cyclops—or scheming how to sail in safety past the perilous islands where the Sirens sang upon the shingle among the whitened bones of men.   Strength, courage, fiery vigour, a sagacity which was never to be found at fault—such was the character of the ancient Wanderer.   And such was the character of Lochiel.

CASANOVA

On the morning of the 25th of July 1755, a prisoner, attended by a gaoler and two archers of the guard, passed across the Bridge of Sighs at Venice to the cells of the *Piombi*. The captive was a man of thirty, tall and strong in figure, with a face of Mephistopheles, an African complexion, and a pair of glittering eyes. His dress was that of a Venetian noble—a flowered coat laced with silver, a yellow vest, breeches of red satin, and a hat with a white plume. The charge against him was a strange one. He had been condemned by the Inquisitors of State as a wizard who had sold his soul to Satan.

This man was Casanova, the tale of whose captivity and strange escape we are about to tell. But first we must glance back at the events to which his present plight was owing. What was the story of this man of magic?

Briefly, it was this :—

His father, Gaetan Casanova, a man of ancient

Spanish race, having tossed away his property at twenty-eight, joined a troop of strolling players, in which he occupied a place so humble that a cobbler, with whose pretty daughter of sixteen he fell in love at Venice, disdained him as a son-in-law. Gaetan, in this predicament, ran off with his Zanetta, and married her in secret; and on the 2d of April 1725 their first child, Jacques, was born. The troop of actors was soon afterwards engaged to start for London, and the child was left at Venice with his grandmother—the cobbler's wife. He was brought up well and kindly; but his constitution was not strong; and at eight years old habitual fits of bleeding at the nose reduced him to a spectre. One of the earliest of his recollections was that of being taken, dripping blood, to the den of an old crone who had the reputation of a witch, of finding the hag squatting on a mat amidst a circle of black cats, of being shut up in a great chest, chanted over by the sorceress, and half-stifled with the smoke of burning drugs. The incantation or the fuming spices seemed for a time to have restored him; but soon the bleeding fits returned more stubbornly than ever. As a last resource it was resolved to try a change of air; and on the day when he was nine years old he was sent to school at Padua. There his life was far from happy. His food was bad and scanty ; and at night he slept, with three or four companions, in an attic where the rats, which ran in swarms across his pallet, froze his blood with horror. But the air of Padua worked wonders ; the fits of bleeding ceased ; his health returned ; his appetite became so ravenous that often he was forced to creep at dead of night into the kitchen, to prey upon the herrings and the sausages which hung drying in the smoke of the great chimney. In school his ready wits soon made him the best scholar in his class ; nor was it long before he knew as much of logic and of Latin as his master, as well as of an art which afterwards proved much more useful to him, how to play the violin. At fourteen, his mother, who had prospered on the stage, placed him in the University of Padua. That great seat of learning then drew students from all parts of Europe ; but Casanova fell in with a set of riotous companions, and added chiefly to his stock of knowledge how to make a bank at faro, .how to run up debts with jewellers and tailors, and how to knock down sentries in the streets at night. Nevertheless, at sixteen he read the Latin theme for his degree of Doctor, and, at his mother's wish, at once took orders in the Church of Rome.

But Casanova was not destined to adorn the Church. Pleasure-loving, giddy, vain, with no more conscience than an imp, the duties of a priest turned out by no means to his taste. The necessity of clipping off his lovelocks hurt him to the soul ; and having, on the feast day of St. Joseph, been selected to pronounce a sermon, he signalised the choice by dining with some gay companions, by drinking too much wine, and by falling headlong in the pulpit, to the scandal of his flock.

It was then proposed that he should spend a period of retirement in a college of theology at St. Cyprian. He entered ; but, as he took no pains to keep the rules of the establishment, he found himself, in no long time, locked up for punishment in the prison of St. Andrew—a fort which stood, surrounded by the water, just at the spot where, on Ascension day, the Doges cast the ring into the sea. It was thought that here at least he would be out of mischief ; but the notion was an error. Casanova merely turned his durance to account to revenge himself with safety on a bailiff, named Razzetta, who had pestered him about a debt. He first pretended to have sprained his ankle, and the surgeon was called in to bind it up ; he then bribed a gaoler to be ready with a gondola, slipped at nightfall from his window, rowed to Venice, caught Razzetta entering his house, thrashed him soundly, tossed him into the canal, rowed back in the darkness to his window, entered and replaced his bandages, and instantly awoke the garrison with piercing cries. He was found, to all appearance, dying of internal spasms; the surgeon was roused up, a drug was administered, and gradually the spasms passed away. Next day Razzetta brought an action for assault and battery. But in vain. The *alibi* was unassailable. Every official in the fort was ready to take oath that at the time when the assault was said to have been committed, the accused was lying helpless in his cell with a sprained ankle and a fit of colic.

Then the Bishop of Martorano, who was acquainted with his mother, promised to look after him, and to push his fortunes; and Casanova, with money in his purse, and with a well-filled trunk, set out by way of Rome and Naples to the Bishop's See. He had, however, only reached Chiozza when he fell in with some boon companions, made a little bank at faro, and lost every coin in his possession. Every gambler is aware that luck must turn. Casanova pawned his trunk for thirty sequins to a Jew, made another little bank at faro, and was again drained dry. By chance he made acquaintance with a monk named Stephano, who was about to beg his way to Rome. The pair agreed to go together; but as the pace of brother Stephano was about a league a day, they travelled like the tortoise and the snail. The monk, moreover, proved to be a reckless thief, who crammed the pouches of his frock with unconsidered trifles, from sausages to truffles, where- ever he could find them; and Casanova, who pre- ferred a safer mode of roguery, and who had no longing to be sentenced to the galleys, at last in- formed him plainly that he was a rascal. Stephano retorted that Casanova was a beggar, whereupon the latter knocked him down and left him lying in a ditch. Five days later Stephano came up with Casanova at a tavern, where he lay recovering from a sprain which he had gained in jumping through a hedge, and about to sell his coat to pacify the land- lord. From this extremity the easy-tempered monk relieved him, and the pair went on together as before.

But at Rome they parted; and thence to Mar- torano Casanova, having no longer Stephano to pilfer for him, was forced to forage for himself. And now a certain natural gift of knavery began to manifest its presence in him. At Naples he came across a wealthy Greek, who had a stock of quick- silver to sell. Casanova took a jar of quicksilver, added secretly some lead and bismuth, and showed the Greek his quicksilver increased in bulk. The Greek, eager to acquire the art of conjuring three jars of quicksilver into four, purchased the secret for a hundred sequins. It was left him to discover, what Casanova had omitted to inform him, that, although he had increased his stock-in-trade, his quicksilver was spoilt.

In the meantime Casanova travelled at his ease to Martorano. Already he beheld in his mind's eye the bishop's palace, gay with company, with books and pictures, dainty dishes and rare wines. He found the prelate in a crazy dwelling, of which the furniture was such that a mattress for himself had to be dragged off the bishop's bed. The whole income of the See was eighty pounds a year. Cowkeepers and market-women were the sole society. Casanova cast a glance upon the congregation gathered in the chapel, besought the bishop's blessing and dismissal, and, sixteen hours after his arrival, started back to Rome.

He carried with him from the bishop a letter of introduction to Cardinal Acquaviva. That great potentate received him graciously, lodged him in his palace, and promised to provide for him. And now, for the first time, his life began to realise his dreams. He had the joy of talking every day with cardinals and cavaliers, and of breathing honeyed speeches in the ears of fair contessas. He was received in private by the Pope himself, and kept the Holy Father laughing for an hour. He seemed, in brief, to have become at once the darling child of fortune ; nor was it this time altogether his own fault that fortune changed her face.

The cardinal had bade him study French. His language-master had a pretty daughter, with whom one of Casanova's fellow-pupils fell in love. As her father frowned upon his suit Barbara put on an abbé's dress, and ran away with him. The old man chased them with a band of guards, and took the lover prisoner; but the false abbé passed unrecognised, and escaped into the night. Barbara came flying up to Casanova's rooms, besought him as her only friend to hide her till the storm was over, and fell fainting at his feet. He consented; but the act of friendship cost him dear. Next day he sent her to the cardinal to tell her story; and Acquaviva, moved to pity, placed her for protection in a convent, until her lover should be free. But Barbara had been noticed as she stole into the palace; and tongues of scandal soon began to wag of Casanova and of pretty girls dressed up as abbés. No scandal was allowed to touch the house of Acquaviva. The cardinal sent for Casanova, and told him plainly, though with sorrow, that he must take his leave of Rome. "Choose any other city you prefer," said Acquaviva, "and I will start you there." Casanova chose the first that came into his head, which happened to be Constantinople. The cardinal gave him, together with seven hundred sequins, a letter to a pasha in that city. And Casanova was adrift once more.

He was weary of the Church. Nature, in his opinion, had designed him for a soldier, and he determined to let Nature have her way. He left Rome as an abbé; but, to the amazement of his friends at Venice, he reappeared there, blazing in a gorgeous uniform, with purple vest, gold epaulets, and red cockade. To account for those insignia, to which his only right was that of having paid a tailor for them, he proclaimed that he had just been serving in the troops of Spain. Nobody believed this story; and he speedily discovered, to his great vexation, that, like the jackdaw in the peacock's feathers, he ran some risk of being laughed at. To stop the mouths of scoffers, he bought an ensignship in one of the State troops, then posted at Corfu; but as he still desired to visit Constantinople, he was granted leave of absence for six months to make a trip there.

Accordingly, he sailed from Venice. The voyage at first was easy; but off the island of Curzola a storm sprang up which put the ship in peril. The chaplain, an ignorant and superstitious priest, took his stand on deck, and, with his missal in his hand, prayed loudly to the demons of the storm. Casanova laughed; whereon the priest denounced him as an atheist, a Jonah who had called the tempest on their heads. The sailors, white with terror, were not long in acting on this hint. One of them crept stealthily to Casanova, watched his moment, and pushed him over the ship's side. Nothing but a miracle of fortune saved him. As he fell, the fluke of the ship's anchor caught his coat and held him swinging in mid-air. There the sailors left him; but a soldier who was on the vessel flung him down a rope and hauled him to the deck. The crew were clamouring to fling him back again, when the priest discovered that the culprit had about him a Greek parchment, which professed to be a love-charm. Here, plainly, was the reason of the tempest. A brazier was fetched, the charm was thrown upon the coals, and, as the burning parchment writhed and cracked, the priest cried out that it was a fiend in torment. Fortunately, at the same time the wind began to fall; the sailors lost their terror; and Casanova was allowed to live.

At Constantinople Casanova, bearing the letter from the cardinal, called on Osman pasha, whose help, however, he no longer needed. The pasha was a curious character. His true name was Count Bonneval; he had been an officer at Venice, but had transformed himself into a Turk to gain the favour of the Sultan. He was now an old man, jovial, fat, and lazy. The sincerity of his conversion to the precepts of the Prophet, especially to that which tells against the use of wine, Casanova had soon an opportunity of observing. The pasha invited him to step into his library. To his surprise, the shelves were screened with curtains, in front of which were iron gratings. Osman took a key, unlocked a grating, and drew aside the curtain. The pasha's books were bottles of choice wine.

This friendly welcome was succeeded by a dinner. At the pasha's table Casanova made acquaintance with a fine old Turk, named Josouf Ali, a man of wealth and a philosopher. Ali conceived for Casanova an amazing liking, repeatedly invited him to his own house, and there, across the hookahs and the hydromel, discussed with him for hours the doctrines of the Prophet. At last this curious friendship reached a climax. Ali possessed a daughter of fifteen, named Zelnie, whose lustrous eyes and skin of alabaster, the ease with which she talked in Greek and in Italian, the skill with which she painted, worked in wools, and warbled to her harp, made her a treasure worthy of a Sultan. He proposed that Casanova should become a Turk, should marry the enchanting Zelnie, and should, at the same time, become possessor of her dowry, a palace, a troop of slaves, and an abundant income.

Casanova was dumfounded. The offer dazzled him; but still he wavered. To be a turbaned Turk, to drink no wine, to learn to jabber a barbaric lingo, to hide for life his brilliance in obscurity, above all to run the risk of finding Zelnie, when the marriage-veil was lifted, not quite the paragon her father thought her — these things made him pause. It was not, however, till the eve of his departure that he decided to decline. Ali, so far from being piqued at this magnanimous refusal, piled the vessel's deck with rich mementos of his friendship—mementos which Casanova, when the ship touched Corfu, immediately converted into cash.

At Corfu, where he joined his regiment, everything seemed in his favour. He was rich, gay, popular among his comrades, welcomed in the best society. He passed there just a year. At the end of that time he had been ruined at the faro table, had pawned his jewellery, was hopelessly in debt, and had lost his chances of promotion. Having made the town too hot to hold him, he arrived at the conclusion that the army was no place for a philosopher. He sold his commission for a hundred sequins, and returned forthwith to Venice.

His new project was to live by gaming — a

strange device for one who, in the effort to be Captain Rook, had so often found the fate of Mr. Pigeon. He tried his luck, however; but in a week he was without a ducat. In order to keep himself from perishing of hunger, he was glad to earn a pittance as a fiddler in the theatre of St. Samuel.

His companions in this new position were the Hectors and the Tityre-Tus of Venice. Their diversion, when the play was over, was to sally, flushed with wine, into the streets, to bully quiet passengers, to skirmish with the guards, to cut the ropes of gondolas, to set the church-bells pealing an alarm, and to send physicians and confessors to the beds of men in perfect health.

Casanova was, for nearly half a year, a ruling spirit of this gang of worthies. But a freak of fortune was again before him.

One night, on issuing from a palace where he had been fiddling at a wedding dance, he saw a signor in a scarlet cloak, who was descending to his gondola, drop a letter on the steps. Casanova restored the letter to its owner, who, in return, on finding that they were going in the same direction, invited him to step into his boat. Casanovo did so, and they started; but as they glided up the long canal, the signor suddenly fell forward in a fit. Casanova sprang ashore, brought a surgeon running in his nightcap, and having seen the patient bled, conveyed him to his palace and took his post at the bedside. The surgeon applied a plaster made of mercury to the sick man's chest, and left him for the night; but by the action of the drug the patient in a little while was gasping in convulsions, and to all appearance dying. Casanova plucked the plaster off again — and by that simple action made his fortune. Next day the patient was much better. He vowed that the doctor was a quack, that he owed his life to Casanova, and that no other should attend him; and thus it came to pass, that when the doctor made his visit in the morning he found the upstart fiddler in his place, and rushed out of the house in rage and horror.

Thus strangely turned into a sage, Casanova set himself to play the part. Signor Bragadin, though one of the most illustrious lords of Venice, was superstitious to the point of mania. Casanova delivered his opinions with an air so solemn, he quoted from the works of learned writers (which he had never read) with such felicity and ease, that Bragadin believed his wisdom supernatural. He hinted this belief to Casanova—and Casanova was ready with a story. He confessed that an ancient hermit, whose cave was in the mountains of Carpegna, had revealed to him the mystery of Solomon's clavicula, which is the art of prophesying by the use of numbers—a secret which he himself was forbidden to reveal, under pain of dying suddenly within three days. Bragadin, to whom the art of sorcery was the most sublime of sciences, panted to consult the oracle. Under the promptings of the prophet it responded, as oracles in all ages have responded, sometimes clearly, sometimes darkly, but never so as to be caught in error. The signor was in ecstasies. As he could not work the augury himself, he resolved to keep possession of the augur; and forthwith Casanova, to his own amazement, found himself installed in rich apartments in the palace, his pockets full of money and a troop of lacqueys at his service, proclaimed to all the world of Venice as Signor Bragadin's adopted son.

He had already been by turns an abbé, a beggar, an ensign, and a fiddler. He was now a combination of quack, prophet, and grandee. Except when called upon to work his oracle, he had no task but to amuse himself. It is perhaps not strange that he was soon in new disaster.

One of his acquaintances, a merchant named Demetrio, whose jealousy he had excited, contrived a trick to make him look ridiculous. Demetrio sawed the plank which ran across a certain boggy trench, with the result that Casanova, who was the

first among a troop of gay companions to pass over,
fell plump into the bog up to the ears. A crowd of
rustics hauled him out with ropes, an indistinguish-
able lump of mud, at which his giddy comrades
screamed with laughing. Burning to requite this
witticism, Casanova crept by night into a burial-
ground, cut off the arm of a dead body, hid himself
beneath Demetrio's bed, and at the dead of night
began to tug the blankets. Demetrio, waking,
cried to the tomfool beneath him, that it was vain
to try to scare him with a ghost ; at the same time
he made a snatch into the darkness, caught the
dead hand, which Casanova suddenly released, and
instantly fell backwards in a swoon of terror. He
had literally been scared out of his senses.

This outrageous act aroused a perfect tempest.
Demetrio's friends burst into vows of vengeance ;
the inquisitors prepared to seize the culprit on a
charge of sacrilege. Casanova was compelled to
fly from Venice. Being well supplied with money,
he wandered from city to city at his ease. At Paris,
where his younger brother, afterwards the famous
painter, was then studying, he resided for some
time ; and as he was a scholar, a talker, and a boon
companion, ever ready to play, to flirt, to spout
Ariosto, or to write a ballad to a lady's eyebrow, the
society of wits and beauties opened to him readily.

He also worked his oracle; and here again he found no lack of people panting to be dupes. Sober merchants consulted him about the safety of their argosies; and a cynic might find food for mirth in the reflection that the Duchess of Chartres herself sent for him to the Palais Royal, and demanded of his oracle how to cure her pimples.

At length, the danger having, as he thought, subsided, he returned to Venice. But in this he was in error. The charge of sacrilege was not revived against him; but reports of his *clavicula* had been noised abroad; he was accused of practising unholy arts; and the spies of the inquisition were upon his track. One of these was ready with a proof that Casanova was in league with Satan; for it had been remarked that, often as he lost his stakes at faro, he never called upon the devil as the cause of his ill-luck. Another spy, who gained admittance to his chamber on pretence of showing him some jewels, observed some books on sorcery lying on the table— *Solomon's Charms, The Conjurations of the Demons, Zecor-ben,* and *Planetary Hours.* Casanova's purse was just then empty; and the spy, under the pretext of selling these rare works at a high price to a *virtuoso,* bore them straight to the inquisitors. The next day he returned them; but in the meantime Casanova's fate was sealed.

A few mornings later, before daybreak, as he was sleeping in his bed, a hand was laid upon his shoulder. He started up, and saw a guard of the Tribunal, with a group of archers, who had come to take him. At that sight a shiver thrilled him to the heart. And he well might shiver, for he was at the mercy of an awful power.

Casanova left his bed, dressed himself with care, and followed the arrester ; and thus in a few minutes he was on his way, as when we saw him first, across the Bridge of Sighs towards the cells of.the *Piombi*.

These cells are the garrets of the Doge's palace,— the name springing from the plaques of lead which form the palace-roof. Casanova was conducted by the gaoler, a rough fellow named Lorenzo, who also, on occasion, served as hangman, along a corridor, from which opened half a dozen little iron-studded doors. Through one of these, so dwarfish that his head on entering was almost on a level with his knees, he was thrust into a cell in which it was impossible to stand erect, and in which the only light that entered glimmered through a narrow grating in the door. The cell was absolutely bare ; but he was told that he might buy himself a chair, a table, and a bed. When these were brought, he was informed that food would be supplied him once a day, at daybreak. And he was left alone.

The time was in the dog-days, and the hot leads turned the cell into an oven, in which, although he stripped himself of every rag, the prisoner was half-melted. At nightfall, when he stretched himself upon his pallet, his rest was broken by gigantic rats which scoured along the corridor, and by the great bell of St. Mark's tower pealing forth the hours. Nor were his meditations more consoling. How long this state of misery might last, he could not tell. He had undergone no trial—he had received no sentence. He might be left there for a week or for a year, or he might wither out his lifetime in captivity.

Day by day went by; August and September passed; and with them passed all hope of swift release. Sometimes the solitude of his cell was broken by the entrance of a fellow-prisoner; first, a count's valet, who had been caught eloping with his master's daughter and a box of jewels; then, a wizen, little red-eyed money-lender, like a screech-owl, who had tried to swindle his own partner. These delectable companions came and went; but the months passed, and Casanova was a captive still. Gradually, his whole thought fixed itself upon another road to freedom. Was there no chance of scheming an escape?

At stated periods, while his cell was being swept,

he was allowed to walk into the corridor, which was secured by a strong door. In a corner of the corridor was a heap of rubbish. Casanova pried into the heap and came across an iron bolt, an inch in thickness and some two feet long. This instrument, together with a fragment of black marble, he smuggled to his cell beneath his coat. There he set himself to grind the bolt into a point upon the piece of marble ; and after a week's constant labour, during which his hands were worn to blisters, a long sharp point was made.

Casanova was well acquainted with the palace buildings. He reckoned that his cell was situated just above the hall of the inquisitors, and he laid a plan accordingly. He resolved to pierce the cell-floor with his bolt, to descend into the hall by ropes made out of strips of bedding, to lie in wait until the door was opened, and then to make a rush for freedom. The project was a mad one; but the ache for liberty had brought him to that desperate temper which is ready for strange deeds—the temper which drove Trenck to burrow like a mole beneath his prison-walls, and Monte Christo in the Château d'If to stitch himself into the dead man's sack, in order to be cast into the sea.

He could not work, however, without light, and the wretched gleam which struggled through the grating lasted only about five hours a day; the rest was pitchy darkness. Casanova schemed again. He possessed a wooden bowl, from which he ate his broth, and a flask of salad-oil was part of his provisions; strips torn off his shirt provided him with wicks, and a scrap of stuffing from his coat with tinder; while, by pretending that he had the toothache, for which a gun-flint steeped in vinegar was esteemed a sovereign cure, he obtained a couple from the gaoler. As soon as he was left in solitude, he struck his flints, and saw, with indescribable delight, his rude lamp flare out bravely on the darkness of his cell.

Armed with his bolt, and lighted by his lamp, he set to work to dig into the planks beneath his bed, gathering, as he worked, the fragments in a handkerchief, to be emptied into the heap of rubbish in the corridor. Except at the hour at which the gaoler visited the cells, he laboured night and day. The work was hard and slow; but in three weeks the planks were pierced, and through a tiny hole, which could be speedily enlarged, he was able to peer down into the hall.

His rope was made; and all was ready; and he was waiting, with a bounding heart, for night to bring the hour of his adventure, when all at once he heard, outside his cell, the bolts which locked the corridor shoot back. His first thought was that he was free — that his order of release had come at last. Trembling with hope, he saw his door fly open. It was the gaoler come to take him to another cell.

Casanova fell into his chair, half fainting. That instant was a bitter penance for his sins. All his work was lost, and it could never be repeated, for the hole would be discovered, and henceforth his actions would be strictly watched. In a stupor of despair, supported by the gaoler, he tottered down the corridor, and along another gallery, at the end of which appeared the door of his new cell. His chair was carried with him by an archer. Under its seat he had contrived a place in which to hide his bolt; and, by good fortune, it was fixed there still.

The gaoler went to fetch the prisoner's bed. Casanova sat there motionless, awaiting the discovery. The result might be to him a case of life and death. What if the inquisitors condemned him to the Wells? Those dreaded dungeons were pits sunk beneath the basement of the palace—dark, deep, and slimy dens, which the rising tides, flowing through the gratings, kept continually half full of water, over which the wretched captive passed his life supported on a tressel, from which he could not stir without the risk of being drowned. Few prisoners issued from the Wells alive. One wretched man, a soldier of the name of Beguelin, who had betrayed his orders, had passed there twenty-seven years of life in death. Casanova called to mind this story. What if such a fate were now before him!

As he sat quaking at the thought, he heard the gaoler rushing headlong back. With eyes of flame he burst into the cell. "Where is your chisel?" he cried furiously; "where did you get it?—who brought it in to you?" An inspiration rushed on Casanova. "You yourself," he answered boldly; "who else has had the chance?"

The gaoler was struck dumb; for if the inquisitors believed this story, which in fact seemed unassailable, he could not set his life at a pin's fee. Tearing his hair, he darted from the cell, stopped up the hole with desperate eagerness, and suffered not a word of the attempt to reach the ears of the Tribunal.

Casanova's wits had saved him from the Wells; but his chances of escape seemed gone for ever. The keeper, it is true, had failed to find his bolt; but how was he to use it? The cell was new—a scratch would have been visible; and, moreover, every morning, when his food was brought, the keeper tapped the walls and floor, to ascertain that they were sound. In truth, his plight seemed hopeless. But fortune, who had tossed him up and down so often, was to give him one chance still.

The cell next his contained two prisoners—an old count, Andro Asquin, and a monk whose name was Balbi. Balbi had a shelf of volumes in his cell, and these, in the spirit of a friendly neighbour, he lent to Casanova one by one—the gaoler, who could not read, and who conceived no danger, being gained by a small bribe to take them to and fro. Casanova let his finger-nail grow long, used it as a pen, and wrote with fruit-juice on a fly-leaf a letter to the monk. Balbi found the writing, and replied in the same manner; and thus a secret correspondence was established.

And now Casanova saw his way again. If Balbi had the bolt, he might make use of it without suspicion; he might pierce the ceiling of his cell, might climb into the space beneath the palace roof, and might make a hole in Casanova's ceiling. Then the pair of them together might break through the roof, and so emerge upon the leads.

The monk agreed. But how was he to get the bolt? Casanova solved this puzzle also. He concealed the bar between the binding and the back of an immense old folio Bible; and the hoodwinked gaoler bore it safely into Balbi's cell.

But how were the operations of the monk to be concealed? Casanova told him. He was to purchase, through the keeper, a number of wooden figures of the saints, tall enough to reach the ceiling of his cell, which was barely six feet high. Balbi gave the order, and the saints arrived. Thenceforward, when the gaoler paid his visits in the twilight of the morning, he found invariably the pious monk telling his beads before St. Philip or St. Francis. Who could have dreamt that the Apostles' heads concealed a gaping hole?

The hole grew larger daily. In ten days the monk had pierced his ceiling, and had worked so far through Casanova's that a few hours' toil would end his task. No trace, of course, was visible in Casanova's cell.

It was Monday, the 16th of October; the monk was working overhead; when Casanova heard again, with freezing blood, the bolts which locked the corridor fly back. He had barely time to give three knocks, their preconcerted sign of danger, when his door flew open, and a prisoner was thrust in.

The new arrival was a little, skinny, ragged rascal, grasping a string of beads, and chattering with terror. Casanova, eager to discover whether this new comrade could be trusted, soon drew forth his story. His name was Sorodaci; he had been a spy, devoted to the saints, and to the holy office; but having, in a praiseworthy attempt to ruin his own godfather, become suspected of false dealing with the Council, he had had the misfortune to find himself locked up instead of his relation. Here was a colleague for the plotters! This reptile, dying for a chance of crawling back to favour, would give his ears to get an inkling of their scheme. A wink or a word to the gaoler, and their hopes were gone for ever.

Their work was at a standstill. For some days Casanova nourished the vain hope that Sorodaci would be speedily released. His fingers itched to throttle the intruder; but after studying his man, who was a ninny eaten up with superstition, he resolved that he would fool him. Accordingly, he wrote to Balbi, directing him to set to work next day at three o'clock precisely. That night, he started from his bed, crying aloud that he had had a vision. The Virgin of the Rosary had appeared to him, and had assured him that an angel would descend to break their prison, and to set them free. At three o'clock that afternoon they might expect to hear him working at the roof above them.

Sorodaci was dumfounded. In vain he made a feint of disbelief; as three o'clock drew near he gasped and trembled; but when, precisely as St. Mark's gave forth the hour, the angel was heard working overhead, he fell upon his face in mortal terror. There was no more danger of his playing false. The angel worked; the gaoler paid his visits; but Sorodaci never dreamt of treason.

Two days passed; it was the last day of October, and Balbi set to work for the last time. At ten o'clock at night a hole appeared in the low ceiling, the monk came tumbling into Casanova's arms, and Sorodaci reeled against the wall in inexpressible amazement at perceiving that the angel had a thick black beard.

Casanova seized the bolt, ascended through the hole, and made a trial upon the palace roof. To his delight, the planks were crumbling with the rot. In half an hour he touched the plaques of lead, wrenched up the fastenings with his bar, and thrust his head out of the hole. To his concern, the moon was shining brightly; but it was near its setting, and by midnight would have disappeared.

Meanwhile the captives met in Balbi's cell. Count Asquin, Balbi's fellow-prisoner, old, fat, and suffering from a broken leg ill set, refused to risk his neck on such a venture. Sorodaci also, whose faith in this strange angel was much shaken, and who trembled at the thought that he might tumble into the canal, elected to remain. He would, he said, invoke St. Francis for their safety. The other two made ready. Casanova bound into a bundle the rich dress which he had brought into the prison; and each carried on his shoulder a coiled rope made out of strips of bedding.

Midnight pealed from St. Mark's tower; the moon was touching the lagoons. The adventurers bade farewell to their companions; and Casanova, bidding the monk follow him, lifted the plaque of lead, and issued through the hole.

The roof was steep and slippery. Casanova, on his hands and knees, digging his spike into the leads to keep himself from sliding, and trailing the monk behind him by his waist-band, crawled snail-like up the perilous slant, and at length perched panting on the summit. No sooner was the monk astride, than, in endeavouring to wipe his brow, he let his hat roll down the slope and plunge into the sea. His maladroitness might have been their ruin; for had the hat rolled down the other side, it would have dropped into the Piazza, and startled the sentries like a bolt from heaven.

The next thing was to fix their rope. But here an unexpected difficulty stopped them—they could find no means by which to fasten it. For a whole hour Casanova crept about the roof, seeking for a point to which to loop his cable, but in vain. He discovered nothing but a mason's ladder, far too short to reach the ground, lying beside a heap of plaster and a pile of plaques of lead. At length he was compelled to change his tactics. Several dormer windows opened on the roof, through one of which they might descend into the palace. To do so was to run their heads into the lion's den; but there was no alternative, and it was possible that, by some rare good luck, the lions might be caught asleep or hoodwinked. Casanova, with his bolt, wrenched off the light iron grill which barred a window, broke the narrow leaded panes, and the monk, while Casanova held the rope, slid down into the room below.

In order to descend in turn, Casanova dragged the ladder to the window; but in the attempt to introduce it, he very nearly put an end to his adventures. His foot slipped, he went rolling down the roof, and in an instant found himself suspended by his elbows over the abyss. Thus hanging between life and death, his only chance was in one desperate effort—if that failed him, he was lost. Collecting all his strength, he writhed his body upwards, and sank gasping on the gutter. Safe, but sick with horror, he lay there long without the power of motion.

At length, his strength returning, he lowered the ladder to the monk, who held it in his arms while he descended. The room in which they found themselves was pitchy dark. They groped and found a door, through which they passed into a room in which were several chairs and a great table, but from which they sought in vain to find an exit. At length they found themselves compelled to wait for daybreak. Casanova, utterly exhausted, threw himself upon the floor, and, with the coil of rope for pillow, fell into a death-like sleep. It was the first which he had snatched for several nights. When he woke, the first gleam of day was stealing in, and the monk, in a frenzy of impatience, was shaking him with violence. In the grey morning light they found the door, and issued through a gallery, the walls of which were lined with niches, wherein the archives of the State were stored in parchment rolls, down a narrow flight of stone steps closed by a glass door, into the Doge's council chamber. The door of this was fastened, but the panels were not thick, and in half an hour the never-failing bolt had pierced a gaping hole at a height of five feet from the floor. The monk, whom Casanova held suspended by the legs, went through headfirst with ease; but Casanova, who had to follow without help, tore his legs and sides upon the jagged splinters, till they dripped with blood. Descending two more flights, they reached the massive doorway of the royal stairway. To their consternation it was locked. To break through it was quite hopeless. They might as well have tried to pierce the marble walls.

Nothing was left but to try stratagem.

Casanova, all in blood and rags, sat down, untied his bundle, and put on his gorgeous coat, his white silk stockings, and his gold-laced hat with the white plume. His rich embroidered mantle he bestowed upon the monk, to whom it gave the aspect of a thief who had just filched it. Then he thrust his head from a side grating, and attracted the attention of some persons in the court. These men called the door-keeper, who, thinking that he must have locked in some one over-night in error, came hurrying up in trepidation with his keys.

Casanova, through a cranny, watched him coming. The instant the door opened, he walked out quickly, followed by the monk; and before the warder had recovered from his stupor, the two had vanished down the Giants' Stairs, pushed across to the canal, sprang into a gondola, and were skimming over the water towards Mestro.

It was a lovely morning; the air was clear and

pure, the sun was rising brightly. The contrast with the scene from which he had escaped struck Casanova to the soul ; and, to the amazement of the stolid monk, he burst into a flood of tears.

They were free. But could they keep their freedom ? The danger, as they knew, was far from over ; the hue and cry was still to come.

At Mestro they hired a carriage for Treviso, where, having spent their stock of money, they plunged on foot into the woods. There, the better to escape detection, they parted company, and each took his way alone.

By two o'clock that afternoon Casanova had walked four-and-twenty miles. His plight was wretched to the last degree ; though dropping with fatigue, and faint with hunger, he durst not venture near a public inn. Finding himself at length in sight of a large private house, he demanded of a shepherd, whose flock was feeding on a hillside, to whom the place belonged, and was informed that the owner's name was Captain Campagne, the chief of the Venetian Guards. At that name of terror, Casanova trembled ; then, by an impulse over which he had no control, and which he was never able to explain, he walked straight down the hill towards the dwelling of the man of whom, of all others, he had the most to dread.

In the yard a little boy was playing whip-top. On Casanova asking where his father was, he called his mother, a young and pretty woman, who informed the stranger that the captain had just been summoned for three days to Venice, in order to hunt down two prisoners who had escaped from the *Piombi*.

Casanova breathed again. The situation was one after his own heart.

"I regret to find my godfather from home," he said; "but I am charmed to make the acquaintance of his lovely wife."

"Your godfather!" cried the lady, "why then you are His Excellence Monsieur Veturi, who has promised to be sponsor to our child—I am delighted to receive you. My husband will be distressed that he was not at home." And with a thousand such civilities Casanova was welcomed into the house and a feast was set before him—after which, as he explained the sorry state of his apparel, his wounds, and his fatigue, by stating that he had had a fall whilst hunting in the forest, he was conducted to the most luxurious sleeping-chamber in the house. From three o'clock that afternoon till six next morning he slept like a stone figure. Then he awoke, dressed himself, walked unperceived out of the house, and went his way—half trembling at his rashness, half laughing at the picture of the captain's face when he should hear the story, and wholly grateful to the captain's pretty wife.

And now the worst was over. Without much misadventure he begged his way to Bolzan, which was beyond the State of Venice, where he could laugh at his pursuers. Thence he dispatched a messenger to Signor Bragadin for a supply of money. The signor sent him all he wanted; and Casanova was once more rich and free.

He was free. His great escape from the *Piombi* was a thing accomplished; and it was this of which we set ourselves to tell. At this point therefore we might leave him; but the colour of romance which wraps the sequel of his story tempts us to let it pass before us rapidly.

From Bolzan he made his way to Paris, where he received an ardent welcome. The fame of his escape was there before him. All society desired to hear from his own lips the details of his unprecedented exploit; and soon, from the youngest page to Madame Pompadour herself, all tongues were talking of the bolt, the lamp, the monk's cell full of wooden saints, and Sorodaci gaping at the angel. For his own part, Casanova was resolved to run no further risk of such adventures; his life in future should be sage and steady. But as his purse grew light, his resolutions vanished. He looked about him for a victim; and in the Marquise d'Urfé, a dowager whose family was of the old nobility of France, he found one after his own heart. The Marquise was, in truth, a female counterpart of Signor Bragadin. Her whole soul was devoted to the magic arts; her library was crammed with books on sorcery; her laboratory contained a never-dying furnace, over which a mystic powder had for fifteen years been glowing in a crucible, in the confidence that it would turn at last into the philosopher's stone. A belief in genies, with a burning wish to have the power to summon them, was Madame d'Urfé's weakness. Casanova showed her his clavicula, which he assured her that he worked by the assistance of a genie of the name of Paralis. From that moment Madame d'Urfé was his slave. Another and still stranger whimsey took possession of her brain; she believed that, by the aid of Paralis, she might be changed into a man. Casanova did not disenchant her; for the preparations for the process were a work of time, and meantime he lived in the old lady's palace, drove about the city in her carriage, sponged upon her purse, and was even reported to be about to marry her in secret.

But long continuance in one mode of living was against his nature. Sometimes in company with Madame d'Urfé, at other times alone, he rambled over Europe. City after city was the scene of his adventures. At Stuttgart he struck up an acquaintance with three officers, who invited him to supper, put a drug into his wine, set up a bank at faro, and in a short time fleeced him of his purse, his watch, a diamond snuff-box, and notes-of-hand for fifty thousand francs. Casanova, drunk to stupor, was carried home at midnight in a litter. But when the winners called next day to cash their notes, he told them bluntly that they were a gang of sharpers, and might whistle for their coin. The officers in fury flew to court and gained the Prince's ear; and Casanova, to his consternation, found himself condemned to pay the whole amount, under pain of having his possessions seized and sold, or of being made a common soldier in the Prince's petty army.

Meantime he was kept prisoner in his rooms. By day, a sentinel was posted in the ante-chamber; at night, his door was locked and the key taken by the guard.

But, poisoned, tricked, imprisoned as he was, Casanova's wits were still his own. One night, before his door was locked, he sent his valet to the sentry with a flask of wine. As the man was drinking, the valet, under the pretext of snuffing the single candle by which the ante-chamber was illumined, snuffed it out. Casanova was upon the watch; shoes in hand, with all his valuables about him, he stole out in the darkness past the sentry, crept downstairs, and darted forth into the night. The candle was relighted; the sentry drank his wine, locked the prisoner's door as usual and departed. When he returned next morning, he found the three creditors waiting for admittance; and the four men went into the room together. They saw a figure resting on the bed. They addressed it—but in vain; they shook it—and a wig-block covered with a wig rolled out upon the ground. Casanova, fearing lest the guard might peep into the room before he locked the door, had left a dummy to befool him.

While his bamboozled enemies, with faces a yard long, were gaping at his proxy, Casanova was *en route* for Zurich. A new desire possessed him; he was weary of adventures; he sighed for a hermit's cell and a life of contemplation.

On the morning after his arrival he left his bed at daybreak and wandered forth into the mountains. Rapt in meditations, he had rambled many miles, when he perceived the grey walls of an ancient monastery, surrounded by the solitary hills. From the chapel came the voices of the monks at matins. Casanova entered. When the service ended he was civilly accosted by the abbot, who conducted him to see the convent; after which, in a luxurious chamber, a dinner for an epicure was set before them. Here was the life for Casanova! He determined to become a holy brother in the service of our Lady of Einsiedel.

The abbot proposed a fortnight for reflection. It was agreed that on its expiration he should call on Casanova at his inn. Casanova returned to Zurich in the abbot's carriage, and passed some days in pious meditations. But the night before the abbot's visit, as he was sitting in his window, he beheld four ladies, one of whom was of enchanting beauty, stepping from a chariot at the door. The party entered the hotel, were conducted to the apartment next his own, and ordered supper to be served. Casanova bribed a waiter, tied a green-baize apron over his scarlet waistcoat and gold lace, put a plate under his arm, and walked into the room. There, while he ministered to his enchantress, he drank his fill of beauty. The sight reminded him so vividly that monks have no concern with starry eyes and lips of roses, that when the abbot called next day he found his devotee a turncoat. Brother Jacques had relapsed into a jack-a-dandy.

The renegade resumed his wanderings. Again he was to be descried at city after city; at Lausanne, visiting Voltaire, and charming the great writer and

his guests with the fire with which he quoted Ariosto
—at Vaucluse, weeping at the fountain—at Rome,
receiving from the Pope, for what merit is not clear,
the cross of the Order of the Golden Spur — at
Naples, blazing amidst courtiers, and kissing the
hand of the child-king—again at the Eternal City
glittering in the carnival — at Paris, wheedling
Madame d'Urfé out of gold and gems.   Then he
took a whim to visit London.   But his experience
of our country was not happy.   The weather was
all fog.   King George III., to whom he was presented by the French ambassador, impressed him
merely as a short fat man with a red face and a red
coat, a plumed three-cornered hat, and a strong
resemblance to a cock.   The people were pure
savages—an opinion which he formed not wholly
without reason, on seeing a play damned at Drury
Lane.   The house shook with yells and cat-calls;
Garrick, who endeavoured to appease the tumult,
was greeted with a storm of cabbage-stalks and
rotten apples; and when at length the curtain fell,
a fierce mob rushed upon the stage and tore the
scenery to tatters.   Nor did his ill impressions end
with these.   An old hag and her siren daughter,
who had fleeced him of some money, brought a
charge against him, of having, in a fit of passion,
thrown a pin-puff at the damsel.   As Casanova

was returning from a ball at daybreak, two watch-
men stopped his chair and carried him before a
magistrate at Newgate. Casanova eyed his judge
with feelings of the liveliest curiosity—a curiosity
which the other, had he known the history of the
culprit, would have returned with interest ; for the
judge was Henry Fielding, the creator of *Tom Jones.*

Fielding bound the prisoner over in two sureties
to keep the peace. His tailor and his wine-mer-
chant appeared for him, and he was set at liberty.
But his ignominious and absurd position was to be
rendered still more galling. The insulted siren
bought a parrot, taught it a phrase of words, and
hung it in a public place ; and Casanova, as he
happened to pass by, heard its harsh voice screaming to a crowd of laughing loungers, " Casanova is
a rascal." It need scarcely here be added that the
parrot spoke the truth.

He had by this time tossed away his stock of
money, and was about to sell his jewels, when he
happened to win a hundred guineas from a chance
acquaintance, Baron Stenau, who paid him with a
bill which bore the name of a respected firm at
Cadiz. Casanova cashed the bill, which proved to
be a forgery. Stenau had vanished ; and Casanova
found himself in signal danger of ending his career
by being hanged at Tyburn.

He fled to Dover, crossed to Calais, and wandered from city to city to Berlin. He had some thought of taking service under the great Frederic—that is, he was prepared, for a sufficient recompense, to glitter like a popinjay about the court, decked with a gold chain and his Order of the Spur. The king offered him a post as overlooker in a college of cadets. Casanova went to visit this establishment, and found a barrack thrust away behind some stables, full of great gaunt rooms with beds of sacking, in one of which apartments, at the moment of his visit, the king himself was flourishing his cane and roaring curses at an overlooker who had left a nightshirt on a bed. This did not altogether jump with Casanova's notions. He turned his back upon the city in disgust, and wandered to St. Petersburg. There he was presented by Count Panin to the Empress Catherine, and had the pleasure of listening to her Majesty's opinions on the reformation of the calendar, and of laughing at the statues in the royal gardens—an assemblage of Apollos humped like Punches, cupids dressed as soldiers, and bearded patriarchs inscribed as Sapphos. But neither here did he obtain the offer of a post to suit him ; and accordingly he left for Warsaw, where he was more successful. King Stanislaus Augustus, to whom he was presented, was struck by some of his remarks upon the classic poets, desired to study Ariosto with him, and would probably have made him his own secretary, but for the event which we have now to tell.

The king's chamberlain, Count Xavier Branicki, a young and dashing officer, passed for the favoured lover of an actress named Binetti, whose charms were just then taking all the town by storm. Branicki, though in error, regarded Casanova as his rival. The two, by ill luck, chanced to come together in the lady's dressing-room. They quarrelled; the count insulted Casanova; and next morning Casanova sent a challenge to the count, which was instantly accepted.

In Branicki's coach-and-six, attended by some officers of the court, they drove to a sequestered region of a park. A trifling incident aided to decide the fortune of the day. One of the officers produced two huge horse-pistols, loaded them, and laid them cross-wise on the ground. Casanova chose one pistol; Branicki took the other, remarking as he did so, "That is an excellent weapon you have there." "I am going to test it on your head," said Casanova coolly; and probably this piece of braggardism saved his life. Branicki was a first-rate marksman; but Casanova's answer shook his nerve. In order to protect his head, he took up a position of constraint, which made his aim unsteady. The two were stationed at a distance of ten paces; the word was given, and the two shots were fired at the same instant. Branicki's bullet shattered the left hand of Casanova. Casanova's shot Branicki through the body.

Casanova hurried to his fallen foe, and raised his head with his unwounded arm. As he did so, the count's attendants drew their swords in fury, and would have cut him down. But Branicki was an opponent worthy of the days of chivalry. He ordered the assailants to stand back and to respect the laws of honour. For himself, he believed that he was dying. "You have killed me," he said to Casanova. "The king will never pardon you. Look to your own safety. Take my purse, and my ribbon of the Aigle Blanc as a safeguard, and fly from Poland for your life." Casanova refused the noble offer; but from that instant the antagonists were friends. Branicki was carried to a neighbouring inn, where, after a long hovering between life and death, he recovered slowly. Casanova stole back into the city, and took refuge in a convent till his wounds were healed, which was not until he had been forced to quarrel with his doctors to prevent their cutting off his hand.

The king, at Branicki's entreaty, forbore to seize

and hang him. But his career was over. He left the city, as he had left so many others, and once more rambled up and down the earth. At length he roved to Spain and to Madrid ; and in that land and city of romance he met with an adventure which the genius of the place might have inspired.

One night—a night of the full southern moon— he saw the window of a mansion opposite his own thrown open, and a young Señora of surpassing loveliness look out, with eyes bent eagerly upon the street. Of Casanova and his open admiration she appeared to take no notice. Presently she gave a start of joy, and Casanova saw a young and handsome cavalier, wrapped in a brown mantle, approach the mansion, open with a key a little door, and disappear within. The lady at the same time vanished from the window; but a quarter of an hour had not elapsed before she reappeared there, holding in her hand a letter and a key ; and now she looked across at Casanova, and signed to him to come beneath her window. He hastened to obey, and the key and letter dropped into his hat. He tore the billet open, and read these words— " Are you brave and secret ? — are you to be trusted ? If so, as I believe, come at midnight to the door. I will be there."

Casanova spent the next two hours in decking

himself for the mysterious assignation. At the stroke of midnight he descended, opened with his key the little door, and found himself in a dark passage. Instantly a low voice whispered, "Are you there?" a hand was thrust into his own, and he was led in silence through a windowed corridor into a magnificently furnished chamber, in which, by the faint gleam of candles, he descried a curtained bed. By the same dim light he saw the lady at his side. She was trembling like a leaf from head to foot, her eyes were wild, her face was white as ashes. In her hand she held a crucifix.

"Swear to me upon this cross," she said, "to render me the service I am going to ask of you."

Casanova, bewitched with beauty, seized the crucifix, and took the vow of folly. His companion laid her hand upon the curtains, and with a convulsive action dashed them back. A dead man lay upon the bed. It was the young and handsome cavalier with the brown mantle.

Then in broken words she gasped out all the story. The dead man was her lover; he had deceived her basely, and she had plunged a dagger into his heart. And the frightful service which she required of Casanova was to bear the bleeding body from the mansion and to cast it into the river near at hand.

Casanova stood in stupor, staring from the lady kneeling at his feet to the dead man lying on the bed. The danger was extreme; but his vow and the despair of his companion drove him on. He raised the body on his shoulder, bore it down the gallery and out into the night, and let it plunge into the rolling stream. Then, drenched with blood, aghast lest any eye should have espied him, he crept back like a robber to his rooms.

And he had cause for trepidation. As he was lying in his bed, a guard walked into his apartment, seized him, and marched him to the dungeon of *Buen-Retiro.* He had been seen staggering down the river bank with the corpse upon his shoulders. That, on such evidence, he would swing, seemed certain. But his escape was to be fit and striking. The Señora, hearing of his peril and heedless of her own, burst into the audience chamber of the President of the Council, and poured the truth into his ears.

Her act saved Casanova. Her family was rich and powerful; the dead man was of evil reputation; the story was hushed up, and the beautiful Delilah, with her family, was suffered to quit the soil of Spain in secret and for ever.

With this romantic episode the curtain falls for a long interval upon that drama of a thousand

scenes, the life of Casanova.   It is to rise once
more for the *finale*; but more than twenty years
have first to pass—years of the events of which
we have no record.   The freaks, the follies, and
the adventures of that long term are wrapped from
us in darkness, till suddenly, upon a certain day in
the year 1789, the curtain of the night again flies
back, and Casanova is discovered to us among the
guests of the ambassador of Venice at Paris.
Another of the guests on that occasion was Count
Walstein, with whom he fell into a conversation
touching the arts of magic and the old clavicula of
Solomon.   Walstein, delighted with his new acquaintance, offered on the spot to make him the
librarian of his castle in Bohemia.   Casanova, old,
poor, and weary of adventures, grasped at the proposal.   The very next day, in the count's company,
he left for Castle Dux, near Toeplitz—the abode
in which he was to spend, in peace and quietness,
the fourteen years of life which yet remained to him.

A librarian is not every day made out of an
adventurer.   But Casanova's character was strangely
mingled.   He was, as the parrot summed him up,
a rascal; he was a mixture of Gil Blas, Cagliostro,
and the Wandering Jew; but he was also a scholar,
a poet, and a wit.   To the count he was in every
way an acquisition.   He had looked with his own

eyes on every side of life; he was the prince of talkers and companions; and the count, and the gay guests who thronged the castle, were never wanting for diversion, when Casanova told, across the wine or round the ingle, the many-coloured tales of his career.

THE END

J. D. & Co.   Printed by R. & R. CLARK Edinburgh